Detective Jack Mitchell is not a people person. After fourteen years dealing with the monsters of society, he has learned to keep people at arm's length. Failing is his biggest frustration, and on the case of his career, he is having no luck hunting down a copycat serial killer...or the one man who survived the original case.

Six years ago, Will Blaikie was taken by a monster who changed his life forever. Narrowly surviving, he has become a prisoner in his own home. Friendless and alone, he watches in horror as a new monster emerges who only wants to copy the murderous deeds of Will's monster...including taking Will.

When these two men are thrown together, and the monster comes for them both, one must learn to feel safe and protected, and the other must learn to feel love and peace.

I0619987

SAVED

Karrie Roman

This is a work of fiction. All characters, places and events are from the author's imagination and should not be confused with fact. Any resemblance to persons, living or dead, events or places is purely coincidental.

Published by
NineStar Press
PO Box 91792
Albuquerque, New Mexico, 87199
www.ninestarpress.com

Warning: This book contains sexually explicit content, which is only suitable for mature readers.

Print ISBN #978-1-945952-88-3
Cover by Natasha Snow
Edited by BJ Toth

DEDICATION

To my husband, Adam, and my extraordinary sons—thank you for supporting my love of reading and writing even though you don't understand it.

Angela, my fellow book clubber, for sharing my passion and cheering me on, thank you.

And to all of the fabulous authors whose stories over the years have delighted me, inspired me, almost broken me, but most of all kept me sane in a mad world: thank you is not a big enough sentiment.

ONE

IF HE COULD have gotten away with it, Jack Mitchell would have broken Constable Morris Harrison's nose with one well-aimed and well-deserved blow. He hadn't been prone to violence since he had grown out of his brash youthfulness, but Jack's frustration and intolerance for fools today was amped up. He was so riled up, in fact, his fists clenched with unrealised anger.

"Was that the fucking media?" he roared, shaking the officer a little as he did so. He hadn't quite gotten there in time to stop the woman, who had to have been a reporter, from getting back into her car and peeling away. He did get there in time to grab the collar of the uniform who was supposed to be maintaining the integrity of the scene.

Jack could see the indecision in the young officer's eyes as he considered his choices. Deny it, admit to it, and grovel for forgiveness, or stand up to Jack. For a brief moment, Jack could see fight flitting through the young man's eyes before it died. Fear rose instead from the smouldering ashes of fight.

"Yes, God, I am so sorry. I don't know what happened. They just turned up and I—"

"Shut it. Christ, you stupid... Did they get a photo?" Jack was livid, just barely holding himself back from thumping this bozo on the nose. "Did they get a fucking photo?"

"Yes." The young officer had wised up enough to keep his head down. His answers were short and to the point as he recognised Jack's complete intolerance by this time.

Jack still had ahold of the uniform's collar when Kate arrived at his side. "What's your name, Officer?"

"Har... Harrison, sir, Constable Morris Harrison."

"Do you enjoy your job, Officer Harrison?"

"Yes, sir."

"Then you better damn well hope you still have it tomorrow. Do you realise what you've done here?" Kate reached over, placing her small hand on Jack's bicep, trying to calm him. Sometimes it worked, but not today. "We didn't want the press to know there is a copycat yet, Officer Harrison, and now thanks to you, some reporter is going to put it together, and we'll have lost our upper hand." Jack could see fight edging back into Harrison's eyes, and he couldn't decide if he wanted it or not. A good fight would release the coil of tension throughout his body. However, he wasn't in the mood for one of Pete's sour looks and lectures about his conduct towards his coworkers.

"I think...well, I think the public should know."

Wrong answer, kid.

"You're not here to think, Harrison. Your job, your only job here, was to protect the scene and afford the victim some privacy and dignity, and you fucking failed. Get out of my sight before I lose my temper and really let you have it." Unbelievably, the damn idiot didn't move.

Kate had watched the incident play out, offering only her touch and composed nature to calm Jack. "For Chrissake, kid, do the smart thing, and get out of here," she snapped. It sounded to Jack as if she'd reached her limit too. Officer Harrison glanced at them both. Defeated, he wandered away, hopefully reconsidering a few of his life choices.

"Well, Jack, I'll say it again. You sure have a knack for dealing with people." Kate shot him a fond look and laughed. "Pete's going to have your balls when he hears about this one."

Jack figured Officer Harrison had more to worry about than him, and right now, he wanted to get back to his case. So far, it was shaping up to be the biggest, most frustrating one of his career.

They had got the call first thing this morning, and it was approaching midday now. If the coroner didn't hurry up, the already oppressive smell from the decomposing body would putrefy even more under the stifling noon sun. January days in Sydney could reach extreme temperatures and today had a forecast in the high thirties. Detective Jack Mitchell was already sweating in his suit.

They had managed to contain the crime scene—until Harrison's bungle. Once word got out about the crosses, and that this was the second similarly mutilated body found, it would only be a matter of time before the words *serial killer* and *copycat* were tangled together and thrown about.

"Much longer, Annie?" He hated to bother her, but the longer the body was out here the greater the risk of discovery.

Annie was an exceptionally thorough coroner. She was meticulous with her work and wouldn't be rushed. Still, it didn't hurt to give her a little reminder that time was ticking away. "Keep your pants on, Mitchell. Another ten and I'll be out of here. How about you go and annoy your partner instead of me?"

"Alright. Geez, can't a man ask a question?" After six years in homicide he knew Annie as well as anyone, professionally. Personally, he never got too close with anybody—except a very select few.

Jack could see his partner, Kate Phelps, had moved away to talk again with, or more likely comfort, the elderly man who had called the police. Discovering a body was always a traumatic experience, regardless of the condition it was in. A murdered body with significant injuries would doubtless scar the old guy for years. He wanted to avoid rejoining them. Living humans were not his thing, and he was the last person anyone wanted offering comfort. Having been dismissed by Annie, there wasn't much left for him to do until the body was removed, so he walked away, leaving Annie under the watchful eye of one of the other uniformed officers on scene. Jack headed over to Kate, reaching her side midway through her conversation.

"No, Mr Daniels, I already told you there is no reward for finding a body." Kate sounded exasperated—so much for the traumatised old guy needing comfort.

With the single-minded focus of the truly greedy, Mr Daniels carried on undeterred. "I bet the media will buy my story. It's not every day a dead body with a cross carved into it is found. I deserve some compensation for the trauma I've suffered."

Left alone, it was probable that Kate would have pacified the man. She would commiserate with David Daniels, subtly manipulating him away from his avaricious line of thinking. Jack did not have the patience Kate had been blessed with, and he'd heard enough. True to human nature, Daniels was after money with little or no thought to the real victim here—he was currently lying in a stranger's field, his throat slit, his body a registry of injuries. There were few less-dignified ways to leave this world, and Jack couldn't bear to listen to this clown try to profit from the as yet unnamed victim's misfortune.

"I tell you what, *sir*, how about, as soon as we identify the victim, I personally put you in contact with his family. Perhaps you can discuss with them a suitable compensation for *your* pain and suffering." Jack could feel the admiring gape coming from Kate as he continued. "Perhaps you may even consider suing them to compensate you for the inconvenience of finding their loved one deceased on your property." Jack made sure to level his most intimidating glare at Daniels.

Daniels recoiled from Jack while his mouth was similarly backpedalling. "I didn't mean... I just thought that... I'm sure you can appreciate this is a very trying time, Detective. I apologise." Daniels turned and fled towards his Ute, mumbling under his breath the whole way.

David Daniels lived on semirural acreage. He had discovered the body early this morning while searching for his dog, Jessie. A well-trained rural dog, she always ventured out, did her business and a brief reconnaissance of the property before returning for breakfast. This morning the dog had not returned. Daniels had made his grisly discovery thanks to the bloodhound-like nose of his cattle dog who had stood guard over her find until her human arrived.

"You know, if this gets back to Pete, he is going to send you to that sensitivity training he keeps threatening you with, Jack." Kate's words were serious, but her tone was light. Kate and Jack got on better than many people who worked so closely together. There was respect and a genuine affection between them. Jack dreaded the day they had to move on from each other.

"Hey, at least I didn't thump him." Two morons in one day and Jack had managed not to strike either of them. Maybe Kate's composure was finally rubbing off on him.

WILL BLAIKIE DIDN'T often watch the news. It wasn't because he preferred to bury his head in the sand about the world. More often than not, he was just protecting himself. He knew very well what happened out there, and he didn't often want to be reminded of it. He had one television in his house, a smallish thirty-four-inch flat screen that was mounted over his fireplace. It was rarely on other than for movies or, of course, for *The Walking Dead*.

Tonight Will needed the background noise though. So he had left the TV on after watching a repeat of last season's final episode before the new *Walking Dead* season kicked off in a couple of weeks. He would proudly admit to being a diehard fan if anyone asked. He could hear the news broadcast begin from the kitchen where he was whipping up a quick stir-fry. There was no point in elaborate and complicated meals if you were only ever cooking for one. The breaking news item immediately caught his attention and left him cold.

Hesitantly making his way to the TV, he picked up the remote and rewound, wanting to have misheard. He hit play when the giant red breaking news banner crossed the screen. Will stood listening as a flawlessly presented, heavily made-up woman, who smiled entirely too much throughout her report, confirmed his worst fears.

"Police have yet to confirm the discovery of a second body with the all-too-familiar cross carved into the chest. Having viewed the body found in a semirural field today, I can confirm that a cross was indeed carved into the deceased's chest. An unnamed police source unofficially confirmed that this was the second body found bearing the cross. Sydney-siders will remember the Beecroft Butcher from six years ago when the city was paralysed with fear during the yearlong killing spree. Twelve men were killed before the killer, Russell Coburn, was finally—"

He only just made it to the bathroom before the entire contents of his stomach came up. Will draped himself over the toilet seat, heaving and sweating as he vomited into the bowl until nothing but bitter bile remained in him. He could still hear the low mumble from the television, but thankfully, no words were clearly audible. He'd heard enough—too much. His entire body shook, and he imagined his mind would look a picture of complete panic and chaos if he could peer inside it right now. He lay on the cool tiles, curling his body around the toilet bowl, unconvinced there would be no more vomiting. He felt a wet nose snuffle against his arm and reached back to give a reassuring pat to Henley. The furry dog took up his position, laying himself practically on top of his master. Protecting him as always, not just from physical harm, but from the mental hurt Will was now threatened with.

An hour and a half later, both Will and Henley were still curled up together on the bathroom floor. Though his body was still wracked with tremors, they were easing as was the chaos in his head. Could this really be happening again?

Two

DETECTIVE JACK MITCHELL was not a people person. At best, he could tolerate a small group of approximately three people in his life that he considered anything close to friends. At worst, he found people to be sociopathic arseholes who got off on inflicting the worst kind of pain on others. On his good days he tried to believe that most were just doing the best they could to make it through this life with some measure of happiness. Good days in his line of work were few.

When you are always expecting the worst in people, it also made for a lonely life, but that suited Jack. He didn't need relationships. Being a cop for fourteen years, the last six in homicide, had cultured his estimation of the human race. He had seen a lot, learned a lot, and he knew there was even worse out there. He placed himself somewhere in the middle of his spectrum of human nature, neither truly good, nor truly bad. He guessed most of humanity could be squeezed into that middle slice of his scale. Some days, though, it seemed as if the scale was tipping dangerously toward the bad.

Right now in top spot of his shitlist was his boss, Pete Delaney. He had just threatened—yet again—to cuff Jack to the bathroom pipes if he didn't calm the fuck down. Pete made this threat so damn often Jack wondered if perhaps it was actually some kind of kink of his.

When he was on a case, Jack didn't do calm and Pete knew this. Especially when he was tied up on a complex, frustrating case. Almost a week had passed since the second body in the case he and his partner, Kate, were working on had been found, and they were getting nowhere. The original case six years ago had been a massive media spectacle—not least because the son of one of the country's most popular media personalities had been murdered by the killer. The Beecroft Butcher, as the media had so charmingly dubbed him, had terrified the northwestern suburbs of Sydney and captivated the rest of the country for a year. In that time, twelve young men had been killed. The Butcher had become famous for carving a cross into each man's chest upon their death.

In the last two months, two bodies of young men, similarly mutilated with a cross carving, had been discovered. The original killer was dead. The coward had hanged himself in his cell before he had even made it to trial. So they knew they were looking for a copycat. Someone who wanted their fifteen minutes of fame, basking in the reflected infamy of the original case.

Aside from looking for the killer, though, they were also tasked with finding the one young man who had survived the original killings. It was this man who was the cause of Jack's frustration today, as they continued to try to track him down—with little success.

Spiralling thoughts were coursing through Jack's mind as he tried to focus, get a handle on the next steps to take. They had nothing to go on in the actual case: no clues, no witnesses of any real use, nothing. They had hit a brick wall. And now they had hit that same brick wall trying to track down the survivor, and it was making Jack feel as though he were mired in quicksand. He was stuck, and he fucking hated it. He was the type of man who needed to be taking action, not sitting on his hands waiting for a lead. Hence his temper tantrum, as Pete had called it, ten minutes ago and the resultant threat of being cuffed in the bathroom. Instead of the cuffing, Pete had sent him for a timeout in the break room as though he were an unruly five-year-old child. After five minutes and a large cup of tea, Jack hated to admit that Pete was right, and he was starting to calm down—not that Pete would ever hear those words.

"Jack, we've found him." His boss poked his head in the door and looked at him with what could almost pass as a grin. Peter Delany was a first-class policeman and boss, but Jack suspected he failed in the 'being human' stakes. According to his soon-to-be ex-wife, he did, anyway. In her words—as she had screamed at him in front of the entire station— he was married to his fucking job and wouldn't recognise a human emotion if one bit him on the arse. It was true Jack had found his boss asleep at his desk in the early morning hours more times than he could count, even before his wife had kicked him out, but Jack had always admired his commitment to the job. Pete's ex was the one who had been at home waiting for him and worrying about him, and that was a lifestyle Jack didn't understand, so far be it for him to judge.

To people such as Jack and Pete, the job consumed them to the exclusion of others around them vying for a place in their lives. The nature of his job was just one of many reasons Jack steered clear of relationships. Many times over the years Jack had looked at Pete and known he was catching a glimpse of his own life twenty years from now—minus the ex-wife.

Jack put his cup in the sink and headed for his desk, Pete following close behind. "About fucking time, Pete. Where is he?"

"Right under our fucking noses." Pete spat in disgust. "Here's the address. And the kicker is he is about four streets from you, Jack." Pete glared at Jack as though he should have known every person who lived within a four kilometre radius of him. Fuck, Jack didn't even know his nearest neighbours to speak to. "You and Phelps go and bring him in, and for fuck's sake, be pleasant, Jack. He's not a suspect."

"I can do pleasant," Jack replied as he grabbed his jacket and sprinted from the room. He was pretty sure he heard several chuckles behind him. *Arseholes.* He barely slowed down to grab Kate at the vending machines on his way out. There was no doubt or hesitation as she pocketed her Mars Bar and followed him out the door. After almost five years as partners, they knew each other better than most.

Jumping in the passenger side—Jack was man enough to admit Kate was a far better driver—he got the address up on Google Maps and buckled up. His leg started bouncing with nerves. He had waited a long time to get this guy, and he was anxious to get this done. Suspects he could deal with, but being pleasant to a survivor of crime was not something he was used to. Nor did he think he'd be particularly good at it if he was honest. He had been told more times than he cared to think about that he had a prickly temperament. Pete had been right to warn him to be pleasant. Kate picked up on his nerves immediately.

"Relax, Jack. We're just going to talk to him. You have spoken to people before, you know." Jack's eye roll was the only response she got.

They were about a fifteen-minute drive away from meeting Will Blaikie, the only survivor of the Beecroft Butcher. Notoriously reclusive and infuriatingly unwilling to talk to law enforcement, it had taken them weeks to track Will down. The address Will had set up for himself on the electoral roll, driver's license, and just about everywhere else they looked had turned out to be a vacant block of land. All his mail was sent to a PO Box. The land, they eventually discovered, belonged to Will's brother, Sean. He was currently somewhere overseas, and all attempts to contact him had failed. Jack couldn't blame Will for hiding away from the world. He knew the original case back to front, and he knew what Will had suffered.

"So what we want is to see if he can help us with any information but also suggest some kind of protection for him... Jack? Hello, Jack. Are you listening?" Kate's voice finally cut into Jack's wandering thoughts.

"Yep. Sorry, Kate. Yeah. We've all read his interviews from back then, but he may have remembered something else, I guess, so I think the main thing is to warn him about what's going on. There's a good chance he could be in danger."

"You'd think he would have contacted us by now. I mean, it's all over the media about the copycat. Common sense should have had him calling us straightaway."

"You know people, Katie. Never can tell what the hell they're gonna do." Could Kate be thinking that Will Blaikie was the killer? Jack knew plenty of people had considered it. The idea galled him, but if he had learnt one thing in his thirty-four years, it was that people always surprised you.

"You okay, Jack? You seem a little off the ball." Kate was an excellent detective; she missed nothing, which Jack did not always appreciate, especially when it came to her keen eyes watching him.

"Yeah, Katie, just tired I guess. Let's do this, huh?" he replied just as they pulled up to a large gate that blocked the entrance to a fairly short driveway. From what he could see, it didn't seem to be a particularly large house, though it was almost entirely surrounded by hedges. The gate and hedges were the speed bumps, meant to slow down anyone trying to get to Will Blaikie. There was no money for proper security. Jack knew Will's financial situation and knew he had never sold his story to make a quick buck as many others might have.

Jack jumped from the car and strode to the intercom on the gate before pushing the button rather impatiently. He glanced around as he waited for a response, checking the area for anything out of place, something that had become habit over his many years on the force. As he lifted his finger to press the button again, he heard a soft voice through the speaker.

"Can I help you?" Will's question was timidly asked yet clear and polite.

"Mr Blaikie? I'm Detective Jack Mitchell. My partner, Detective Kate Phelps, and I would like to come in and talk to you for a short while. We—"

This time Will's voice was neither timid nor soft when he abruptly interrupted Jack with an unwavering "No."

"Mr Blaikie, we need to talk to you as a matter of urgency for your own safety. Please, may we come in?" Jack kept his tone calm yet firm. And Pete didn't think he could do pleasant? This was being damn pleasant.

"If this is about the young men being taken again, then you don't need to warn me, Detective. I am very aware of what is going on, but I don't know anything that could help you. I'm sorry." Jack found he enjoyed the timbre of Will's voice. It was soothing and masculine yet not aggressive. It kind of reminded him a little of Liam Neeson's. It was the kind of voice you could close your eyes and listen to for hours, regardless of the topic.

"Please, Mr Blaikie. I know this is difficult for you, but if we could just have a few minutes of your time?" Silence answered him, and Jack thought for a moment that Will had perhaps decided not to answer until they had no choice but to leave. Just as he turned to head back to the car, he heard the intercom crackle to life again.

"Am I a suspect?"

Jack didn't miss the indignation or the hurt in Will's voice. Technically he wasn't an official suspect, but anyone even on the periphery of this case needed to be questioned and ruled out. "No, but it wouldn't hurt if you could let us know where you were at certain times in question." Jack winced at the request, feeling like dirt for even asking, but that was his job.

"I don't know you, Detective, and I don't trust people. Please...leave now. I will check you out and come to the station to talk to you, but you are not coming in here. Do you have a business card?" Will didn't even address the issue of being a suspect.

"Yes I—"

"Please just leave it in the mailbox and go."

Jack smirked, secretly pleased with the exchange. Will Blaikie was a sensible and cautious man, no doubt born of his traumatic experience, but it was good to know they weren't dealing with a fool. He considered arguing but in the end decided that he wouldn't get anywhere.

"Okay, we can do it your way. We'll be at the station tomorrow, so show up anytime and we can talk. Alright?"

"Thank you."

"See you then, Mr Blaikie, and please...please be careful." Jack turned back to the car, sliding into the passenger seat to the sound of his partner's soft chuckles.

"Ah, Jack, you have a way with people. 'Please, please be careful.' I didn't know you cared so much." Kate's grin spread from ear to ear. She was a beautiful woman. Not in a glamorous movie star sort of way, but she had a warmth and friendliness that, to Jack anyway, was infinitely more appealing. Fortunately, looks could be deceiving because she was also tough as nails and the kind of partner you wanted to have at your back when the shit hit the fan. Kate Phelps was also a huge pain in Jack's arse as she seemed to take absolute delight in busting his chops over every single little thing.

"Just drive, Lucille." Kate bristled at the use of her hated middle name, which was why Jack used it every chance he got. Guess he could be a gigantic pain in the arse too.

AS SOON AS the two detectives left, Will Blaikie sank to the floor of his living room, knees drawn up to his chin and arms wrapped protectively around himself. He stayed there for close to half an hour, desperately trying to calm himself. Shivers wracked his body until it ached. His breath caught right down in his lungs so that his entire chest burned with the effort of trying to expel the trapped air. He tried all the different breathing techniques he had been taught by various shrinks over the years, but it took longer than usual to clear his head of remembered terror and fearful thoughts of the future.

When finally he calmed enough to get himself off the floor, he moved to his favourite armchair and curled himself into it. Will wasn't stupid. He had known that there was a copycat after the first two murders. Even before it had been officially confirmed, aspects of the cases felt familiar, especially to someone with such intimate knowledge of the original case.

The arrival of Detective Mitchell and his partner had made the copycat case distinctly real. No longer were the recent murders something he could pretend didn't touch him. For weeks, Will had suspected that the police were probably looking for him. He was ashamed to admit he'd stayed hidden, but there was nothing he could do. He didn't know anything about these cases, and he never wanted to rehash his past.

Every day he was thankful that his monster was dead, but after the detectives' visit, he knew it was time to accept that another monster was out there. Would there always be another monster? Will didn't want to think about the recent killings. He knew what those poor men had gone through—maybe not the details, but the terror they had experienced. He knew the bitter taste of fear intimately.

Some mornings he still woke up, and for just a brief moment, he would think he was still there in the dark, the captive of his monster. On those days, he was so terrified, so utterly overcome with fear, believing he was back there with another day of unrelenting pain to endure. Back to another day of never knowing what would happen, but always hoping that today would be the day his torment was finally over, whether through death or rescue. Until the time came when hope finally started to fade. That had been the worst time—when hope was gone—when he had started begging. Many days during his captivity he'd begged for death, but his monster had never given it to him—some would say fortunately. Will wasn't always so sure.

God, he wished it would all just go away, or he could go back in time and not go out that night, or maybe just go back and die with the others. Anything rather than live with the memories. But he couldn't think that way; he wouldn't think that way. Years of therapy had taught him he was better than that, stronger. He was still alive, and despite everything he had been through, he had learned to love his small world—the amazing stories he read and movies he watched, his beloved dog, his beautiful garden, the decadent flavour of rich, dark chocolate, the clash and flash of a good Sydney lightning storm. Though he lived his life essentially in one small house, it was still a beautiful world, and he was grateful he was in it—mostly.

For now, he had to think about what he would do about his visit to the detectives tomorrow. The idea of going in to meet with the police filled him with dread. Leaving his house was never easy, but venturing somewhere new was going to be extra challenging. Yet he knew without question he had to do anything he could to put a stop to this new monster.

First on his list was to check out Detective Jack Mitchell. The events of his past had left him with a healthy dose, maybe overdose, of paranoia, and he didn't intend to be fooled by anyone again. He picked up his iPad and googled Parramatta Police Station—he wasn't quite ready for a trip outside his front door to get the detective's business card. Finding the contact details he needed, he reached for his phone.

His call was answered on the third ring by an incongruously jovial-sounding officer thanking him for his call to Parramatta Police Station.

"Ah, hi," Will responded. "Could you tell me if you have a Detective Jack Mitchell working there please?"

"Yes there is. Can I put you through to him?"

"No, no thanks. I just wanted to check. Thanks for your time." Will ended the call without waiting for a reply. So he had established there was a Detective Jack Mitchell, but was it the same man who had come to his door?

Will opened up Facebook and searched for any Jack Mitchells. Several came up who were apparently in the Sydney area, but none of the photos matched the image of the man Will had seen through his security cameras. And he didn't think the one with the faces of several small children for his profile picture quite fit the man who had stood at his gates. He tried googling Jack. There was mention of a Detective Jack Mitchell in connection with the homicide death of a young woman Will remembered reading about not that long ago, but there were no images. He had exhausted his detective/IT skills. Hercule Poirot he was not. Now he had to consider if he was willing to go into the station tomorrow without confirming his visitor was actually Detective Jack Mitchell. In the end he knew he would—lives were at stake, maybe even his own.

Will went to the kitchen to make himself a snack and a milkshake, because sometimes indulging in a childish treat from your past was the best calmative. Moving about his kitchen he pulled different ingredients and utensils from drawers and cupboards. He wondered, as he sometimes did, what his life would look like if evil had never come calling for him that night six years ago. He could never manage to grasp a clear picture of that other life though, and perhaps that was a good thing because that life was gone for good. Will had always been somewhat of an introvert, something that was exacerbated by his captivity. So he knew he would never have been out living the dream, or what some would call living large, even if he had never been taken. Perhaps one day he would find the courage just to live amongst other people again.

IT WAS ALMOST 5:00 p.m. by the time Jack and Kate got back to the station. Officially they got off at five, but Jack wasn't looking forward to another lonely night at home, pacing the floorboards trying to produce a clue out of thin air to catch this killer. He thought about going out to pick someone up, work off some pent-up frustration—it had been a while, but he couldn't work up any enthusiasm for it. He could not get his mind off this case.

"Hey, Jack, you okay?" Kate was using her soft, motherly, 'I want to fix this for you' voice, so he must still look out of sorts. This was the second time today she had asked if he was okay, and that was unprecedented. He must look Godawful, not just out of sorts. "You're too still, Jack, and we all know that's not a good thing. Can I help?"

"I'm still sometimes," he blatantly lied. The only time Jack wasn't moving was when he slept—hell not even then if past bedmates' complaints were anything to go by. "Sorry, Kate. Yeah, I'm okay, just thinking. Are you outta here?"

"Yeah, Phil is on nights so I need to get home to the little swine." Jack wasn't sure if it was appropriate for a mother to call her kids *swine*, but Kate always did it with such affection, and he knew she loved the hell out of those kids.

"Okay, I'll see you tomorrow. I think I'll read over the files again before I head out. Give those babies a big kiss from Uncle Jack, hey?"

"Uncle Jack? We both know you are trying to teach them that your name is Tony Stark. Although why I don't know. Tony Stark is an arrogant... Oh wait...yeah, I get it." She smiled and winked. "You do know that by the time they're old enough to figure that one out, there will be some new whizz-bang superhero," she replied with a gentle kiss to his forehead.

"Hey, Iron Man will NEVER be out of fashion!" he yelled to her retreating back. "And I am not arrogant!"

After picking up the files, he retreated to the break room, figuring he would be much more comfortable curled up on the lounge in there and desperately needing a cup of tea. It was a source of great amusement to his coworkers that the six-foot-three-inch, hard-as-nails Jack Mitchell drank tea, especially green tea, but there was something so calming about a nice hot brew. Besides, he never did the dainty china tea cups and pinkie thing like a society matron, so he figured his masculinity was secure.

The break room was empty. After making his mug of tea, he got his little area set up, dragging a chair over next to the couch to use as his table. He removed his shoes, and despite his large frame, managed to curl himself up on the couch. He flicked through the file, bypassing the latest cases and, instead, pulling out the file on Will Blaikie. Jack wanted to be sure he knew everything before meeting him tomorrow. Or perhaps his curiosity had been peaked after *almost* meeting Will face-to-face.

He put aside the photos taken immediately after Will's rescue—they were seared into his brain. He didn't need to look at them again. The brutality of Russell Coburn was evident in the photographic evidence left behind. According to the reports, during his month in captivity, Will had been starved, beaten frequently, cut, and burned repeatedly. Nothing life-threatening, but... Jack suspected that the psychological scars left on Will would have been far harder to heal, if in fact they could be.

Will had also been forced to watch the brutal torture and murder of two other men. According to the police interviews, both Will and Russell Coburn indicated that Coburn had come to believe Will could become his willing accomplice, almost as though he had developed an infatuation with Will. Coburn believed he had been teaching Will, in effect grooming him, by making him watch. At the time, they believed that was why Coburn had taken two men at once for his last victims— one for him and one for Will. According to the reports, Will had refused, and he had suffered for it.

When he finished the official interview notes, he hesitantly picked up the notes added by detectives and psychologists with their more personal thoughts from the time. He knew what was in there; there was some suspicion that Will was indeed a willing participant and was a danger to society. That suspicion was in the minority, and not one piece of evidence had ever been found to support it. Jack had never bought that theory, though he guessed it was understandable, considering. However, it still annoyed him, given the state Will had been in when rescued. Who would have blamed Will for doing whatever he had to do to end the torment? Yet he hadn't done it. It took a brave man to endure a punishment he could have avoided.

Sitting quietly, reviewing the notes of Will's case, he considered the other theory being floated: that Will was the copycat. Logically, Jack could see how some people could make that leap, but it just didn't work for Jack. There was no evidence to suggest it was true, but there was no proof to discount it either. It was another reason the department had been so eager to track him down, just in case. He thought back to the voice he heard today, soothing, quiet, and nervous. No, he didn't believe Will was involved. Though it was one of the first things he had learned about being a detective: never shut the door on a suspect until you can unequivocally rule them out.

A sharp poke to his chest several hours later woke Jack from his sleep.

"Get the hell out of here, Mitchell. You're cluttering up the place...again." Bill Hodges, the night cleaner, was a kindly man, jolly and quick-witted. He too seemed to enjoy busting Jack's chops. He reminded Jack a lot of his grandfather.

Jack had lost his small family through the years—first his mother to illness when he was only a young boy and lastly his beloved grandfather just a few years ago. He'd also lost his father suddenly in between them. He watched Bill as he continued to sweep the floor of the small break room, the white of his hair almost identical to his grandfather's. His pa's hair had been that colour for as far back as he could remember, and Jack recalled once asking him why his hair was so white. Jack must have only been about eight at the time, sitting beside Pa on the couch, watching the football as they did every Sunday afternoon. Jack wasn't a diehard fan, and he didn't care who won, but he yelled at the referees and the players right along with his grandpa. It was their thing, and Jack loved every minute of it. One Sunday during a break in the yelling, Jack had asked his grandfather why his hair was so white. His Pa had taken a sip of his beer, looked Jack straight in the eyes, and told him his hair had turned white the day Jack was born. Jack had frowned in confusion. The old man had laughed and told him he didn't know if it was the shock of having the most beautiful grandson in the whole world or fear of now being old enough to have a grandson that had turned it white. He missed his pa every day.

"Sorry, Bill. I'll be out of here in a minute." After cleaning up his mess, Jack slid the file under his arm and walked back to his desk. He grabbed his keys, keeping the file under his arm. Even though he had fallen asleep, he knew once he got his sorry arse home, sleep would evade him.

THREE

IT WAS NEARLY three o'clock and still no sign of Will Blaikie. Jack had moved beyond antsy; he was tired and damn cranky. He'd been right and sleep had not come to him when he got home last night; in fact, Mr fucking Sandman had not come to him until nearly three this morning. Since waking at six thirty, he had barely sat down for more than five minutes at a time. He was either up pacing with a growing impatience or doing little errands that Pete, rather suspiciously, kept asking him to do. He suspected it was to try to keep him from annoying the crap out of the rest of his coworkers. Kate had started throwing things at him an hour ago every time he went to stand, and Pete threatened to cuff him to the bathroom sink again if he paced in front of his office one more time. That man really did have some kind of kink for cuffs going on there. He considered the pile of paperwork he was working through, his knees bouncing, hands twitching. Perhaps another cup of tea...

"No, don't even think about it. Sit your arse down for ten whole minutes, and I will think about letting you get another cup." Did Kate just growl at him?

"But I just thought—"

"No. What is up with you, Jack? Why are you so uptight?"

"I don't know, Kate. I wish I did. This case is just pissing me off. No reason, just one of those things you know?" He couldn't explain it. He knew he just had to ride it out and work his arse off to close this case. He glanced up from Kate's earnest face and noticed Pete talking to a tallish man, whose back was to him. He wore a nice-fitting pair of blue jeans and navy-blue T-shirt. His hair was dark brown, almost black, and it stuck up at the back in a double cowlick. His arms, though not huge, were nicely shaped and hung stiffly by his side, but his hands were almost flapping against his thighs. Pete reached out to grab the man by his left arm and turned him to face a now openly staring Jack.

Jack was straight-up bisexual—dick, pussy, muscles, breasts—he didn't care; it all turned his shit on. From an early age, Jack had been equal opportunity, finding both men and women attractive and enjoying the company of both in his bed. So it was no surprise to him that he found the man now walking towards him incredibly attractive. His stomach actually fluttered when the man stopped in front of him. His reaction wasn't troubling at all; he had worked with, or had to deal with, plenty of people he found attractive in the past. This man was just one of many. Jack did have an appreciation for beauty, and he found beauty to admire in many people. Profound he was not.

"Detective Mitchell?" Ah, that voice. So this was Will Blaikie? He had changed considerably from the damaged young man in the file photos. A little broader in the chest and carrying more weight, obviously because he hadn't been near starved for the last month. He had lost any hint of boyhood and was now most certainly all man, a very appealing man.

"Mr Blaikie." Jack finally took the proffered hand. Will's grip was warm and firm, suggesting a certain confidence. Although his gaze fell away from Jack's almost immediately, revealing the truth of his nature. Will was putting on a good show, but he was nervous and a little timid. It was unsurprising given his past. "Call me Jack."

"Jack. Please call me Will. Sorry I'm so late, it just took... I mean, I..." Will floundered and left off his reply, gaze darting around the room instead.

"Had something better to do?" Jack finished sarcastically for him. "This is my partner, Detective Kate Phelps." Jack indicated the now standing Kate who also took Will's extended hand while glowering at Jack. That had been rude and unnecessary, and Jack knew he was better than that, and Will was deserving of better than that.

"Good to meet you, Will. Sorry about the circumstances. We can step into one of the interview rooms for a little privacy if you would prefer." Kate gestured towards the interview rooms. "We'll try to get through this as quickly as we can." God, Jack loved his partner's ability to easily deal with people and make them comfortable. Many times they had played good cop–snarky, irritable, slightly socially incompetent cop with a suspect. Jack could literally see Will start to relax under Kate's care.

Kate led Will to one of the nicer interview rooms available and indicated a seat for him to take. Jack trailed behind, feeling a little disoriented, as though he had lost control of this meeting already. Caught up in his own thoughts, he missed whatever it was Kate was asking him because both she and Will were looking at him with frowns, or rather in Kate's case, it could have been a little smirk.

"Sorry, what?"

"Tea, Jack? I was just going to get one for Will and thought you might like one too," she replied, her smirk growing almost to a full-on grin.

"Thanks. I'll get them, Kate. Your usual?" Kate nodded her reply. "And you, Will?"

"I'll take a tea please, black no sugar."

A man after his own heart. It wasn't unusual for him to make the teas. Kate was a great cop but Godawful at making tea. How you fucked up pouring boiling water in a mug was beyond him, but it had been Jack's unfortunate experience that Kate could. Today, though, he had needed to get out of that little room, and so he left Will and Kate talking as he escaped the room to get his head on straight. Christ, maybe he did need that holiday Pete was almost forcing him to take once this case was done. Everything about this case was messing with Jack's head; he felt at sixes and sevens, unable to get his act together.

With the teas made, Jack headed back into the interview room, gaze immediately landing on Will. The man was absolutely beautiful. Dark-chocolate-brown eyes, big, soulful, puppy-dog ones framed by thick, dark lashes were staring into Jack's own brown orbs as he handed over the tea and offered a bikkie. Christ, he had always thought his own eyes were pretty damn nice, but compared to Will's, his just looked the colour of swamp water. Will's lips were full and rosy, if one could call lips that. They were the deep red of youthful lips, almost as if he wore lipstick. Jack was pretty sure he knew several women who would be envious of the natural beauty of those lips. A barely noticeable scar ran from the corner of Will's left eye, almost reaching to the corner of his lips. Rather than spoiling his looks, Jack thought the minor imperfection gave Will a slightly dangerous appeal. *Fuck, get it together, Mitchell. He's not here for a fucking date.*

Handing Kate's tea over, Jack switched back to what his partner was trying to get through his scattered brain. "I was just reassuring Will that we don't need him to rehash every little detail. If he can try to think if there is anything he may have remembered over the years that he may not have told us originally or any thoughts he may have, no matter how small, that may help us," Kate suggested.

"I try hard not to think too much about it. I...um...well, it messed me up, but I have been seeing someone for a while, so if you wanted to talk to them I don't mind. I'd like to help." It took Jack a moment to realise

Will was talking about seeing a therapist rather than seeing someone as in dating. He mentally slapped himself at the ridiculous relief he felt. He caught Will looking his way and, shaking himself, jumped into the interview, trying to finally be the professional he supposedly was.

"So why are you talking to us now?" Jesus, that's not even what he meant to ask, let alone the snarky tone he'd used. He needed to ease up on the poor man; he was in here about to talk about his horrible past, and Jack could barely be civil to him.

He noticed Will's slight flinch as he lowered his eyes, and Jack silently rebuked himself for his shameful behaviour. "Well I just thought, I mean I want to help. I don't want anyone to have to go through what I, well you know...and I just wasn't sure what I could do..." Will trailed off, a flush now covering his face and reaching down his neck past the collar of his T-shirt.

Kate was outright glaring at Jack now, and Will was still looking down, apparently fascinated by his own feet, a frown on his lips. Jack scrambled to fix his mess.

"Of course, sorry, of course you want to help. It's just you know you've never really talked..." *Oh for fuck's sake.* He was making a mess of this. "Well, thank you, I mean, it probably won't be necessary for us to talk to your therapist, but thank you for offering. We were just hoping that maybe there was someone that Rus...ah, Coburn may have mentioned, or maybe even if there was ever anyone else there while he had you? We know Coburn had no living family but maybe a friend he might have mentioned? Perhaps there has been someone trying to get to know you recently, maybe plough you for information about what happened? Or, as Kate said, if you have remembered anything else new. Something along those lines." He finished up hopefully, looking at Will for any signs to indicate he hadn't totally fucked this up. Those dark-chocolate eyes were looking back up to his face now, but the frown was still there.

Will's eyes lowered again, something he seemed to do as though to gather his courage before speaking. "He um...my monster never spoke about stuff like that. He only ever told us what he was going to do or wanted to do to us. Nothing friendly or personal you know, just...just bad stuff." He was looking right at Jack now; he had found his courage.

They sat for a moment, looking at each other. Jack at a loss for words and Will seemingly challenging him to find some, with one eyebrow arched and his lips now pulled tight together. Well, evidently, Will had come to the popular conclusion that Jack was an arsehole. Not really a shocker there, but Jack was not yet sure what to make of Will. He was hard to peg. He was quiet, shy even, and easily flustered, yet Jack knew there was confidence there, strength. There had to be to survive what Will had. *My monster,* Will had said. Jack couldn't even begin to imagine. Will intrigued him, but was that because of what he had experienced or because of the man himself? Perhaps it was both. Or perhaps this case was just royally fucking with his brain.

Interrupting Jack from his thoughts, Kate cleared her throat. "Will, we hate to ask this of you, but please try to think about it, and let us know if you recall anything. I can't imagine how hard it is for you, with all these bad memories being brought up, but I do thank you for wanting to help. Right now, I want to focus on you. There has been no threat made that we know of, but as you know, the media at the time went, well frankly, crazy about you. They reported everything they could about what happened in the case, and they made it clear that you were somehow special, I guess, to Coburn. A copycat is likely going to want to recreate your involvement too. That may mean he chooses someone special to himself, but it could mean that he comes after you. The department may be willing—"

"No. Thank you, but no." Will left no room for argument or persuasion. "I don't want protection or anything. I would rather those officers be on the street trying to catch him." There was a steel backbone to Will that Jack had known had to be there for him to have survived what he did.

"Are you sure? Are you taking precautions, making sure you're safe?"

"Kate, I have been doing that since I was rescued. No one could be more cautious than me." Finally, a hint of a smile from Will.

"Will, I live about four streets from you, so if you don't mind, I will be driving by a fair bit just to check out the street, look for anything unusual. I could be at your place in about five minutes; hell, I could run there faster than that if you needed me." *What the actual fuck...* Oh, yep, he could see by the look on her face that he was going to cop shit for this from Kate later. Jack didn't know who in the room was more shocked and horrified by his words, but it brought things to an uncomfortable standstill.

Will's gaze was back on his feet, Kate was doing some mix between a grimace and a smile, more flustered than he had ever seen her, and Jack was now rubbing his temples with finger and thumb, trying to figure out what the hell just happened. The absolute silence and awkwardness in the room was becoming oppressive.

Strangely, it was Will who broke the silence. "Well, thank you, Jack, that's...um, comforting to know, but I'm sure I will be okay and won't need you to *come running*." Was he mocking Jack? Yep, the little shit was. Jack could see the grin on his lips, now that he had lost all interest in his feet. "I have your card, though, and if I think of anything else, I'll be sure to call."

Will stood to leave, Kate rising with him. Jack stayed in his seat, possibly a little shocked by his behaviour. He reached up to shake Will's hand before he walked to the door with Kate leading the way. Will stopped suddenly and reached into the pocket of his jeans, pulling out a crumpled sheet of paper. He turned to Jack and threw the paper on the table in front of him. "I forgot this," his teasing tone gone, replaced with...perhaps bitterness.

Jack opened the sheet of paper to see every date since the first victim had gone missing listed and beside each date was written 'at home, alone.' Jack didn't think it was possible for him to feel like a bigger heel at that point. As the interview room door shut behind Will's retreating form, Jack dropped his head smack down and then rocked it side to side on the table. He closed his eyes and willed the day to start again.

Not five minutes later, the door flew open, and Kate and Pete walked in laughing their collective arses off. Jack lifted his head to glare at them before dropping it back down with another thud. "You watched?" His voice was muffled against the desk.

"Oh I watched alright, Mitchell. Care to explain?" replied Pete, the amusement obvious in his voice.

"Nope." Jack stood, gathering what remained of his dignity and stalked past his boss and his partner without a backwards glance. "I'm going home. See you both tomorrow." He could hear the laughter continue until he was well out of the office.

HIS MEETING WITH the detectives had left Will shaken. As a rule, authority figures such as cops had always intimidated him in spite of the enormous respect he had for them. Even though he had left Detectives Mitchell and Phelps over an hour ago, Will's pulse was still slightly elevated and his breathing fast. He needed to calm down. He contemplated giving Dr Granger a call but didn't think he was actually in the mood to have the doctor poking around in his head right now. He needed to talk to someone, though, and as much as he loved him, Will didn't think Henley's furry ears would cut it as a sounding board today. He had no friends and Sean was... God knew where. The only other person was his cousin, Del, so named after the love of her father's life, Delvene Delaney. Apparently Aunt Joyce had no problem with her husband's obsession with another woman as she always joked it had given her some peace and quiet whenever Delvene was on the telly. Perhaps a catch-up with his favourite and only cousin was just what Will needed.

Del answered on the fourth ring in her usual jovial manner.

"Will? God, it's good to hear from you. How the hell are you?" The tension in Will's shoulders started to unknot immediately. They spent the next twenty minutes filling each other in on the boring day-to-day of both of their lives. Until Del got tired of the dance and demanded to know what was wrong.

At thirty-six, Del was quite a bit older than Will, but they had always gotten along very well. The day after Will had been rescued, Del had turned up at the hospital and promptly told him that he looked like absolute crap. Everyone else in the hospital room that day had been mortified, but Will had felt such relief. For the first time since he had been taken, he had been treated as a normal person rather than a sadist's plaything or a fragile man made of glass that may shatter at any moment. After Del's visit Will actually thought that just maybe he would be okay.

"There's a copycat, Del."

"Shit, fuck. Okay, what's being done?" Del was level-headed as always.

"Well, I went in to see the cops today. They just wanted to know if I had any ideas or knew anything that might help them." It was harder than he thought just to talk about the possibility of what might be going on, but he had worked too hard to fall apart so he pressed on. "They said that maybe I was in danger." Will spoke so softly he wasn't sure Del even heard him.

"And what are they going to do about it?" Del was angry.

"They mentioned protection—"

"And you took it." It was a statement, not a question. The silence stretched on. "Will, tell me you took the protection."

"No. No, I didn't. I don't think it's necessary yet."

"Will, honey, you listen to me. You take that protection. You've been through enough, and if there's even the smallest chance you might be in danger, then you have to do whatever it takes to protect yourself."

"I'm being careful, Del. I just don't think I need police protection yet."

"What if you come visit me for a while then? It's beautiful here in Perth at the moment, and the cricket will be on at the WACCA in a few days. We could go." It was tempting. Del was what some might call a little alternative. With dreadlocks halfway down her back, multiple piercings, and a penchant for homemade dope cookies, Del lived her life exactly as she wanted. Will admired her so much for that. He also found her company calming.

"You know I can't leave Henley, but thanks, Del." It was a half-truth, but he knew he didn't have to make the humiliating admission to Del that a trip to Perth would be unbearable for him; she understood.

There was a dramatic sigh through the line and Will knew he had won, for now. He also knew he could expect frequent calls from his cousin for the foreseeable future.

"What about Sean? Have you told him?"

"No. I don't... It's not his problem. He's happy where he is...wherever that is." He tried to tease a little about his absent brother, but it fell flat. He would give anything for Sean to be here now. He suspected, by Del's mumbles about inconsiderate, something, something, dicks, she knew how much he needed Sean.

"So tell me, how were the cops? Anyone you know from...before?"

"No, no one from before. They seemed nice. It was a lady and a man, and they both seemed very...nice."

"Nice... Will? Tell me."

"Well, the lady was lovely. The man was a bit of a dick, but he seemed competent and he was...hot." Will's cheeks flamed at the admission.

"Reeeally? Do tell, cousin."

"You know tall, muscular, brunet, beard, voice all gravelly. Masculine."

"What are we talking here, Will? Above six foot?" Del had an unrelenting passion for tall men.

"Ah, I'd say about six two, six three."

"So the mother lode then...hot, masculine, protective, built. Tell me again why you didn't take their protection?" Del giggled. It had been comparatively easy when Will had come out. He'd never had that many friends. The ones he did have either didn't care or were struggling with their own teen angst to have much energy to spare worrying about his. No one in his family had a problem with it as such, but he never could have talked about men with Sean or his mother. Del, on the other hand, loved men and loved talking about men, especially with her gay cousin, of whom she was inordinately proud for the rather underwhelming feat of being born gay.

"Yeah, he was something else, but so far out of my league."

"Don't do that, Will. Any man would be lucky to have you. You're sweet and loyal, funny, intelligent, and this may be a little icky, but you are a damn fine-looking man. So don't you sell yourself short."

"Thanks, cuz. Look, I should get going, but thanks for the talk. I mean it. I don't know why I spent so much on those damn shrinks when a chat with you is the best medicine."

"You know it. Take care, Will, and if you need anything, you call. Promise me?"

"Promise." They said their goodbyes, and after hanging up, Will knew that he had absolutely made the right decision. A chat with Del had worked wonders: he felt calmer, infinitely more relaxed than he had half an hour ago. Surely everything was going to be fine.

FOUR

THE NEXT WEEK went by without incident, or rather, a serious incident. The whole station seemed to have somehow heard about Jack's offer to run to Will's aid. Being the complete pricks they were, his colleagues had teased him mercilessly. It started out small, *Oh, Jack, I need my lunch. Could you run it over to me? Oh, Jack, I need help. I can't get the paper in the copier. Could you run over here and help me?* But frustration at the lack of progress on the case allowed things to turn to the ridiculous with high-functioning, stressed men and women looking for an outlet. It started one morning when Jack had walked into the office to the blaring sound of the *Superman* theme playing over the building's PA system. Next, a photoshopped image of Jack as Superman had mysteriously appeared on every screensaver in the building. The final humiliation had been a pair of Superman undies flying like a flag from the antenna of his car. The least they could've done was compare him to Iron Man, for God's sake. He didn't know how, but someday, some way, Kate would be paying for this.

The night of what he referred to as his brain snap, but Kate had called the *beginning of the big thaw of your ice-cold heart*, Jack had run the gamut of self-recrimination and appeasement. He had gone home, berating himself for his stupidity, before consoling himself and finally convincing himself that he was on the brink of crazy. No other explanation possible. After a few pick-me-up drinks, he even considered making an appointment with the department's shrink. By morning's forgiving light, he had vetoed the visit to the shrink and decided to forget about the whole sorry incident. Treat it as a simple brain snap and move on. There was nothing wrong with offering to run to someone's aid, after all. That's what cops do. It just wasn't Jack's MO. He was protective and would do anything he could to help someone else. But Jesus, to actually offer to run, literally run on his own two feet, to their aid the way he had? He had sounded like an absolute twat. Perhaps he was getting too old for this job at the ripe old age of thirty-four.

Needless to say, he had heard nothing from Will Blaikie. He was either still laughing at Jack or at home fearing that Jack may burst through his window at any moment to come to his rescue.

Time passed and Jack was still working hard on *the* case as well as finishing up paperwork on old cases. He also began helping out on other cases to give himself a break.

By the ninth day post brain snap, things had settled down and the incident was all but forgotten, and then came the phone call. Any calls to detectives not to their mobile went through reception first, and then they simply transferred the call. Of course Shane Jenkins, on reception today, was the biggest arsehole out there. Jack suspected he was responsible for the *Superman*-theme music. He was also suspiciously close to Amber in IT, which would explain the screensavers. So rather than simply transfer the call, Shane rose from his desk to his full height, obviously to get a better view of the fallout. He barked into the PA, "There's a call for you, Detective Mitchell, on line two. A Mr Will Blaikie. He wouldn't say what it was in regards to, but he may need you to come running."

A pin could be heard dropping in the room of twenty-odd, usually boisterous, police officers. You could also safely say that close to half of those present were vulnerable to whiplash, given the speed with which their heads turned to Jack. Shaking his head, Jack reached for the phone, mumbling something about funny arseholes.

"Detective Mitchell here," Jack spoke, determined to be nice and professional.

"Ah, hi, Jack, this is Will Blaikie. I'm sorry to bother you, but I wondered if I could speak to you?" There was a trace of hesitation in Will's voice, almost as if he wasn't quite sure if he should be bothering Jack. Well, they had told him, no matter how trivial he thought something, he should give them a call, so...

"No trouble, Will, what can I do for you?" At the sound of a snigger, Jack looked around to find his fellow officers still staring, apparently having nothing better to do. "Could you excuse me for a minute please, Will?" He didn't wait for a reply before standing and—covering the mouthpiece of the phone—yelled, "Alright arseholes, I'm sure you all have more important things to do. Crimes to solve, bad guys to arrest, for example."

This was met with a room full of people shaking their heads and several replies of "No" or "Not at all." Not one soul in the office moved. *Jesus, where was the fucking respect?*

Rolling his eyes, Jack turned his attention back to the phone call. "Sorry, Will, go on."

"Well, it's just that I got a letter today and it...on the back of the envelope it has the sender as Russell Coburn. It's happened before over the years, and I know he's dead and there are plenty of sickos out there, but with what's been happening, I just thought, well, maybe I should..." Will trailed off, no doubt waiting for some sort of reply from Jack. When no response was forthcoming, Will tentatively went on. "Jack, are you there?" Jack's silence seemed to have weakened Will's resolve. As though the silence confirmed that he shouldn't have bothered Jack.

"Will, listen, put the letter down and stay there. I'm on my way." Jack slammed the phone down and reached for his jacket. Across from him, Kate also stood. Catching Jack's gaze, she grabbed her stuff. A cacophony of wolf whistles and catcalls followed them to the door. Kate didn't join in—she knew the look in Jack's eyes.

Speeding along towards Will's place, Jack was agitated, and from the looks of Kate, she was too. Jack had filled Kate in on what was going on, and she was equally concerned. Maybe it was nothing, but a good cop always listened to their gut. This could be it. This could be contact with their killer. This could also be very bad news for Will.

"I'm worried for him, Jack. I think we should insist on protection, especially if this letter is legit. He's quite a big guy but timid, you know?" Kate wasn't telling Jack anything he didn't already know.

"We can't force him, Kate, but we can damn well try to be more persuasive." *Or we could just tie him up and drag him somewhere safe.* Now there was a thought.

After pulling up in front of Will's, Kate barely had the engine stopped before they both jumped out of the car, all but running to the gate. They hadn't even pressed the button when the gate started opening. Walking up the path past the hedge barrier, Jack glimpsed Will's home clearly for the first time. It was more a cottage than a house. Painted a light cream with white trim, it was well maintained. It was only a small cottage, the block it sat on more lawn and garden than house. It was unusual for the northern Sydney suburbs where more and more oversized minimansions were squeezed onto tiny blocks—your nearest neighbour almost within touching distance of your outstretched arm. Jack could see Will holding the front door open for him and Kate to enter. He was pale and those gorgeous dark-chocolate eyes were wide and staring directly at Jack. Kate walked slowly up the stairs—as though she was afraid she may startle Will. She lightly squeezed his shoulder in support as she passed.

Jack followed, stopping in front of Will, finding and holding those eyes with his own. "It's okay, Will. Come on, let's look at this letter." A slight nod was the only reply he got.

After closing and locking the door, Will brushed past the two officers and motioned for them to follow him into the cosiest living room Jack had ever seen. He wasn't one for home decorating, but this room was warm and instantly made him feel comfortable and safe. One entire wall was lined floor to ceiling with shelves that were overfilled with books of all kinds. Also on the shelves were some collectors' items: a Han Solo figurine and several *Walking Dead* bobbleheads. And mounted on one of the shelves was a dagger Jack thought looked similar to Sting from the *Lord of the Rings* movies. The wall opposite was almost entirely a window, giving a spectacular view of the little garden and grounds outside. The wall in front of them had a fireplace that was more than just decoration—in fact, it looked well used. Two comfortable armchairs with a couch between them faced the fire.

Will indicated for them to take a seat and then reached down to pick up the innocuous-looking envelope resting on the coffee table. Before he could grab it, Jack interrupted him. "Will, don't touch it," he cautioned, removing gloves from his coat pocket. He pulled them on and then walked to where Will was standing, seemingly frozen in the act of picking up the letter. "Sorry, I just don't want anyone to touch it now without gloves."

"Of course, sorry." Will crumpled into the armchair closest to him.

Jack carefully opened the sealed envelope and pulled the contents from it. There were two printed photos and what looked to be a sheet of paper with writing on it. After a quick glance at the photos, Jack placed them face down on the coffee table, feeling there was no need for Will to see them. Jack could feel the bile rolling through his stomach. He didn't even need to read the accompanying letter to know that it was unquestionably from the killer. The photos were enough. Jack glanced at Kate before opening the sheet of paper. The handwriting was elaborate, fancy, and even romantic. It was, in truth, a love letter of sorts to Will. Jack read it through before glancing again at Kate. She got his message.

"Ah, Will, I could do with a nice cuppa if that's not too much trouble. And Jack here...well, let's just say things turn ugly if he goes too long without his tea. Do you mind popping the kettle on?"

One look at Will showed Jack he wasn't fooled for a minute, though he calmly stood, nodding his head as he withdrew from the room. Jack immediately picked up the photos and showed Kate whose soft "*Oh, fuck*" Jack barely heard. She reached for gloves of her own and took the letter from Jack. After no more than thirty seconds, she folded it and placed it back in the envelope where Jack had put the photos. Kate leaned closer to Jack and whispered, "Jesus, Jack, he's in real trouble here. We have to get him protection."

The letter lovingly declared the killer's intention to return Will to where he belonged. It had been sent to the PO Box, so presumably, he didn't know where Will actually lived...yet.

"Yeah...yeah I know. Fuck." Jack didn't deal well with frustration or helplessness, and he had been feeling a good deal of both lately. It was too much, and he needed to take back some control of this case. Photos of the two victims, post mortem, sent to Will, plus the letter. It was clear now that Will was in trouble.

He could hear Will moving about in the kitchen, and his frustration rapidly boiled over into anger. Will didn't deserve this shit; he had survived one madman and now another was coming after him, but Jack was for damn sure not going to let that happen. He stormed into the kitchen, grabbing Will's arm as he was reaching for God knows what in the pantry, and whirled him around until they faced each other almost nose to nose.

"Listen, Will, I know what you said about protection and all that shit, but you are damn well going to take it. I don't—"

"Okay." The soft reply was practically just a puff of air onto Jack's chin. Jack stared into those eyes, fear staring back at him, and he knew Will meant it. He would take their offer of protection this time.

"Damn right, okay." Jack's reply was gruff.

"I can't go through that again, Jack. I just can't." Will was visibly shaking now but took a moment to gather his courage before addressing Jack again. "Could I ask one thing though? Can it be here? I feel safest here, and well, there's Henley to consider, and he's a bit fussy and demanding, and I just don't think he would manage if I left, so I would have to bring him too, and he's um... He's not the best house guest, you know. He's grumpy and smelly and still chews just about anything he can find, so..." God, Jack thought it was adorable when Will rambled. Most of the time he was quiet, saying only the few essential words required, but every now and then words seemed to tumble out of him, almost as though he couldn't turn off the tap from his thoughts to his words. And then they flowed out of his mouth without a great deal of thought behind them, his gorgeous eyes appearing to grow wider the further he got into his ramble as if he was astonished by his own ability to put a few sentences together. Jack loved it.

"I am assuming this Henley is some sort of animal?"

"Yeah, my dog. He just lost his brother, Don, a few weeks ago." Jack raised his eyebrows at this. "Yep, Don Henley, I'm a fan. Anyway he's pretty down about it, so I'd prefer to stay here if possible."

"I tell you what, Will, we'll speak to the boss and see what we can come up with, okay?" Will's lips curled into a hint of a smile at this, and his shoulders seemed to relax.

"Jesus, oh fuck, what the hell is that? Oh my fucking God, what is that?" Kate cried from the other room. Jack took off at a run but could hear Will's laughter behind him. He entered the room where Kate stood with her hands covering her mouth and nose, tears streaming down her face. It took no more than a second for it to hit him. The smell was unlike anything he had smelt before; it brought tears to his eyes, and he was pretty sure he might have thrown up a little in his mouth. As a homicide detective he had encountered his share of dead bodies but fortunately he usually had his little bottle of miracle Vicks to help counter the odour. Now though, his nostrils were on their own, and it was not good.

Will entered the room, still laughing, and gestured behind one of the armchairs. Jack could see something brown and furry poking out beside the chair. "That is Henley. I told you he was smelly. Poor old man, aren't you?" He crooned as he knelt down to actually touch what surely had to be the rotting remains of Henley. Nothing living could smell that rank. Henley made a soft wuff in reply to Will, his tail thudding on the floor. "Sorry, he's old and a bit flatulent. He can't help it though, can you, old man? No, he can't." Will was occupied talking to the dog now, so Jack indicated the door to the kitchen and followed Kate out. They were both taking huge gasps of clean air as they fled into the kitchen.

"Christ, I didn't even hear the dog come in. Talk about a stealth weapon."

Jack sniggered and began to explain to Kate what had been discussed between him and Will. He could tell Kate was pleased, and she left, throwing a goodbye over her shoulder to Will and grabbing the envelope on the way out. Jack had agreed to stay with Will while she left to go talk to Pete about the protection.

Jack found Will still kneeling on the floor beside Henley, and he knelt beside him, keen to get a better look at the source of that amazingly unpleasant smell. A large German shepherd mix lay still in front of them, and for a moment, Jack wondered if the dog was actually dead after all. Twitching ears and soft wuffling disproved that theory. Will turned to him, still lightly stroking the dog's flanks. "So, what now?"

"Well, Kate has gone to speak to our boss about protection while I stay here...protecting you. We'll have to wait to see what happens, but I promise you won't be alone for now."

WILL STUDIED JACK for a short time before rising to his feet and holding his hand out to help Jack do the same. Jack glanced between the hand and Will's face before taking the assistance.

"How about I finish that tea, Jack. I know I could do with one about now."

"Sure that would be great, thanks." They looked at each other for a moment before Will turned away towards the kitchen.

The scary truth was Will found it intense to be around Jack, and he would have chosen something a little stronger than tea if he had anything in his cupboards. Will's experience with men was exactly one kiss with Mark Sutcliffe behind the school hall in grade twelve. It had been awkward and clumsy, as first kisses often were, and neither of them had ever mentioned it again. Will's experience with women was exactly zero, and he intended to keep it that way. He had nothing against them—they just didn't do anything for him. He didn't believe in love at first sight, but he believed in lust at first sight, chiefly now that he had experienced it with Jack Mitchell. Well, technically it had been lust at second sight—his first view of Jack had been through the grainy image from his security camera, and it had not done justice to Jack's hotness.

At the police station where he had met Jack face-to-face, Will had channelled Garth, best friend of Wayne from *Wayne's World*. His vision ambled in slow motion every time he watched Jack move, but rather than hearing "Dreamweaver" in his head, he heard Ginuwine's "Pony." Christ, the way Jack rolled his hips when he walked—no, swaggered—had Will's mouth watering. Will wasn't quite sure what it watered for, perhaps a taste of Detective Mitchell, but damn, he just found the man hot as fuck. Will laughed at himself as he finished making the tea. He had never thought of anyone as hot as fuck; in fact, he was pretty sure he had never put those three words together in a sentence before. Meeting Jack Mitchell was either going to be a huge disaster for Will personally, or quite possibly, it would be the greatest adventure he'd ever been on.

Will hadn't been able to get the tall, muscular detective, with the hint of ginger in his neatly trimmed beard, out of his mind. Jack had a body to die for, as the saying goes. He had broad shoulders, a trim waist, and long, long legs. Jack was the type of man whom everyone—gay, straight, bi—would appreciate for his beauty, and many of them would fight to get him into their beds. Perhaps if Will were a little more assertive he would try to land Jack for himself. But Will was happy to content himself with just looking.

With the tea made, Will prepared to go back into the living room where he knew Jack waited. He marvelled at his ability to even think about such things, given the dangerous situation he now found himself in, but the mind had an amazing ability to protect itself. It didn't hurt that he was feeling such a strong attraction to someone, which was a novelty for Will, and for once, he just wanted to be normal and enjoy it.

JACK SETTLED INTO one of the armchairs—not the one harbouring the odious Henley—and stared into the fireplace while he waited. He couldn't help but think how cosy it would be curled up with a book, a steaming cup of tea, and maybe even a special someone's head in his lap as they lazed on the couch together in front of the fire. Filling the last hours of the day reading, sharing heartbreakingly intimate quiet times with someone you loved, before turning in for the night with some slow and gentle lovemaking. *Oh Christ, you're such a sap, Mitchell.* He didn't care though; it sounded too damn good for him to worry about seeming like a sap. He'd never thought about long-term before, never considered having it all, never wanting it all. Of course, if he was truly honest with himself, that wasn't strictly true; he had just never allowed himself to think about it. He was a worker; he had his job—his very important job—so having that long-term happily ever after just wasn't in the cards for him. But God, it sounded good and sometimes he wanted it—coveted it even.

"Here you go, Jack," Will said, holding a steaming mug of tea out to Jack.

"Hmm, Earl Grey?" Jack questioned upon sniffing the mug's contents. Will smirked and gave a small nod in confirmation.

"One of my favourites, though a good green tea with jasmine is particularly calming," Jack ventured, conversationally. Jack was often lost in the fine art of small talk, but he figured tea was a fairly safe topic.

Will looked up from his own mug. "That's my favourite, though I don't drink it much. It tends to bring on a migraine."

"Oh I didn't know you suffered with them. Are they frequent? I've never had one, but I hear they are painful."

"Pain's a funny thing, Jack. Migraines hurt, sure; but there are worse pains, and you know it's going to pass; it's nature isn't it? You know it's a physical pain your body can't help. It's not meaning to hurt you. There are other pains that may not hurt as much physically, but are far harder to bear."

Jack figured that Will knew all about pain. And right then he looked to be in a bit of it, pain of the uncomfortably embarrassed kind.

"I'm sorry, um, I got carried away. So in, ah...in short, the migraines are manageable."

Jack sipped at his tea, back to being at a loss for words. He sure as hell didn't want to make Will uncomfortable. So perhaps tea wasn't such a safe topic. Perhaps a broad topic where Will could choose a safe path. "So tell me a little about yourself, Will. Tell me about what you do. I mean I know you work, right?"

"Yes I do, actually. I...after what happened, I had some problems going out in public and dealing with people, so I had to find something to do where I didn't have to...go out I mean. Or actually deal with people, so I became a proofreader. I work from home and get to read lots of different things. I love to read—just in case you hadn't noticed, Detective." He gestured to the shelves filled with books. "I was about halfway through an ancient history course when I was...when I was taken. I had planned to be an historian, specifically on ancient Rome. But after...well, I haven't managed to get back to that yet."

God, Jack admired Will. There was not a trace of bitterness in his voice when he spoke about how his life had been so dramatically changed because of the actions of another; it was simply a matter of Will accepting this had happened to him, and so his life had to be this way now. Will Blaikie was a fighter, a survivor.

"Did you always want to be an historian?"

"No, actually when I was little I wanted to be a cop or a journalist. With maturity, I realised I didn't have the personality for either of those, but I loved reading, and I loved history so...ta-da, historian." Will's accompanying grin came out as more of a grimace, and Jack suspected, like much of his past, his failed aspiration was still a painful topic.

Two hours later, Will had regaled Jack with what he apologised for as "all the tediousness of my job," and he had given Jack a tour of his bookshelves. They shared some common literary tastes though Jack couldn't quite wrap his head around Will's interest in romance novels. Will had explained that he used books as an escape, to live the lives that he never would in the real world. Jack had laughed and said he knew he did a similar thing when he picked up a Matthew Reilly or a Lee Child book, because honestly, it was not plausible he would ever end up saving the president of the United States or fighting off killer whales.

Henley had been sleeping quietly and harmlessly all that time, but now both men were treated to another release of his noxious gas. Henley poked his head out in the aftermath with what Jack swore was a grin on his face. Jack held his breath and fled the room, Will following him into the kitchen.

"You get used to it, Jack," Will said, when he caught up to Jack, who had his face pressed to the open kitchen window, clearly trying to breathe in as much fresh air as he could.

"How could you get used to that? I think he's in there laughing his arse off at the poor humans right now," Jack replied.

Will laughed, a genuine sound, and Jack couldn't help but think it had been an oddly pleasant afternoon, foul smells notwithstanding.

They had yet to hear from Kate, but just as Jack said he'd give her a call and reached for his phone, they heard the telltale buzz of the intercom. Glancing up at the monitor, Jack could see Kate's face, her watchful eyes scanning the area. Will pressed the button to open the gate, and they sat there silently waiting for whatever news she would bring. Moments later, Kate walked into the room giving Will a smile, Jack an eye roll, and something between a glare and a look of fear to Henley who regarded her with absolutely no interest at all before thumping his head back onto the floor. She held a bag in her hands.

"Is that my go bag?" Jack asked, incredulously.

"Well, I've got good news and bad news. Pete has okayed protection, but the department won't fork out for twenty-four-hour protection, so... Pete and I figured that you could do the nights, Jack, to save on the cost."

"What the fuck? Why me? Did Shane put you up to this? Are you all laughing at me?" Jack rambled out question after question. He could see Will was standing, a deer caught in headlights, his eyes darting between Jack and Kate in apparent disbelief. How could this be happening? He couldn't be in the company of Will Blaikie every night and survive it, could he? Will was a quiet and cautious person, but Jack was...well, he wasn't, and Will was so damn hot. Will was offering a few stuttered attempts at a refusal before Kate interrupted both he and Jack.

"It makes sense, Will. We can pay for an officer to be here during the day, but Jack can stay here at night. He has no family or social life to speak of, so it's no inconvenience to him, and that way you have twenty-four-hour protection at half the cost. I took the liberty of bringing Jack's bag for him, so he's all set for the night." Kate kept her face turned from Jack's, aware of and no doubt a little frightened of, the look she knew she would get. Jack couldn't stop thinking about the time he and Will would be spending together. What would they talk about? What would they do? What if he made a colossal fool of himself? Would he get to see Will shirtless? Jesus, for the foreseeable future, Jack and Will would be spending their nights together, and the thought of it both terrified and thrilled Jack.

FIVE

THEIR FIRST WEEK together progressed better, no doubt, than both men had expected. They seemed to enjoy each other's company and liked to spend their time together either quietly reading or having casual yet often intimate conversations over a pot of tea in the living room. It was just as Jack had imagined it that first day he came to Will's house and looked around the cosy living area, but without the lovemaking.

Will was entering the room with a pot now. Jack put down his latest Jack Reacher, curled his legs under himself, surprisingly, looking forward to one of those chats.

"First day on the job?" Will had a rather odd conversation style, randomly throwing questions at Jack almost game-show style. The first time he had done it, he had surprised Jack by looking up from his book and asking, "Fictional characters you have fallen in love with?" It had taken a moment for Jack to realise, firstly, Will was asking him a question, and secondly, he had indeed fallen in love with some fictional characters. At six foot five with a take-no-shit attitude, who could resist falling for Jack Reacher, though that little fantasy had been ruined by the Tom Cruise movie fiasco, and of course, then there was Iron Man, though that was more hero worship, and then there was Lara Croft, who was kick-ass, and of course, Aragon with that damn smoking-hot beard, not to mention the way he wielded a sword. Yes, once he had got going, his list of fictional infatuations was long and varied and, according to Will, made him "a very fickle man indeed." Jack reached over to pick up the mug of tea—chamomile with honey and lemon that Will had just poured for him—and considered his answer. Will asked him a lot about his job, but Jack tended to censor his answers. Will had seen evil and horror up close; he didn't need to hear about any more of it.

"Well, it's certainly not the oddest thing I have seen on the job, but for a first day, it kinda made me wonder what I was getting myself into." He took a quick sip of his tea. "I was walking the beat with my partner, a very surly and surprisingly uncomplicated man by the name of Ted.

We were patrolling around St. Mary's Cathedral in Hyde Park. There were hundreds of police from all over Sydney out that day; the pope was due in Sydney the following day, and we were doing the rounds, checking for any sign of trouble.

"It was early evening, just on dusk, and we came across this man bent over in the gardens of the church. So we approached him to see what he was up to. He jerked when we announced ourselves and stood with a guilty look on his face." He chuckled a little at the memory. "So we asked him what he was up to, and he hemmed and hawed. He seemed guilty of something, so my partner asked him to empty his pockets. Slowly, you know, just in case. Anyway, we're standing there, and I'm thinking that it's the first day on the job, and we were going to stop some arsehole from assassinating the pope, and I was going to be a big hero. We even had our hands hovering over our guns, ready to draw, sure he was going to pull some sort of weapon from his pocket. Next minute all these bits of plants and bulbs and dirt fell to the ground, and as we were looking at the mess on the ground a boiled egg landed with a thud on top. The three of us just looked up at each other, not quite sure what to say. Turned out he was just some eccentric plant lover out stealing from the church gardens, with a boiled egg in his pocket, I guess in case the hard work of theft made him hungry." Jack smiled fondly again at the memory. At the time, his disappointment had quickly turned to relief that it hadn't been something more serious.

Across from him, Will gave a little snigger before turning sad eyes on Jack. "My brother loved plants. When we were younger, he often took me walking at night to be lookout for his own petty theft of plants from our neighbours' gardens, especially old Mr Pratt's. God, he hated the Blaikie boys. You'd think we killed his cat, not swiped a few cuttings." Jack remained silent, hoping to encourage Will to continue talking about this brother Jack was aware of but knew nothing about.

Will didn't talk much at all about his past or family. Jack knew that, much like him, Will didn't have a lot of family. His mother had passed away a few years ago, and from what he could gather, his father had never been in the picture. But every so often, as though he had dropped the wall he'd built around himself, he would surprise Jack with a peek into his private world. Jack loved those moments; they felt special, made him feel proud that Will had trusted him with a little bit of himself. It had happened a few times over the last couple of days, and Jack could see the surprise that flashed over Will's face every time, as though he couldn't believe a couple of bricks had been knocked out of his keep wall. That surprise was there now, but Jack didn't want him to clam up this time, so he decided to push for more.

"What's he like?" he asked gently. "Your brother. What's he like?" he repeated when Will remained silent.

"Sean..." Will's reply was little more than a whisper. "He was, or I should say is, a couple of years older than me. He was...he is a great brother. I remember one Boxing Day we went over to Manly on the ferry with Mum to see some friends of hers, and there had been a summer storm the night before. When we got out to the Heads, the waves were enormous, and the ferry was bobbing around like a cork in the water." Will's face lit up as he continued with his story. "I would have been about seven, so Sean would have been nine. Everyone on the ferry was green, some were vomiting, and one old lady was saying the Lord's Prayer over and over. But Sean was up the front of the ferry hooting and hollering like he was on the best ride in the world. That's how he is...fearless and happy. At least he used to be... I haven't seen him in a couple of years. He lives somewhere overseas, Scotland somewhere I think. It's hard to keep up actually; he moves around a lot. I'm not really sure what he's like now."

Jack easily picked up on the trace of sadness and maybe shame in Will's tone and was curious what had happened between the brothers. He hesitated, unsure whether to push for answers or leave it for another time. Before he could decide, Will answered for him.

"We don't speak much. He blamed himself for what happened to me. I was only nineteen when I was taken, and it's stupid, but he was the older brother, so he thought he should have protected me. Anyway, he's so riddled with guilt he can't even look at me; my presence makes him uncomfortable, or so my therapist says. So he stays away, and we barely speak." Surely Will didn't blame himself for the brothers' falling out. Was that the reason for the hint of shame Jack had noticed a moment ago?

They fell into a thoughtful silence, Jack pondering the unfairness of Sean not manning up to be there for his little brother and his own oddly angry reaction to the situation. Will was probably wondering how more personal information kept falling out of his mouth. Breaking the strange mood in the room, Will stood and tidied the tea things up.

Turning on his way out the door, Will quietly spoke, as though reading Jack's thoughts. "Shitty things happen, Jack. My grandma used to say if you're sitting at a table with others, and you all put your troubles in the middle to exchange, you'll always want to pull your own back out. Life's not fair, Jack, so don't worry about me. I have learnt that lesson." Will's smile was anything but happy; it was sad and resigned, and Jack wanted nothing more than to see a genuinely happy smile on that man's face, and even more *he* wanted to be the one who put it there.

MORE OFTEN THAN not, when he and Jack were talking, Will was left profoundly shocked by what came out of his mouth. Notoriously shy all of his life, he had never felt this kind of ease around another person, and he was greedy for more of it. Usually when Will had to deal with people, he found it exhausting. There was the constant fear he was making a fool of himself: never knowing what to say or how to act. Most of the time, it just didn't seem worth the trouble. His mother had always told him he would grow out of his shyness, but he suspected his experience at the hands of Russell Coburn may have derailed that. People made him even more nervous now than in his youth.

It was different with Jack; his shyness was pushed down and out of the way, allowing him, for the first time ever, to actually show himself to another person. The freedom to be himself made it an exhilarating experience to be in Jack's company. It was easy and effortless spending time with Jack, not to mention Jack was, without question, the hottest man Will had ever known.

Will had begun his fascinated cataloguing of Jack's body the first night Jack had stayed over. Will had watched him intently, while he selected a book from Will's collection, acutely interested in what he would pick. It wasn't until Jack had picked up the third book that Will had noticed his large, masculine hands. As if the hands weren't enough, Will had later noticed the perfect half-moons on the nail beds. Never before had Will actually noticed anyone's half-moons, but he found himself strangely fascinated with Jack's. What kind of desperation had him noticing tiny markings on another man's fingernails?

The following day he worked his way up to what he—at the time—had thought to be the absolute sexiest thing about Jack: his arms. Will had never considered himself an arm man—not that he had any experience with men—but he always stuck with the more obvious...a nice arse, or in his less-shallow moments, a beautiful smile to look at. Over the last few days though, Will found he couldn't take his eyes off Jack's arms. Whenever Jack was in a T-shirt, or better still, the singlet he wore to bed, Will almost always swallowed his tongue. He didn't think he would ever tire of the arm porn he was treated to whenever he caught Jack doing his push-ups or sit-ups.

Yesterday, Will's interest had moved up to his current preoccupation, which was with Jack's amazingly broad shoulders. They left Will wondering if Jack had been a swimmer to develop shoulders like that.

Whenever he could muster the courage though, he found himself pleasantly fixated on Jack's eyes. They were brown like Will's but far lighter. The colour reminded Will of the caramel filling in Caramello Koalas. They were stunningly beautiful, and Will knew if he ever had the audacity, or the chance, he would happily stare into them for hours.

It was late, and Will should let Jack get to bed, but as was becoming more frequent, he didn't want his time with Jack to end. He left the dirty crockery in the sink and went back into the living room, again squeezing into the small space Henley had left for him on the couch. "Why police?" he asked, looking up into those eyes.

Jack remained silent so long Will wondered if he was going to answer at all. Eventually, Jack's soft voice broke the silence.

"I just knew it's what I should do. At school, I was always getting in fights with the bullies. I wasn't the biggest kid, but I was fearless or maybe just stupid. If someone was being bullied, I'd step in, usually fists first. My dad was always being called into the principal's office for my fighting, but I never told them anything about why I was fighting. One day Dad got so mad at me, he told me he didn't want a thug for a son, and he was so disappointed in me. That night I told him why I was fighting. He never said a word, just nodded and got on with whatever he was doing. Next time he got called into the principal's office, my dad tore the principal a new one, told him he should be thanking me for protecting the kids where the adults were failing to and told him if I got detention again, when the bullies didn't, he'd be going to the education department so fast it'd make the man's head spin. Dad stood there in that principal's office and told me he was so damn proud of me he thought he may just burst." Jack's eyes were closed as if watching these events replay behind his closed lids, the hint of a smile on his face. "The principal was left floundering; Dad had a way about him for sure. He told me that night to never change, and he quoted Winston Churchill to me...you know the one about evil prevailing when good men do nothing. I guess I've kind of lived by that ever since. Law enforcement was a natural choice."

"I bet your dad is very proud of you."

"He was, yeah. He died a few years ago. He was a truck driver and fell asleep at the wheel."

"I'm so sorry, Jack." Will leant over and laid his hands on Jack's in comfort, the lump in his throat choking off further reply.

"Thank you. Fortunately no one else was involved; Dad would have hated that. He was a good man."

"So is his son," Will said softly, afraid of how his compliment would be received. He never gave compliments, aside from the obligatory social niceties he had taught himself to utter as a teenager, because he never had the courage to give overt, optional compliments. Jack raised his eyes to meet Will's, and as they sat looking at each other, it felt as though they were looking into the very soul of the other, and it wasn't long before Will started shifting uncomfortably. This closeness with another person was new for Will, and as comfortable as Jack made him feel, the intimacy of holding eye contact for any length of time was still challenging for him.

An ill-timed passing of gas from Henley broke the spell and sent the two men fleeing to the kitchen for fresh air, their laughter echoing through the house.

When the laughter died, awkwardness seemed to fill the space around them. As much as Will didn't want to leave Jack's company, he didn't have the wherewithal to manage the unease he felt. Flight had always worked well for him, so with a hasty good night, he retreated to his bedroom. What did Jack make of his behaviour? Many people simply didn't understand those who had trouble in social situations, often thinking of them as snobs, when in reality nothing could be further from the truth. Will was usually quiet or fled because he simply didn't know how to handle the situation, and flight seemed the best choice.

Safely in his room, he settled under the covers of his bed, hoping sleep would come quickly, though he suspected not. The conflicting emotions that had been churning through Will since news of the copycat and the arrival of Jack Mitchell on his doorstep made getting a sound night's sleep increasingly challenging.

SEVERAL HOURS LATER, Jack sat in the dark, steaming tea in hand, listening to the sounds of the night. He could hear the tiny insects that came out in the safety of nighttime, and he could hear the occasional car driving by. The only other sound seemed to be the growling snores of Henley and the thump of Jack's own heart. Will had gone to bed hours ago, but as Jack had crept past his closed door, he could see a sliver of light underneath it. He wondered if Will was still up or if he left the light on for comfort and a sense of safety. He was tempted to knock and offer the other man a cup of tea but thought better of it. If Will was finally getting some peaceful sleep, he didn't want to disturb him. He heard him most nights pottering around his room well into the early hours of the morning, or worse, he heard the tormented screams from the occasional nightmares that sometimes haunted Will's sleep.

With the moon so bright tonight, he could see the grounds clearly out of the window facing him. It was bright enough he would spot an intruder walking around the house. Will's gardens were indeed lovely. In fact the more Jack saw of Will's house, and the more he got to know the man himself, the more impressed he was. He thought back over the last few evenings they had spent together, and it dawned on him that he had not had such a good time in someone else's company in a long time. They were similar in some ways and so very different in others.

Jack didn't have time for many people, and he had few friends, but he enjoyed being around Will. Behind the quiet nature was a wicked sense of humour and a remarkably resilient man. Jack admired him a great deal. He was still suffering from what he'd endured, but he didn't complain. He didn't use his suffering to excuse a bitter attitude or allow himself to fall to pieces. He was a decent man doing the best he could with what life had given him, and that impressed Jack.

Henley lifted his head slightly, giving a soft wuff before lying back down. Jack didn't need to turn to know that Will was up; his soft "It's okay, boy" to Henley gave his presence away. After receiving no acknowledgement, Jack figured Will was unaware of him sitting there, curled up as he was in the giant armchair facing the window. Staying in his place, he finished sipping his tea. He could hear Will softly moving about the house somewhere and thought he would ask if he wanted a tea, perhaps it would help him sleep. Moving quietly through the house, he headed in the direction he thought the soft sounds Will had made came from. The laundry, he thought. He turned on no lights, the moonlight adequately lighting his way. Rounding the corner into the laundry room, Jack immediately froze when he caught sight of Will.

Will had his back to the door, the washing machine lid was hanging open, and he was lifting his T-shirt over his head. After tossing the shirt in the machine, his hands went to the waistband of his sweatpants, tugging them down before stepping out of them. Then he crouched to pick them up and tossed them in the machine too, leaving Will in nothing but a pair of tight boxer briefs. Jack couldn't tear his eyes from the sight before him, though he knew he should. The moonlight cast Will's near-naked body in a shadowy, silvery glow that highlighted the scars crisscrossing Will's back, and Jack knew he had never seen anything more beautiful than the man standing before him. Will took his breath away.

Jack itched to reach out and stroke his hands all over the lithe body, tracing each and every scar. He closed his eyes, desperately trying to manage some control before he crossed a line he knew he shouldn't. He wanted to cross it though. Hell, he wanted to leap right over it, to touch, to lick, to kiss, anything Will allowed. When Jack opened his eyes again, Will was stretching his body, his long arms reaching toward the ceiling, legs stretched up on tiptoes. All the muscles of his body were pulled taut, defining each muscle in an erotic display for Jack's eyes only. He wanted to feel that tight body under him, to run his hands up his strong back and down his well-defined arms, feel the muscles bunch under his fingertips. And damn, Will's arse was perfect—tight and high above his thickly muscled legs. Will was not a huge man, but at around six feet and in excellent shape, he was a powerful-looking man, and he was turning Jack's shit on. Backing away before Will noticed him and sent their relationship to a whole new level of awkwardness, Jack knew he was in trouble. He wanted too much; he wanted what was not his to have. Tomorrow he would see about getting someone else in; it was time to put some distance between himself and Will Blaikie.

SIX

THE NEXT DAY Jack left extra early to go home and shower before heading into work. He had told Will he needed to go home to see to a few things and would shower there. Then he had practically run from the house as soon as his replacement arrived, leaving a startled Will in his wake. The truth was he had gone home to jerk off. After lying awake, half-hard, most of the night, unable to rid his mind of the image of a gloriously, almost-naked Will, he had desperately needed to take matters in hand, literally. He felt guilty enough that he had watched Will during the night; he sure as hell wasn't going to make matters worse by pleasuring himself to thoughts of him in Will's own home. When he stepped into his shower, it had taken just a handful of strokes before he found his release—he had been that damn turned on.

By the time he walked into Pete's office an hour later, he was already feeling antsy again. Apparently one handjob was not enough to slake the lust he was feeling for Will. He needed distance and maybe a good fuck to get his mind off Will. A night or two away would surely calm him the fuck down before he went right ahead and did something stupid. Something along the lines of pushing Will up against a wall, his hands wandering all over that gorgeous body, finally tasting... Christ, this was so not helping, and now he was painfully aware of the hard-on he was sporting in his boss's office. Thankfully, Pete was still on the phone, his back turned to Jack. Jack pushed the heel of his palm to his erection, willing it to subside before Pete turned and was confronted with more of Jack than he would ever want to encounter. Jack was so focused on Aunt Serena and the disturbingly long hairs that sprouted from her chin, in his attempt to get rid of his ill-timed erection, he didn't hear Kate enter the room.

"Morning, Jack. How goes the babysitting?" Slapping his arm, Kate took the seat next to him.

"Fine, fine, though I thought I would like to have a few nights off, if we can organise someone else. I need to go home, get a few things done, and have a break. Sure, Will's a nice guy, but I'm not used to living with someone and am starting to feel a bit closed in. Need to get out and about, see some people, relax, you know." *Oh for God's sake, shut up.* He mentally slapped his own forehead. Jack was rambling and rambling was never good—it was always a giveaway. Jack could tell by Kate's expression she was on to his shit.

Leaning in to Jack, she whispered, "Starting to feel closed in or starting to feel?"

Jack fumbled for a reply, managing only to splutter a few ums and ahs as an answer. He was saved from further humiliation by the low rumble of Pete, finally off the phone and calling for their attention. He did not have good news.

"It looks like he may have taken another man. A Stuart Bates has been reported missing this morning. His father called it in. Apparently Stuart went out with friends last night, somehow got separated from them, and has not returned home. His father says this is out of character, and he was in the area the other men have gone missing from." Pete shook his head, clenched his fists, and carried on. Jack knew the signs of frustration well. "I want you to head over there and talk to family, the friends he was with last night, and everyone you can find. I know this is technically not even a missing person case right now, but it could just be one of our copycat's, and I don't want to waste any time if it is."

Kate grabbed for paper and pen and jotted down the address of Stuart Bates's parents, and together she and Jack walked to their car. As always, Kate drove, allowing Jack to jot down some ideas in his notebook. They both knew this could be nothing, a miscommunication or misunderstanding, but they also both knew this could be something far more sinister. Usually Jack spoke to families after they had received the worst of all possible news about their loved ones, or even worse, he had to deliver that most devastating news to families, so he was uneasy about how to deal with Stuart Bates's family. He knew enough not to make promises he couldn't keep, grand statements that he would get Stuart back alive, but nor could he remove hope altogether. It was a fine line to tread, and not for the first time, he was glad to have his more socially capable partner along for the ride. He was also selfishly grateful that this news seemed to have drawn Kate's interest from his relationship with Will. *Will.* Damn it, Jack had forgotten to speak to Pete about a replacement for tonight. Surely Pete would organise something, especially if Jack was going to be working his arse off tracking down Stuart Bates.

It turned out that Roger Bates was a first-class, homophobic prick. From the moment they set foot inside his home—or as Jack thought of it, his enormous, cold, 'look how much money and stuff we have' display piece—Roger had regaled them with his theory that his son would be home safe and sound if not for his 'lifestyle'—the *disgusting* was implied. Roger Bates was undoubtedly used to intimidating people into agreeing with him. He was a large man, whose cheeks were turning redder and redder as the conversation progressed. He was all bluff and blather—a bully, nothing more, and Jack knew how to handle bullies.

Mrs Fiona Bates sat quietly at her husband's side, neither condemning nor defending her son. Where her husband was large and blustery, Fiona Bates was small and almost fragile-looking. She kept her eyes down and her mouth closed, and Jack suspected that if he so much as looked at her funny, she may splinter apart. It was clear to Jack that Stuart Bates only remained in the family home because Roger Bates did not want to break his wife's heart even more, or what was more likely, he didn't want to cause a scandal in his picture-perfect world. After yet another outburst about the immorality of his son's sexuality, Jack could bite his tongue no longer.

"Mr Bates, I appreciate the fear and anxiety you must be feeling at the moment with your son's whereabouts unknown, but there is nothing to indicate that this is in any way a hate crime. At this point we're not even sure that it is a crime. Now, perhaps it is fear that is making you say some, let's be honest, pretty derogatory things about your own son, and I am sure that you love him more than anything, so how about we concentrate on getting some facts that may actually help get your son home safe to his mother." Well, who knew he could be so polite while giving a bit of a smackdown to such an arsehole? Pete would be proud; perhaps that sensitivity class he had forced on Jack *was* worth it.

Seemingly unmoved, Roger Bates surged on, though in a calmer tone and with perhaps a hint of shame behind his eyes, but men such as Roger Bates didn't concede easily. "Detective, I'm no fool. I am aware that this could be related to those murders, and I know that those victims were homosexual men also—"

"No, actually not all," interrupted Kate. She glanced at Jack, with pride on her face, and then she sat next to Mrs Bates, taking her hand

and continued on addressing Mrs Bates directly now. "Not all of the men were gay, Mrs Bates. We know one man identified as gay but another man had a girlfriend at the time and no known history of any relationships with men. So while we have certainly considered the hate crime angle, we also consider that it may be something else entirely. But Detective Mitchell is right. The most important thing now is to get some facts, timelines, who he was with, friends' names, etc. Do you think you can help us with that?"

Mrs Bates timidly nodded her head, and from that point on, Mr Bates was effectively neutralised. He spent the rest of the interview alternately glaring at Jack and fussing over his progressively upset wife. By the time they walked back out the door, they had several names and contacts of Stuart's friends.

Once back in the car, Kate called Pete, informing him of their progress and where they would be headed next. Jack listened to her side of the conversation, filling in Pete's replies based on his knowledge of the man. Once her report was finished, it seemed Pete had more to say that Jack couldn't quite figure out. He could hear Kate's 'Yes', 'Sounds good' and 'Yes, I think so', but he couldn't figure what Pete was saying. After hanging up, Kate turned to Jack.

"Well, he's happy with things so far, and we are good to go and talk to whoever we feel we need to. Nothing new has come in about Stuart. Holmes and Kassel are still talking to the venue owners and other staff who were there last night, so we can get on with friends and family. Pete wants us back in the office by seven tonight for a debriefing with the others. He also said he has organised one of the newbies to stay with Will tonight." There was a hint of uncertainty to her tone at the end as though she wasn't quite sure Jack would be happy about not staying with Will. Just what did she think she knew about what was going on anyway?

A feeling of disappointment wound its way through Jack as he realised he wouldn't be seeing Will tonight before he remembered that was exactly what he wanted and what he had been going to ask Pete anyway. Still, he knew he would miss the quiet intimacy they had created between them.

"Should you call him, Jack?"

"What? No. I mean I'm sure Pete will let him know." *Should he call?* Christ, they weren't boyfriends, not even friends. Except maybe they had become friends. He cared about Will, more than most people he had known far longer, but because he did care, he should call. Fuck, this was why he stayed the hell away from relationships—too complicated, too confusing. He was lost, feeling his way in the dark, desperately trying not to trip up and fall flat on his face. "Actually, yeah I should call. That's the right thing to do, hey?" Kate, bless her, didn't mock him or laugh; she just nodded and patted his arm.

Feeling a need for some privacy, he stepped out of the car, palming his phone and calling Will's number. He tapped his other hand against the roof of the car nervously and waited. Will picked up on the fifth ring.

"Hello." God, Jack could listen to that voice all day. And Jesus, would the longing for someone who wasn't his ever end?

"Will, it's Jack. Listen, I just wanted to let you know I won't be there tonight. I'm going to be working late, so Pete has organised another officer to stay." After a few moments of silence from Will, Jack blurted, "Should I have called? I don't really know what..."

"Yes, Jack, you should have called. Thank you, it means a lot. I know you are working, so..." More silence, and then a deep breath in. "I think, well, I think I'll miss you tonight." And didn't that just about bring Jack to his knees. Unexpected, but now that they had been spoken, he realised those words were something he had secretly desired to hear.

"Yeah...yeah me too." Clearing his throat, Jack could think of nothing else to add; he was so out of his depth here.

"I should, um, get back. Officer Moore is currently wiping the floor with me at Monopoly. I think he may want to consider a career change to property tycoon. Take care, Jack—I guess I'll see you when I see you."

It took a moment for Jack to recognise what that pinch in his gut, that flare of anger towards Jim Moore, was. Jack was jealous, damn jealous. He loved his nights he spent with Will, but now it occurred to him most of their time together was spent sleeping—separately. He was aware that the day guys got to spend hours around an awake Will, doing God knows what, but absolutely spending more conscious time with him than Jack did. And just what did they do all day? Holy hell, he was jealous, enough that he was ready to march over there and kick Officer Moore the fuck out, despite the fact that Jim Moore was a fifty-five-year-old, happily married grandfather. *Well this is new.*

"I'll be back as soon as I can." Hell yeah, he would, and he was going to be there during the day if he could manage it. "Take care, Will." He finished off, echoing Will's own advice to him.

Not looking at Kate, he stepped back into the car and buckled up. Apparently she didn't get the memo about not talking about it though, smiling fondly at him as she told him how proud she was of him. He searched for the angle, waited for the joke that was to come at his expense but found none. He wasn't sure whether to be pleased Kate wasn't laughing at his expense or concerned.

The first name on their list was Kyle Sandler. The twenty-year-old student was, according to Mrs Bates, Stuart's best friend. They had gone to high school together and were both now studying engineering at Macquarie University. If anyone knew the things Stuart would keep from his parents, it would be Kyle.

It took less than ten minutes to get to Kyle's family home. Unlike the grandiose McMansion that the Bates occupied, the Sandler family home was a low-set, modest family home. It looked as though Mr Sandler had done his own modifications and extensions to the house. It was a hodgepodge of styles both outside and, as Jack was soon to discover, inside. Where the Bateses would easily be described as snobby, well-to-do elitists, the Sandlers were comfortable, wannabe hippies. Not quite living off the land, holding sit-ins about the state of the environment hippies, but they were what Jack's father would have called *floopy tree-huggers*. Where Roger Bates was a cold bastard who barely tolerated his son, Mr and Mrs Sandler sang Kyle's praises and showered him in love. Jack was amazed at how people could live in such a close geographical area yet seem to come from a different planet across the known universe.

By the red rims and dark circles around his eyes, Jack could tell Kyle Sandler had a sleepless night and likely a tearful morning. He knew that Kyle had been the first to raise the alarm, notifying Stuart's family that they had been separated during the night, and he was worried because this was out of character for Stuart. He sat quietly between his parents, answering questions as they were asked. Desperation and something else Jack couldn't quite peg rolled off him in waves.

"We go out every Wednesday night to the Bull and Bush, ten-dollar-steak night and happy hour till seven." In response to Kate's gentle prodding, Kyle began describing, in considerable detail, the night before with Stuart. "Anyway, it's usually Stuart, Bryce Grantly, Joe Foster, and I every Wednesday. Occasionally, some others from uni join us, but last night it was just us four. We had dinner and the others had a couple of beers. I was driving. It was just a normal night. We played a couple of games of darts and didn't really talk to anyone else except the staff." Kyle's voice was getting progressively quiet as he got towards the end of his story. He was getting choked up and seemed to be stuck for the words to continue his tale.

"Kyle, did anything seem odd up until that point? Did anyone take particular notice of your group? Was there maybe anybody there who just didn't seem to fit?" Kate was calm and reassuring.

"Not that I noticed. I didn't pay much attention. Everything seemed normal. Then Stuart got up to go to the loo, and he just didn't come back. Bryce said that maybe he picked someone up, went home with them, but Stuart wasn't like that. He was quiet, safe, you know, never did anything risky, and he wasn't real comfortable...with himself." Having met his father, Jack could understand that.

"Any chance Stuart may have disappeared of his own accord?" They needed to know. Jack didn't want to be wasting time searching for someone who wanted to be missing when there was a killer out there ready to strike again.

"No, no way. He would have at least told me. Stuart has plans and dreams and running away wouldn't have helped him. His dad's a dick and his mum is...useless, but he would have told me." A sob escaped Kyle, and immediately both parents moved to embrace their child, mother and father wrapping him up between them, doing their best to shelter him from what was quite possibly his first real encounter with the horrors that lurked in the world outside the relative safety of their front door. Kyle pushed his head above their encircling arms and continued through his now freely falling tears. "I should have gone with him. I should have been watching. I don't know, something...something I should have done and maybe..."

Four adults all began speaking at the same time, each choosing different words but the message was the same— *You did nothing wrong. There was nothing you could have done.* Jack recognised the emotion he couldn't name before. Guilt. He hoped Stuart was okay because Kyle Sandler would be living with misplaced guilt for the rest of his life if he wasn't.

After making a time for the Sandlers to come in to the station for a formal statement, Jack and Kate headed off to talk to the other two young men who had been out with Stuart last night.

Neither of them could add much to the information they already had, though Joe Foster claimed to have felt something he believed to be *evil* all night. Jack dismissed this as the dramatics of an excitable young man. It was just after seven by the time they finally made it back to the office.

Holmes and Kassel were with Pete in his office when they walked in. As second leads on this case, they looked every bit as drained as Jack felt. Pete waved them in and offered them coffee or tea. When everyone had their fortifying beverage, they took turns sharing the information they had collected during the day. The basics of the case seemed similar to the previous two confirmed murders, a rather unremarkable young man out with friends, separated from them and not seen again. The friends and staff had seen nothing unusual.

The team knew from post-mortem results that if Stuart Bates was a victim of the copycat, they had approximately fourteen days to find him and no clue where to start. Formal statements would be taken tomorrow, but Jack and Kate would be out on the streets, canvassing the area, hoping to find something or someone that could lead them to Stuart.

AFTER THE CALL from Jack, Will had gone straight to speak to Officer Moore. Jim Moore, the usual day officer assigned to protect him, was a pleasant man of about fifty. Will enjoyed playing poker and other games with Jim, and they spoke often, though far less intimately than he and Jack. Their conversations were usually related to Jim regaling him with stories of his family or his frequent sharing of his thoughts on the latest *MasterChef* travesty. Will wasn't in the mood for any culinary disasters today; he needed to know what was going on, though he suspected he already knew.

Jim Moore confirmed that another man had possibly been taken. Will took the news almost as he would have felt a physical blow, his body breaking into a fine sheen of sweat, his limbs weak and trembling. Rational or not, Will had this reaction every time a man went missing. Unbidden, the thought popped into his head that he may have handled the news far better had Jack been here so he could seek comfort in his company. But Jack wasn't here. Jack was where he needed to be, trying to stop the killings. It was selfish of Will to wish otherwise. So Will concentrated on his breathing, using it and sheer force of will to bring himself under control. He thought of calling Del, but he knew he would need more than a friendly chat with his cousin this time. As hard as he had worked, and as much progress as he had made in recovering from the ordeal he had endured, Will still needed what his therapist referred to as a tune-up every now and then. Will had needed these tune-ups more frequently since the appearance of the copycat.

Will excused himself from Officer Moore and took his phone into his bedroom. He put a call through to his therapist, knowing he would likely be with another patient but also knowing Dr Granger would call him back as soon as possible. Surprisingly, his call was put straight through.

"Will. Excellent timing, I have no patient right now. How are you?"

"Another man may have been taken, Ben."

"Shi— I see." Ben Granger was a consummate professional, and though not Will's favourite therapist, they were nonetheless a good fit, and Ben could always talk him through his crisis.

"Did you do your breathing exercises to relax, Will?"

"Yes."

"And physically, how are you feeling now?"

"I'm calmer, a little trembling, but no dizziness." Dr Granger believed the body had to be calm and under control before work could begin on calming the mind.

"Excellent, Will. Let's talk about this latest kidnapping. What does it mean for you?"

Will allowed his eyes to close, concentrating wholly on his mental reaction to the new kidnapping. What did it mean for him? He let the silence stretch, Dr Granger allowing it, knowing that Will was thinking deeply and right into the heart of the matter. Finally, Will replied, "I feel selfish because I'm glad that it wasn't me who was taken. I feel afraid because this could mean I am one man closer to being taken again, and I feel guilty because I am feeling these things rather than concentrating my concern on the missing man."

"Do you feel that you don't care about this man?"

"I care, of course, very much. I would do anything to help him, but I can't stop thinking what this means for me."

"Will, all of your thoughts and feelings are normal, understandable. They don't mean that you are selfish or you don't care. We are all a little grateful it didn't happen to us when we hear about a tragedy. People tend to think they can have only one thought, one reaction, about a situation when, in fact, we have many feelings that fluctuate during any event or crisis or piece of news. Allow yourself to be glad it wasn't you; allow yourself to be frightened and to be concerned for this man. Your reactions are appropriate."

"I don't know if I'm strong enough to deal with all of this again."

"I think you are, and I know you are smart enough to call for help when you need it. You will get through this, Will. Any nightmares?"

"No more than usual. I've had police here for protection."

"That must help you feel safer."

"Yes. I...well, actually, I think I've made a friend." Will spoke shyly, hesitantly.

"Excellent. Tell me about them."

"He's one of the detectives on the case, and he stays here at night for my protection. We talk and he makes me... I don't feel anxious around him. I feel normal or like I want to be normal."

"There is no normal, Will. There's nothing wrong with the man you are."

"I just mean I want to have a normal friendship with him, I guess. You know, maybe be able to go to the football game with him if that's what he likes to do or the movies or even just for a beer at the pub."

"We can work on that if you want. And let me say how happy I am about this, Will. Not that you should change for another person, but that you're hopeful and ready to try to get back a little more of who you were before your kidnapping."

They spoke for only a short time longer, making arrangements for an extended session to begin working on Will's goals before Dr Granger had to start his next session with another patient. Will was feeling better after his brief chat. Logically, he knew all the doctor had said was common sense, but it always helped when someone validated the thoughts he was having regardless of how crazy or awful he thought they were. Will was hopeful of a sound night's sleep tonight. He could feel a fledgling hope of a real friendship with Jack grow within him now that the seed had been planted.

SEVEN

THE NEXT FEW days were a frustrating blur of pounding the pavement looking for witnesses and watching hours and hours of CCTV footage hoping to catch a glimpse of Stuart Bates or his kidnapper. They had found no trace. Several of the cameras appeared to be off during the time in question, and it would seem nobody had seen anything of interest. Jack was beyond frustrated, but the silver lining was that he'd been far too busy to give too much thought to Will and the growing attraction he seemed to be developing for him. He knew Will had protection, and he knew that if the copycat followed the timeline of the original killings they still had plenty of time before Will would be in the real danger zone. Regardless, he couldn't help worrying about Will when he had a spare moment, and he just plain missed him. Downtimes, which were few at the moment, left him open to thoughts of Will, so Jack had been taking on every task and studying every angle of the case. He sat in the interview rooms whenever the witnesses came in to give their formal statements, and he went back over the statements regularly, looking for anything that may help them.

For his part, Will had sent Jack a few texts, complaining that his replacement didn't even like tea and claiming outrage that the young officer preferred the movie version to the book version *of everything*, something that dismayed both Jack and Will. Despite the twinge of jealousy each message caused, Jack wondered if, or rather hoped, it was Will's way of reaching out to him, letting him know that he missed Jack.

The station was quiet today; it was Sunday, after all, but Jack, Pete, Kate, and a handful of others were still there working on the case. They had their own individual methods, but each worked quietly, trying to look at the case from their unique perspectives, desperately trying not to miss anything that might save lives. Carol Forbes worked the front desk on the weekends, and Jack could see her leading a rather terrified-looking young lady through to their desks in the back of the bullpen. Carol understood people and usually knew which officer to take a witness to so they'd be made to feel most at ease. That's why she headed towards Kate, who stood immediately to greet them, but Carol made sure they could all hear her when she spoke.

"Detective Phelps, this is Lyndsay Bordin, who thinks she may have some information for you about Stuart Bates." Carol smiled encouragingly at Lyndsay before handing her over to Kate. Despite her obvious discomfort, Lyndsay managed a handshake and a self-assured greeting to Kate.

Kate led Lyndsay towards one of the smaller interview rooms with Pete, gesturing for Jack to follow. Jack knew Pete and the others would observe from outside since it was less intimidating for Lyndsay that way. Once they were settled, Kate began to gently question Lyndsay.

"Ms Bordin, could you tell us what you know, please?"

Despite voluntarily coming in, Lyndsay almost looked as though she had been dragged in for interrogation. Constantly fidgeting, her eyes darted back and forth between Jack and Kate. To Jack, she almost looked shifty, though he knew it was more likely fear and nerves. Not many people aspired to find themselves in a police interview room, especially if there was a homicide involved.

"Well, it could be nothing, and I am very sorry if it is, but I thought about it, and I had to tell you. I couldn't live with myself if I could have helped and didn't. You see, it's my neighbour. His name is Russell Andrews. He has lived there for about a year, I guess, but he seems off lately." Lyndsay took a small sip out of the glass of water Kate had passed to her, and Jack hoped that an off-seeming neighbour wasn't all she had for them, though the name Russell did peak his interest. "So he has always been a bit creepy, I guess, but the last few months he has been even weirder. He used to have a bit of a chat if we ran into each other, but lately, he won't even wave hello. He never told us much about himself, but I don't know. It's like...he shut himself off. Some days it's...he's looking right through you, ya know?"

"When did this start?" Jack interjected.

"About three months ago, I guess. I just thought maybe we had pissed him off or something, and if that's all there was, I wouldn't be here, but about three nights ago something strange happened, but it didn't seem important till I was watching the news this morning." Another sip of water.

Jack knew witnesses had to be allowed to tell their story at their own pace, but he was getting impatient, feeling a prickle travel up the back of his neck. There was something to this; Lyndsay was not a frivolous attention-seeker, and she had made herself come here because she knew it was important. Jack was nearly bursting to get going on this potential lead.

"I saw him. It would have been Thursday afternoon. He was unpacking some groceries from his car. I waved and said hello, and he ignored me as usual these days. But then as he was pulling some bags out of the boot, something fell on the ground. He dropped everything he had in his hands to grab whatever it was and throw it back in the boot. And I mean he dropped his bags...some jars smashed and things started rolling down the driveway, and he didn't care. Just as weird, he then turned to me and started talking; just nonsense about all the old stuff in his car he needed to clean out, like he was making an excuse for what had fallen out. Then he practically ran inside, didn't even pick up the bags he'd dropped or the fruit rolling away. Nothing." There was a gleam in Lyndsay's eyes that signalled to Jack that the real crux of the story was about to come out. "The thing that fell out looked like a red cap. So why would he be so scared that I had seen it? I mean he had acted like he'd dropped a porno movie or something. Then this morning I saw a story about Stuart Bates on the news and they said he was wearing a red cap when he disappeared. It's not much, I know, but I just had a feeling like I should tell you guys straight away."

Jack and Kate glanced at each other, giving a small nod acknowledging that, yes, this could be something.

Kate took Lyndsay's address and continued questioning her while Jack left the room to check on Mr Russell Andrews. Cases were often blown wide open with the smallest lead, the tiniest detail that most people may overlook, but people as switched on as Lyndsay Bordin trusted their gut, and in Jack's experience, that was usually the right thing to do. He began a search on the property owners of Lyndsay's street. There was no Russell Andrews; in fact, there were no Andrewses at all. According to council records, the owner of Lyndsay's neighbour's house was a Mr and Mrs Haigh. He had their contact information within minutes. He also discovered that the property was in fact a rental property, and the resident's name on the electoral roll was Joan Johnson. Lyndsay had not mentioned a female in the house, and he was sure she would have, but nevertheless, he would check with her. He ran a search on Russell Andrews in the city and expanded that to the state on a hunch that the Russell Andrews they were after would not be quite so easy to track down. Kate joined him while he was still compiling a list of known Russell Andrews names in order of proximity to Lyndsay Bordin's address.

"Damn, Jack, can you feel it?" Excitement was fairly bursting out of Kate.

"I sure do, Katie. We need to get a physical description and check that there were no females living there. The house is owned by the Haighs and a Joan Johnson is on the lease."

"How 'bout I get a sketch artist in to see Lyndsay, just in case, and then you and I can go pay a visit to the Haighs? Pete has sent a couple of patrolmen to do a drive-by to check things out at the house, though Lyndsay said she hasn't seen Russell Andrews since that incident on Thursday. Could be that he got nervy and has bolted already."

Jesus, Jack loved this part, when things were cracking open, and you could almost smell that the hunt was on. He hoped they were in time to save Stuart Bates.

They entered Pete's office to quickly update him on their strategy. He gave them the thumbs up, reminding them to check back in with him before the end of the day.

Jack headed for the printer to collect the paperwork on his searches while waiting for Kate to finish up organising the sketch artist, who no doubt would be none too pleased about being called in on a Sunday. He was waiting rather patiently, he believed, for her at the car when he heard the notification of a text message. Eagerly he looked at the screen and was pleased to see it was from Will.

Will: Just found out... 2nd Jack Reacher movie being made☺

Jack smiled while replying as fast as his one-fingered texting would allow.

Jack: Heresy! Not with Cruise again?

Will: Afraid so.

Jack: When will it end? Should have been Ray Stevenson... He had the height.

"Am I interrupting something?" Christ, he hadn't even heard Kate approach. Trying not to seem too eager when the notification of a response sounded again, Jack casually got in the passenger seat. He situated himself and got his seat belt fastened before reaching for his phone.

"Oh, for fuck's sake, just look at the damn thing, Jack. You're as see-through as a Hollywood starlet's dress."

Jack didn't know what the hell Kate was talking about. "What?"

"Just answer your damn phone, man." Kate was exasperated and Jack could hear her mumbling something about damn stupid man. Best to stay out of her way, he figured and turned his attention back to his phone.

Will: Anyone over 5 ft 7 has the height over Cruise☺

Jack couldn't help his laugh and quickly fired off a reply, telling Will he had to go before Kate had his balls for slacking on the job.

"He's a nice guy, Jack." Kate's soft voice broke the silence.

"Yeah he...ah, who?" It was a painfully weak attempt at covering his tracks and they both knew it.

"Will is a nice guy, Jack. You should go for it."

"Go for it? What, are we in high school?" Unexpectedly, Jack felt uncomfortable talking about this. He wasn't ready to explore whatever he felt about Will Blaikie, let alone discuss it with Kate. Knowing Kate though, he didn't think he'd be let off the hook quite so easily.

"I'm just saying...ugh, you are so difficult, Mitchell." Kate mock banged her head on the steering wheel in frustration while they sat unmoving at the traffic lights. "Look, Jack, Alijah's birthday party is coming up...the one you promised to attend, before you even think about trying to get out of it. Why don't you bring Will?"

Was she kidding? Ask Will on a date, to a six-year-old's birthday party? "You're kidding. Right?"

"No, Jack, I am not kidding. It'll be great."

"No. No way. That's...not even. No." Jack held up his palm in the universal talk-to-the-hand gesture when Kate tried to salvage the idea. Thankfully she let it go, though Jack suspected it wasn't the last he'd hear about it.

By the time they arrived at the Haighs' residence half an hour later, Jack was just about climbing the walls. They had heard from Pete that the house on Baker Street was locked up tight; no one there and nothing suspicious on the outside. He was working on a warrant to get a look on the inside.

Mr Haigh answered the door on the fourth knock. He paled when Kate introduced them as homicide detectives, showing their IDs. It was a fairly common reaction to a couple of homicide detectives landing on your doorstep. Adam Haigh apologised for the delay in answering the door and led the two detectives into what could only be described as organised chaos. Mrs Haigh was surrounded by three small children, all in various states of undress, and all talking at once. Jack's head immediately began throbbing; he loved children as much as he loved grizzly bears: cute to look at, but he definitely didn't want to get too close. He could handle kids one-on-one, but put them in a pack, and it was every man for himself as far as Jack was concerned.

Mr Haigh motioned for them to sit on the couch and introduced them to his wife, who seemed to straighten up and steel her spine immediately, no doubt expecting bad news. She hurriedly finished dressing the children and then led them to a small room off to the left and put them, all three, with the modern-day babysitter. The TV was just low enough not to distract the adults from their conversation.

"What can we do for you, Detectives?" Adam Haigh's voice hardened the moment his children left the room.

"We need to ask you about your property on Baker Street actually," Jack replied.

Adam Haigh exchanged a puzzled look with his wife. "What about it, specifically? We've owned it for about three years, and we leave it in the hands of the property managers at Ray White Real Estate. We have actually only seen it twice, and that was when we first bought it."

"I understand tenants have to be approved by you as the owners. Can you tell me anything about the current tenants?"

"Well, there is only one tenant there. I can't think of her last name off the top of my head but first name is Joan and she's a teacher, I believe. Is that right, Kyls?" Adam turned to his wife.

"Yes, I think her surname was Johnson or Jones, something with a J anyway, and yes, I think she was a primary school teacher. Has something happened?" Kylie Haigh turned her attention to the two detectives.

Without answering her question, Kate continued. "If there was another tenant there, would they be on the lease also?"

"Damn well should be," replied Adam, "though I know it happens a lot, but that is the sort of thing the real estate property manager is supposed to look for during their inspections."

"Mr and Mrs Haigh, we suspect, in fact we know from neighbours that a man is living there, and he goes by the name of Russell Andrews. Does that name mean anything to either of you?"

Both Haighs mutely shook their heads and waited for more.

"We believe that there is no Joan Johnson. In fact, there are no females at all living at the property, according to neighbours. We believe that a suspect in one of our cases may be living there." Kylie Haigh paled and Adam Haigh clenched his jaw, visibly angry at the situation.

"Fuck," Adam swore softly. "What can we do?"

"Well, as a first step, we are going to talk to the real estate manager first thing tomorrow, find out what they know, and go from there. We will keep you informed of what's happening, and if you think of anything, please give us a call," Kate answered.

Jack could feel his phone vibrating in his pocket and excused himself to answer it. He reached the front door just in time to answer to the sound of Pete yelling into the phone. For once Jack was not on the receiving end of that little tirade; apparently someone named Mosley was a *horse's arse* today.

"Jack, is that you?"

"Yeah, Pete, what's going on? And why is Mosley a horse's arse?"

"Jack, someone came after Will Blaikie. Jim Moore has been shot; he's on his way to the hospital now. Will's okay, shaken up pretty bad. There was an officer-involved shooting with the perp. I thought you and Phelps should get over here."

Jack's stomach had lurched with the words *someone came after Will*. He had started trembling and had to reach for the wall of the house to try and steady himself. He felt slightly better knowing Will was safe, but he was also just plain livid. One officer shot and Will—Jesus, had Will watched it all? Had he witnessed violence yet again? He managed to get the words 'on my way' out through gritted teeth, before storming back to Kate and all but dragging her to the car, leaving the puzzled Haighs in their wake.

EIGHT

JACK COULD SEE Will's slumped body and bowed head through the group of officers who stood encircling him. His shoulders shook, noticeably illuminating his fear for anyone who cared enough to look. No one approached Will. In a room of eight men and women, Will Blaikie was utterly alone; he may as well have been on a deserted island for all the comfort he was deriving from the assembled crowd. As much as anything, Will's isolation hurt Jack's heart. Will had earned comfort; he deserved everything good in this world. Pulling himself from his thoughts, Jack stalked towards Will, unsure of his intention until he stood before him. The desire to pull him into his arms was overwhelming. Jack gently reached out his hand to Will's chin, and then he tipped his head back so Will could see it was him. Working on pure instinct now, Jack lightly brushed his lips to the tip of Will's nose before pulling him into his arms. A soft hitch of breath came from Will before he lowered his head onto Jack's shoulder. Jack could feel the length of Will's body against his own and the slight shudder that coursed through them both. God, it felt so right to hold him. He didn't ever want to let go.

The men and women who joined law enforcement usually had a protective streak a mile wide, and Jack was no different, but never had it blazed as strongly as it did now. He could feel it, a palpable fire raging in the pit of his stomach, consuming him. If he could, he would tuck Will away—somewhere no one could get to him. He would fight the whole world, burn it to the ground if he had to, just to be sure Will was safe. The thought of what almost happened here had Jack's own breath hitching, and for one horrifying moment, he actually felt tears well up. He had to get ahold of himself; bad enough he had actually kissed Will, but to start crying? Jesus, what was going on with him? He admired Will, his fighting spirit, his quiet humour, and fuck, the man was gorgeous, but getting teary and dropping soft kisses on noses, well, that just wasn't Jack.

Will stepped back, wriggling from his arms but not quite letting go of Jack. "You came." It seemed that just getting those two words out was an effort, but he didn't look away from Jack's steady gaze.

The knot in Jack's throat got tighter. "Well, of course. Pete would hand me my arse if anything happened to you." He tried for humour to calm them both.

"He shot him, Jack. He just... I..." Will broke off, and then hugged Jack again, sobbing into his neck.

"I know, Will. I know. But he's not going to get you. I'm not going to let that happen. Okay, roomie?" Jack could see the relief in Will's eyes when he looked up, realising what Jack was saying. Jack could see the panic and fear easing. It seemed as though he would be placing himself squarely back in the tempting presence of Will Blaikie.

While crime techs, and seemingly every officer from Jack's department, filed in and out of Will's home, testing, searching and inspecting every inch of the place, Jack and Will sat huddled together on the couch. Will alternated between lying his head on Jack's shoulder, leaning close into his body, and sitting almost ramrod straight, staring at nothing at all, but never moving far from the comfort Jack's presence seemed to be giving him. For his part, Jack merely allowed Will to do as he needed, murmuring soft words to gentle him when Will's panic seemed to escalate.

Jack had needs of his own, though, and his primary need was to touch. It cost him a small piece of his hard-won calmness whenever he couldn't feel some part of Will under his hands. Whether it was stroking his back or just laying his fingers on Will's arm, Jack needed to touch him, to feel the warmth of his skin, to feel life still flowing through that body, that man Jack could no longer fool himself into thinking he didn't want, didn't care about. If his colleagues noticed what was going on between them, they either didn't care or didn't want to risk an arse-kicking for commenting on it. And frankly, Jack just didn't care what they thought; nothing was more important than offering comfort to Will.

Kate was with Pete, questioning Officer Mosley; Jack should be questioning Will, but he just couldn't right now; he selfishly didn't want to know how close he came to losing him. He knew Will would tell him in his own time.

EVERY TIME WILL closed his eyes, he could see the usually warm eyes of Jim Moore going wide with shock and pain, and he could see Jim's body fall. Nathan Mosley had moved fast, dragging Will bodily into the bathroom and shoving him roughly into the tub. Most of what happened after that had been a blur of commotion. Will remembered sounds and smells more than clear images of what had happened. He remembered the sound of a gunshot as the monster had tried to shoot the lock off the bathroom door, the sound resonating exponentially on the noise-amplifying tiles. He remembered the smell of gunpowder, the iron stench of blood. He had seen none of this, but he experienced all of it while hunkered down in the tub—Officer Mosley standing over him, gun drawn. Will wondered if it was the first time the young officer had actually had to draw his weapon.

Sitting here in the safety of Jack's arms, he could feel the phantom remnants of the overwhelming sense of relief he had felt when he heard the distant sound of sirens. He remembered looking up at that point and seeing the strain almost visibly seeping from Nathan Mosley, when he recognised the sirens, realising he wouldn't be standing alone anymore, his shoulders slumping as the tension drained. A complete sense of security, though, had come to Will only with the arrival of Jack, who sat here quietly with him now, shoring up his defences against the rising comprehension of his reality. Another monster had come for him.

Every now and then Jack murmured nonsense into Will's ear as though he could feel when Will's anxiety rose. Perhaps he could.

"Do I...do I need to answer some questions, Jack?" The thought of talking about the attack left Will cold, but he knew he had to tell the police whatever he could to help as soon as possible, while it was fresh in his mind. He watched strangers moving through his home in their easily recognisable crime scene technicians' jumpsuits. They were the good guys, and Will had done nothing wrong, yet their presence still felt like a violation. He could hear Henley whimpering outside, unable to come into the house in case he contaminated their crime scene.

"When you're ready, Will, but the sooner you can, the better. We can do it here or go down to the station if you would feel better. Whatever you need, okay?" Jack continued rubbing small circles into Will's shoulder as he spoke.

It had to be done, and he knew he could do it with Jack there. "Okay. Let's do it now." There was something he wanted first though. "Jack, would I be able to go out to Henley?"

Jack turned his head towards the sound of Henley's whimpering, looking slightly startled. Obviously, in the commotion, he had forgotten about the dog. "Shit. Yeah, of course. Sorry, Will, I didn't even think." Jack seemed abashed at the oversight though he shouldn't.

They moved towards the patio door, watching as Henley just about shook his body in half with the excitement of his master's approach. Jack slid the door open far enough for them both to squeeze out before the excitable pooch could launch himself in to the middle of a crime scene. Will immediately dropped to the ground, and then pulled the dog into a fierce embrace. He was rewarded with copious amounts of slobber from the constant canine kisses bestowed upon him. Will could hear Jack chuckling as he stood above them, watching the affectionate spectacle. Reaching up with his free hand, Will grabbed Jack's hand and pulled Jack to join him on the ground. The irrepressible Henley seeing fit to bestow a few of his kisses on Jack, whose disgruntled noises made his displeasure clear. Until tonight, Henley had merely tolerated Jack, but his part in reuniting Henley with his master must have upped him in the friendship stakes.

After what had happened to him years ago, Will had learnt to relish the joyful times. Watching big, tough Jack Mitchell covered in slobber, trying to disentangle himself from an over-exuberant mutt, was one of those times.

Once Henley had wriggled and slobbered and cavorted himself to exhaustion, Will sat with his back to the side of the house, Henley lying contentedly with his big furry head on Will's legs. Jack sat on the opposite side of Will, clearly trying to stay out of range of the big, slobbering tongue. "He never saw it coming, Jack." It was harder than he thought to get the words out. "He was at the door with a big smile on his face one minute and the next minute..."

"It's okay, Will. Take your time."

"It's a bit of a blur. I remember coming out of the kitchen just as Nathan was opening the door. Jim was standing there about to walk in, and then there was this bang and Jim was falling. By the time Mosley got to me, the monster was there, and he just stepped over Jim's body. How does someone do that?" Despite witnessing the worst of it, human nature still baffled Will. "Mosley just grabbed me, and we ran, and the next thing I knew I was in the bathtub."

"Did you get a good look at the guy?"

"Not really, just a passing glance. I couldn't take my eyes off Jim, and then I had my head down in the tub. He seemed average-looking. It's just an impression more than anything, but nothing about him stood out." It amazed Will that real monsters looked so normal rather than the malformed imaginings of childhood monsters.

Jack was sitting motionless, staring out at the night sky. He was calm and that gave Will courage. "What happened once you were in the bathroom?"

"I had my head down, and then there was a gunshot, and it was so loud. I looked up and Mosley was standing in front of the tub, guarding me. He stood there solid as a rock with his gun, but his hands were trembling. He was so brave, Jack, and he's so young." Will was in awe of the courage it took to stand so stoically in the face of danger.

"He did very well, Will. Thank God." There was a tiny unmistakable wobble in Jack's voice.

"After the gunshot, there was a thud on the door. I think the monster was trying to break in at that point, but that's when we heard the sirens."

"Why do you call them 'monster'?" Jack's voice pitched up at the end of his question, and Will suspected that hadn't been what he'd intended to ask.

"What else are they? I can't think of them as human. They don't deserve it. We're not supposed to be like that."

"I never thought it was you, Will. You know that, don't you?"

On some level, Will had always known that, but it felt good to hear Jack confirm it. "Yeah, I know."

"Good. It's important to me that you know I never thought you were a monster. In fact, I think you..."

Will waited with hopeful anticipation. What did Jack think of him? Could it be even remotely in the same ballpark as what he thought of Jack? Why had he stopped? He turned to Jack, who still sat staring up into the night sky. He would have given anything to know what was going through Jack's mind at that moment.

Finally Jack continued. "I think you should perhaps try to get some sleep."

Will did his best to school his face into a blank, unreadable canvas. On the inside, he felt only bitter disappointment. For a brief, shining moment he had thought...what? Had he really thought he could have Jack? Yes, he had. He knew there was something there... Jack had kissed his nose, for God's sake. The way Jack had held him tonight and cared for him... It might have been foolish, but Will was going to hold onto his hope.

IT WAS IN the early morning hours when the last of the officers finally left. Kate had gone home about an hour ago, on Pete's orders, and two of the uniforms were staying in a patrol car outside. Jim Moore was resting comfortably in hospital, his gunshot thankfully missing major organs and arteries. The veteran officer would make a full recovery. Jack had sent Will to bed just after Kate left and then had quietly spoken to Pete just outside Will's door. Pete had told him that Jim Moore had come to the house to relieve Mosley; he hadn't even stepped through the open doorway when their perp had shot him through his right mid-back. Thank Christ, Mosley had reacted quickly, hauling Will into the bathroom, the most defensible room in the house, to protect him until backup arrived. Not before Will had witnessed Jim's shooting though. He would owe Mosley for the rest of his days for keeping Will safe.

Unfortunately, Mosley hadn't been able to positively identify the attacker as the same man in Lyndsay Bordin's sketch, since his line of sight had been all wrong, with the offender too far back and hidden mostly behind Jim Moore. By the time he had emerged, Mosley had turned and grabbed Will, and they were on their way to the bathroom. Jack had asked Pete why Mosley was a horse's arse, and Pete had shaken his head in disgust while telling him Mosley had tried to refuse a visit to the hospital, not realising he had been nicked by shrapnel from the blown-out wall trim during the shooting that had followed their retreat to the bathroom. Thank Christ, the perp had been a poor shooter and had missed blowing out the lock. Pete had suggested a sedative for Will. He had refused, but he appeared to nod off fairly quickly after coming down from the adrenaline rush. They had also decided it would be best to move Will. Tomorrow morning, they would pack up and go to Jack's place. Being on the eighth floor of a high security building would afford Will more safety than his current situation.

Jack stood at the door, watching Will sleep and, frankly, feeling a little creepy about it, but he couldn't bring himself to look away just yet. Will was tossing and turning a fair bit, no doubt troubled in sleep by his past horrors or conjuring nightmares of what might have happened today. Not for the first time, Jack wished he could take the horror and the memories away from Will. He remembered Will telling him about monsters and his complete lack of understanding of how people could do what they did, just a short time ago. The almost childlike naiveté, despite what Will had experienced, had broken Jack's heart.

He watched now, Will's body twisting in the dark. He could faintly see a grimace forming on Will's beautiful face, but he was unprepared for the scream that wrenched itself out of Will's now painfully contorted body. Without thought, he rushed to his side.

"Will... Will, wake up... Come on, baby, wake up." Will's body was hot to the touch and dripping sweat, his breathing frantic and tortured. The tumult of Will's body stopped when his eyes flew open, and he sat bolt upright. Jack wasn't sure if reaching for him would frighten him more, so he stood beside the bed, hands clenching and unclenching with annoyance at his inaction.

Blinking a few times, Will looked up at him, reached for his arms, and pulled Jack into an awkward embrace. Jack sank onto the bed, arms curling even tighter around Will's body, and held on. He could feel Will trembling, feel the dampness of his skin and his still heavy breathing. Their positions were awkward and uncomfortable, but neither let go or spoke for some time.

Finally Will began to pull back from Jack, and he could see silent tears falling from Will's eyes. Growing up, he had always been told that men shouldn't cry. Whether it was his father, friends, or the media saying it, the message had been the same—real men did not cry. He knew now that was utter bullshit. Will had earned these tears, and by God, he could feel his own eyes moisten. He lifted a finger to gently wipe at a tear falling down Will's scarred cheek and was astounded by an overwhelming urge to taste it. Gorgeous, dark-chocolate eyes watched him as he lifted his finger to his mouth and licked away the salty tear. Realising what he had done, Jack turned away from Will, unwilling to show him the hunger he knew would be obvious in his eyes.

"Sorry, Will, I don't know what I was thinking. I shouldn't have done that." Jack was nothing if not honest, and he had no reason not to be now. It could be a huge mistake, but he decided that Will needed to know. He wouldn't risk a misunderstanding. "I...uh, well, I want you so damn much, Will, and I think you know that... Maybe you even want me too"—Christ, he was sweating bullets—"but I can't do this. Not now. I'm on a case, and I can't be distracted. Maybe when—"

Will stopped his words with a finger pressed to his lips. "I know, Jack. I do." Jack could see the blush creeping up his neck. "I'm sorry I...um... I think I might go and have a shower, and maybe we can have a cup of tea? I don't think I'll be sleeping again tonight."

Will appeared embarrassed and uncomfortable, but there was also a certain resignation to his bearing as he brushed past Jack towards the bathroom. And Jack hated it. He had fucked up. He'd hurt Will.

"And for what it's worth, Jack...I do want you too...desperately." He didn't turn to look at Jack when he spoke the words.

Will wanted him. He wanted him, and fuck, if that didn't go straight to Jack's balls.

NINE

WITH THE EXCEPTION of the recalcitrant behaviour of Henley, the move from Will's had been efficient and fast. Neither of them had mentioned what had happened during the night, busying themselves instead with preparations for the big move. Will had packed a single bag for himself the morning after the attack. Henley, on the other hand, required two bags and, inexplicably, two different beds in order for him to comfortably settle into his new temporary abode. The two beds sat side by side in the corner of Jack's living room, though Henley only ever slept in the rattiest-looking one, the other remaining unused.

For the first day of their stay, Henley had expressed his displeasure at the upheaval through an almost constant discharge of flatulence and the chewing destruction of both a pair of joggers and the corner of Jack's couch. Jack and Will had spent most of that day crammed onto Jack's tiny balcony, enjoying the fresh air. Jack tried not to laugh every time Will stammered through a mortified apology for his dog's gas problem, blaming it on his old age and nerves. What Jack found absolutely adorable, though, was Will's explanation for the second bed. His face aflame, he had told Jack that the second bed belonged to Don, Henley's late brother. Apparently Henley couldn't sleep without it being close by. Jack wasn't sure which was sweeter: Henley's devotion to his lost brother or Will's willingness to do whatever he could to make his beloved pet happy.

It still seemed strange to him: coming home to his unit and finding it occupied rather than the empty space he was used to. Occasionally he would walk into a room or simply look up from whatever he was doing, and see Will and, for a brief moment, be startled by his presence. Jack had never had someone stay with him. Even when he had brought someone home to fuck in the past, which was rare, they were usually gone by morning. Despite always having planned on being alone, Jack kinda liked the company— even the stinky Henley was growing on him.

Six days after Will's attack, no leads had panned out, and the case seemed once again stalled. Jack stood staring out the kitchen window at the city lights, while listening to the kettle coming to boil. He had the mugs ready with their favourite tea while Will showered. They had followed the same routine since they had moved to Jack's unit, settling back into cosy chats and quiet reading. It was domestic and Jack had never experienced anything quite like it. Knowing Will wanted him too, Jack had expected things to be awkward between them, but surprisingly, it was not. He desperately tried not to imagine Will under the shower right now and began busying himself with their late-night snack as a diversion. Nothing went better with tea than a few bikkies and a hedgehog brownie slice for Will. The fact that he knew so many insignificant details about Will surprised him sometimes. He was never cruel or deliberately hurtful to his lovers, but he had just never cared enough to bother learning the little things about them. They were either one-hit wonders or casual acquaintances 'with benefits'—never had they been intimate beyond physical release. Now, with Will, he had the intimacy but not a physical relationship. Could he do this with Will? Could he pursue something more, something like an actual relationship? For the first time in his life Jack thought maybe he could.

Rousing from these thoughts, Jack became aware of the silence. The kettle had boiled, and the shower was off. He turned toward the living room to find Will standing at the kitchen door, only a towel wrapped around his slender hips, his eyes wild with desire. Jack damn nearly choked on his tongue.

"Please, Jack... I need—" Will didn't finish the sentence before Jack was on him, his arms coiled so tightly around Will's body that Will gasped for breath. Jack gave him just enough time to draw air in before he closed his lips over Will's. Rather than the sweet and gentle kiss Jack had imagined for their first kiss, this was desperate and almost brutal, teeth nipping and tongues duelling. Jack could tell Will lacked experience, but he more than made up for it in enthusiasm. He could feel Will's hands on the back of his head, his fingers tugging on his hair, and that drove his own desperation. It was as if they couldn't get close enough to each other.

It could have been minutes or hours—time seemed irrelevant—when Jack finally broke away. Both men were panting, and Jack could feel Will's cock, long and hard, pressing against his own. He cupped Will's face, looking into those eyes, the pupils blown, and the hunger in them matching Jack's own.

"Jesus, Will, I..." Jack found himself stuck for words. What should he say? What should they do? He didn't want to fuck this up, he wanted a real shot with Will. He could admit that to himself easily now. But was now the right time?

"Jack, please. I know we shouldn't do this. I know the timing is bad, but I..." Will's face was flushed, his eyes downturned now, and he was trembling. "I need you... Please."

How do you say no to that? How do say no to something you want almost more than your next breath when it's being offered to you? How do you say no to the person you want most of all when they are offering themselves to you? Jack sure as shit didn't know. Will had found the courage to ask this, to ask for what he wanted, and Jack wouldn't turn him down again. Jack nodded and reached for Will. He felt Will's hand slip into his own and tug him towards the bedroom. Will tossed the towel as he entered the room, and Jack had a close-up view of his perfect arse.

It struck Jack that this was reality, and it was going to happen, and all of a sudden, Jack couldn't think of a single reason for it not to. Will turned to sit on the bed, but Jack reached out to stop him. Shaking his head slightly, he dropped to his knees and took Will's hard cock into his mouth, almost to the root in one swallow. Will's hips bucked at the sensation, and Jack felt the head of Will's cock touch the back of his throat. He hummed softly before pulling off and licking into the slit. Above him, he could hear Will cursing and could feel his fingers tangling through his hair. Fuck, he loved sucking cock. He gave a lick up the length of Will's shaft before taking him to the back of his throat again and again. Will's hips were pumping almost uncontrollably now, the grip on Jack's hair so tight it was bordering on painful, and Jack loved it. Will's taste was a-fucking-mazing. He felt Will's cock swell even further, before his hips seemed to lock into place, and Will came down his throat. Jack kept sucking, swallowing every drop until Will begged him to stop. Will's body was shivering and oversensitive, and Jack helped him down onto the bed.

Jack lay down beside Will and tried to take him into his arms, but Will pushed him off and, instead, began to undress him. Will's eyes never left Jack's as he lifted the T-shirt over his head and urged Jack to lift his hips so he could drag Jack's sweats down over his own throbbing erection. Jack took Will's face into his hands and placed a gentle kiss to the tip of his nose. He had never been so gentle with a male lover before. He wasn't overly rough with them, but that was one of the joys of being with a man—not having to hold yourself back, letting your passion take you over, getting or giving a good, hard pounding. With Will, though, Jack found that each gentle touch gave him such pleasure, not just physical, but a satisfaction in his very soul, and now that he was allowed to touch Will, he found that he couldn't stop, didn't want to stop.

"You don't have to do this, Will," he whispered against Will's face. He could feel Will quivering and wondered again at his experience with other men.

"I want to, Jack. It's just... I don't know how." Will's eyes were downcast as he spoke, and Jack knew then that Will was doing his 'fake it till you make it' routine again. Outwardly trying to come off as confident, but inside, well, Will had once described it as being mentally curled in on yourself, hoping that people couldn't see the terror you were actually in. He didn't want that with Will; he didn't want Will to be terrified with him.

"Look at me, Will." Will's gaze slowly rose to meet his own. "You don't have to pretend with me. If you're scared, be scared. If you have never done this before, that's okay 'cause I promise you I am going to love it, whatever you do, and if you're not ready, then we just lay here, and I will hold you all night if that's what you want. Do you understand?"

"I just want to be normal, you know. I want to stop being terrified of everyone and everything, and I know...I *know* I can do that with you, but I... After what happened I couldn't be around people, and I just closed myself off. I used to be braver than I am now, better at dealing with people, though never extroverted, just reserved. Anyway, I have only kissed one other person before, but I want to be with you, Jack, like normal people. I just don't know how to do it. Would you... I mean could you, tell me what to do?"

"Ah, baby, you just do whatever feels good, whatever feels right." Jack answered. He knew exactly what to do, and lay back on the bed, spread out for Will. "How about you start by just touching me, anywhere, any way you feel comfortable, okay? If I don't enjoy something, I'll tell you."

Will sat up and peered down at Jack through hooded eyes. He reached out to touch Jack's face and placed a gentle kiss on the tip of his nose, just as Jack had done to him moments ago. Slowly, he began tracing his fingers down Jack's body, his touch lightly feathering over Jack's neck and shoulders before reaching his chest. Jack gasped a little when those fingers traced around first one and then the other nipple, his eyes rolling back in his head when Will tweaked and pulled until the little nubs hardened. He could feel his cock hardening again and caught Will's quick glance down as he, too, registered Jack's excitement.

Perhaps emboldened by the reaction he was getting, Will leant over and flicked his tongue around one nipple while his fingers kept up the torment of the other. Jack couldn't hold back the groan the duelling sensations caused. When Will raised his head again, his lips were curved into what Jack honestly believed was the dirtiest smile he had ever seen. Christ, Will was a natural. Dropping his head again, Will then trailed his tongue down from Jack's chest to curl around his belly button. Will twisted his tongue around and then sucked a little on his navel, the head of Jack's cock brushing on Will's cheek. Jack's hands fisted the sheets beneath him in an almighty effort to remain still when all he desired to do was reach out and maul the man leaning over him.

"Will, feels so... Holy shit!" Jack cried out when the tongue that had been tormenting his belly button unexpectedly flicked over the head of his cock. Will's hand gripped around the base of Jack's cock while his tongue kept licking around and up and down his shaft. Without question, this was the most exciting encounter of his life. There was no real skill to what Will was doing, but he was licking at Jack's cock like it was the best damn thing he had ever tasted, and Jack quickly decided that expertise was overrated. He much preferred Will's wholehearted passion.

But, as much as he wanted to come down Will's throat, Jack knew there was something he wanted more. He reached down to pull Will up to him, finding his lips for a slow, gentle kiss. Will stretched his body out alongside Jack's and fell into their kiss, never releasing his grip on Jack's shaft, holding it as though it was his new favourite toy, and he was never letting go. After a moment, he pulled away from the kiss and looked solemnly into Jack's eyes.

"Was that no good?" Will whispered.

"Oh no, no, it was perfect, Will, too good. But I want to come with you," Jack answered. He reached out and took ahold of Will's rock-hard cock with one hand and pulled his hip over with the other so their cocks were now flush. "Like this."

Will tried to release his grasp, but Jack covered his hand with his own and guided both hands to wrap around the shafts that had started to rub together seemingly of their own volition. Will's hand was touching the hard flesh, with Jack's hand covering his, guiding his movements. Will's eyes had widened with the contact, and Will seemed to be unable to look away from the sight of them jacking each other off together.

"Oh fuck, Will, so good," Jack managed to groan out. Will responded with a breathy "Yes" just before Jack started to feel Will's cock harden and pulse, sending Jack into his own blinding orgasm. Twin streaks of come spurted over both bellies, the suddenness of his orgasm leaving Jack reeling. Will's head flopped onto Jack's shoulder as they both tried to settle their breathing. Jack's other hand rubbed small circles over Will's back, and in the silence, Jack barely made out the whispered "Thank you" that fell from Will's lips.

WHEN JACK HAD admitted several days ago that he wanted him, Will had been over the moon. It was a quick trip and a long fall back to earth when Jack had told him—almost in the same breath—that nothing could happen between them. Will had tried for six long days and nights to stay away from any thoughts about Jack other than friendship. Officer Mosley was back protecting him during the days, but nights...nights were all his and Jack's. And it was hard. It was very hard to stay away. It was hard not to touch Jack again after the way Jack had held him following the attack. His entire body yearned for Jack, went up in flames from a mere glimpse of Jack. Every night, he had woken up coming in his damn sleep pants from vivid dreams of Jack. Tonight, in the shower, he had tried desperately to get himself off before going back out into Jack's company. He couldn't do it. When his own hands had gripped his shaft, stroking, trying to find release, it had felt so hollow and so unfulfilling. He'd needed more. He'd needed Jack, and he'd left the shower with concrete-like determination to have Jack.

Of course, Will wasn't that embarrassingly naïve he didn't know most people generally thought of sex as the best thing ever. Now that he had experienced it, he could see why. The way Jack made Will's body feel, the pleasure he had experienced with Jack, was breathtaking. A thousand times better than his fumbling efforts to pleasure himself. He and Jack had known each other for a few weeks now, and they had spent a lot of quality time together. Neither of them watched much TV. Reality TV disgusted them both, and it seemed that was pretty much all that was on the idiot box these days. So they spent most of their time together reading or talking, getting to know each other better than most people ever did. Will wasn't sure about Jack, but he knew he had never known anyone as well as he knew Jack. And, fuck, if they could do more of what they had done together tonight...well, Will knew he would be one lucky son of a bitch. His lack of experience concerned him, but he didn't think it was anything that couldn't be helped by a little googling.

Will disentangled himself from Jack's body and slid quietly out of bed, Jack barely reacting when Will had moved, only muttering a few indecipherable words and wrapping his arms around a pillow in place of Will's body. Will padded towards the bathroom. He closed the door once he entered before switching the light on. He went to the sink and stood looking solemnly at his reflection. He couldn't notice any differences in the person who stared back at him, and he found that to be unbelievable, considering how very different he felt. Will wondered if other people would see the difference—would they look at him and know that he'd had sex now? Was it even called sex if there was no penetration? Were they going to do that again? Would they do more? Will had no experience, no blueprint to guide him.

As he had done so many times before, he wished Sean was here to talk to. He was so far out of his depth, yet when he thought of Jack lying naked in his bed, he didn't get nervous or scared. Not now, not after that. Instead, he felt what he thought may be trust—a building trust that he could talk to Jack about these things, about anything. He trusted that he could be safe with Jack. It was a fantastic feeling.

TEN

THEY WERE VERY careful with the information they released to the media. It was always a balancing act. Releasing just enough information to keep the public alert and allow the tips to flow in but not releasing too much and scaring both the public and the perp. They didn't want him to go to ground, but they did want him shaken up enough to slip up and attract attention. They had given details of Stuart Bates' disappearance—the when and where, the lack of CCTV footage. In fact, they had pretty much told the media everything they knew at the time of his disappearance. They didn't release information about Russell Andrews and the red cap, but they were all starting to reconsider that. Perhaps that would get the tips flowing again, even though they knew it was risky. In truth, Lyndsay Bordin's story didn't amount to anything in the way of hard evidence of this man's involvement in the crimes. So there was a chance they would be holding an innocent man up for public condemnation.

They also didn't tell the media about the attack on Will. The media had reported an officer had been shot, but no mention of Will or the connection to the copycat had been made. Sometimes the media worked for you; sometimes they didn't. Jack was all for people having a right to know, but sometimes the people had to wait to know, in order to help their case. He remembered the press at the time of Will's rescue. They had been in a frenzy to get the true story of what happened from Will. Jack could recall his own disgust at the actions of some members of the media. Trying to sneak into Will's hospital room and shoving their mics under his nose as he was finally released from the hospital after a three-week stay. Journalists like that were fucking vultures as far as Jack was concerned. Jack could also picture how frail and frightened Will had seemed under the glare of the cameras. Yet he had conducted himself with such calm dignity, refusing to speak of what had happened. Jack had a true love-hate relationship with the media.

They watched the house on Baker Street, out of sight, hoping that Russell Andrews might return, but no one had been near the house in days.

It was damn somber at the station today because everyone knew that if Stuart Bates had been taken by their killer, then his time was almost up. Typically, the victims had been killed around the ten-to-fourteen-day mark. Everyone involved was now essentially waiting for his body to turn up, and they all hated it.

Jack was feeling absolutely mystified by his life at the moment. His reality had always been so clear to him. Work, work, work, and the occasional hook-up on the side. And now that things had changed, he couldn't quite fathom how people could function with the duality of a gratifying relationship in their personal life and such frustration and anger in the workplace. He guessed—having no real experience—there would be times when that was reversed. Perhaps there were even times when things went smoothly—or badly—in both parts of your life. And yet, here he was right now, elated with how things were working out with Will. Last night had been passionate and remarkably tender. When he had awoken this morning, with a naked Will still wrapped in his arms, he had been mesmerised by the sight of Will, so peaceful in his slumber. Jack had never felt such warmth smouldering inside of him and such a longing for another person. But more than anything he had felt at peace, a true peace unlike anything he had experienced before.

However, at work he was frustrated and angry that they were having no luck with their case. He was desperately sad for Stuart Bates and his family and friends. For the first time ever, Jack's professional life was not giving him the satisfaction it usually did. He wanted nothing more than to get the fuck out of the office. He wanted to get home to Will. Just thinking *Will* and *home* in the same sentence left him bewildered.

The problem with working with detectives was that you could never hide anything from them. As soon as Jack had seen Kate this morning, he knew that she knew something was going on between him and Will. He didn't bother trying to pretend otherwise; he had simply asked how she knew. She had laughed, patted his arm, and told him it was so bloody obvious even a first-year constable would have known. When he persisted, she had simply replied, "You're smiling, Jack." Since then she had occasionally lifted her head from her work, a smile on her face, sighing a little while shaking her head at him and getting back to work.

By noon, Jack was seriously considering violence against his smug partner. Three things stopped him. First, he knew Kate could, and would, kick his arse. Second, he would never, ever hit a woman—his grandpa had taught him that, and Jack was pretty sure he'd come back from the grave to kick the ever-loving shit out of him if he did. And third, his captain's booming voice was calling them into his office.

"You were considering knocking my block off just then, weren't you?" Kate asked him as they made their way towards Pete's office. Jack stayed silent. "You know I would have kicked your arse don't you...Iron Man?" She laughed.

Jack took the high road, trying to salvage some dignity by once again staying silent though he couldn't help the grin that tugged at his lips. God, he loved this woman.

"Kate, Jack, get your arses over to Ryde TAFE. There is a Michael Collins there who says his IT teacher got students to turn off CCTV cameras as an assignment, and can you guess where?" Pete was actually grinning. Jack and Kate didn't even reply, but Pete would know from the gleam in their eyes that they got it. "That's right, boys and girls; apparently Mr Collins is a bit of an amateur sleuth. He watched the special on the murders a few nights ago, and he put two and two together and came up with his teacher...Mr James *Andrews*."

Jack thought Pete may have still been talking when he and Kate sprinted out of his office.

Michael Collins met them at the administration office of Ryde College of Technical and Further Education, TAFE. With him was an administration officer, Bevan Malik, who looked decidedly stricken at the predicament he found himself in. They were led to a small meeting room where Collins launched straight into his tale without any prompting from either of the detectives.

"James got us to turn off a couple of cameras each over several different nights, always at the same time of night, and one of those nights was the night that man went missing. It seemed strange to me because it shouldn't have been an actual assignment or anything—the TAFE would never allow that. I mean it's not that difficult if you go in through an open port in their Wi-Fi network and just DDOS that mother—" Collins seemed to have become aware that not everyone in the room was as enthusiastic about the technical intricacies of what they had done. "Anyway, James just said it was a cool class activity. When I watched that special on the news the other night, and they said how lots of the CCTV cameras were off, well, I realised that one of my cameras was near that bar, the Bull and Bush, so I spoke to some of the others in the class and realised that between us we had switched off nearly every camera in that particular area." Collins took a deep breath and paused for what Jack could only imagine to be dramatic effect. "Now, I think that James did it so that it would be hard to trace back to him, and none of us would realise what he was doing." There was an excited gleam in Michael's eyes that frankly creeped Jack out.

"Is that common for this type of course, Mr Malik?" Jack interrupted, turning his focus to the TAFE administrator before Collins got his second wind up.

"No, it's..." Michael Collins's words died on his tongue with the withering glare Jack sent his way.

"Um, no, no, not at all," Malik inserted. "We absolutely do not encourage this sort of illegal behaviour. It's hacking, among other things. James Andrews would have known that. This is an advanced course, but still, that's way out of the standard curriculum." Malik was fidgeting, no doubt already worried about the potential fallout of this on the TAFE.

"And where is Andrews now?" Kate asked.

"Actually, he hasn't been in for a few days. He called in sick, but we haven't heard any more from him."

"We're going to need his contact details and any files you have on him. Does he have an office or classroom?" Jack asked.

"I can get his file for you now. James is part time here, so there is no office, and teachers share classrooms and use different ones on different days." Malik seemed less nervy now that he had been given a job to do.

"Michael, Mr Malik, can you tell us if this sketch looks anything like James Andrews?" Kate asked, pulling out the sketch artist's impression of Russell Andrews.

"Shit, shit, yeah it does. That could definitely be him though his nose is a little bigger and his chin a little pointier."

Jack and Kate shared a glance.

"So this is real then?" Collins was practically vibrating with excitement. "I mean it could be him, and we might have helped him, and oh, God..." he groaned. Finally realising the enormity of the situation, Michael Collins got defensive. "We didn't know. Oh, God, will we be charged with being an accessory? I mean surely you don't think the whole class... Oh, they are gonna hate me for dragging them into this."

Jack tuned Collins out as he continued to ramble. He caught snippets of Kate trying to appease both men now that Malik had joined in pleading the TAFE's case as soon as Collins had mentioned charges. Jack examined the room, continuing to ignore the increasingly loud pleadings of Michael Collins. Jack watched Malik as he left the little room they were in to get James Andrews's file. Kate touched Jack lightly on the elbow and gestured towards the door. He followed her out, shutting the door on Collins, who was still muttering about his innocence.

"What do you think, Jack?" Kate asked although Jack knew it was just a formality. They both knew this was another piece in the puzzle. Another step closer to catching their killer and, hopefully, saving Stuart Bates.

"I think we're hot on his heels, Katie. I think he's tripped up, and I think we're close." Murder investigations were often two steps forward, one step back. Patience was needed. It was hard not to get excited when a new lead opened up, though. Jack reminded himself they still had a long way to go.

"I think so too, Jack, but I think we need to be careful. He needs to know we're on to him, or we may lose him. We talk to the media, allude to the fact that we are close. Maybe get his image out there but hold back on the names and where we got the information. That way, he knows we're looking, but he doesn't know our noses are practically right up his butt."

Jack nodded in response. "You have such a way with words, Kate. Such a lady. Your mother must be so proud."

"She is," Kate replied, perfectly serious.

Jack wondered what this meant for Will. Would Andrews make a desperate grab for him, or would he walk away, go underground? He hoped neither. Best case, he and Kate went to his residence now and picked him up. But Jack knew *best case* was a rarity in his line of work.

Malik was quick to return with the file and was clearly desperate to see the end of this little meeting. He could barely muster an invitation to call him if they needed anything more before fleeing back the way he had come. Michael Collins's goodbye was similarly unenthusiastic, despite their repeated assurances that he was not in trouble. Jack and Kate were laughing as they left the grounds of the TAFE.

NEITHER ONE OF them noticed the man watching them, safely hidden from their sight behind the tinted windows of his SUV.

ONCE BACK AT the station, Jack, Kate, and Pete went carefully through James Andrews's files. They didn't want to miss anything. There was an address in the file that was not the one on Baker Street. Pete immediately dispatched some uniformed officers to the address. There was a contact number for Andrews that went straight to a generic message when they called.

Leaning back in his chair, feet casually laid across his desk, Pete sent the file flying out of his hands in frustration, maybe disgust. "I think it's time we released the sketch to the media. There's no next of kin listed in his file—not one other person we can talk to about this man—he's like a ghost. So I think we get his image out there."

"I agree. Now that we have a second witness confirming that this guy is suspicious, we need to at the very least get his face out there to warn the public," Kate responded. "Jack, what do you think?"

"Yeah, it's time. Somebody must know more about this guy, and so far, we have two different names and two properties where he should be, but nothing has turned up. There has got to be more properties we don't know about or he is staying with someone. Either way, this guy is smart, and we need help from the public."

"Agreed. I'll get in contact with our media liaison, and I'll give the academy a call, see if we can get some cadets in to man the phones. Christ knows how many nutjobs we'll have calling in once this gets out there." Pete was all business now. No cop wants an unsolved case on his watch...especially a serial killer case.

Leaving Pete to organise the media release, Jack and Kate headed to the address for James Andrews.

They found the uniformed officers standing at the gate when they arrived. The officers informed them no one had answered their knock to the front door, and it appeared no one was home. Jack and Kate walked around the property, spotting no other buildings. If this was where their killer lived, he either did his dirty work inside, or he had another location he used. Pete was working on a warrant to get them access, though Jack suspected it would yield them nothing—just as their search of the Baker Street house had. Until then, their hands were tied.

"How about we try the neighbours?" Kate suggested once they had toured the property. The house backed onto a park, so there were only two direct neighbours to talk to. One house was empty, but in the other, they found an elderly gentleman who was happy to talk to them.

After five minutes, Jack concluded that the old guy had nothing useful to tell them, only that he hadn't seen his neighbour in a couple of days. It did take them forty-odd minutes to extricate themselves from the company of the lonely old man, though. They then called through to Pete, who advised them he was just now emailing a copy of the warrant he had finagled, so they were free to enter the property. Jack approached one of the uniformed officers and requested his lock kit. It was an old house with a feeble lock, so they were in within minutes. Jack supposed that if you were a serial killer you weren't terribly worried about other people breaking *in* to your home.

It was sparsely furnished, featuring one plastic outdoor chair facing a small television in the living room. The kitchen had a bar fridge, toaster, kettle, and one set of cutlery and crockery. The fridge was empty except for an out-of-date bottle of milk, one carrot, and some butter. The pantry was similarly empty but for some biscuits and a few cans of baked beans. Only one of the bedrooms contained anything at all—a single mattress on the floor covered by a filthy sheet—no pillow and no blanket. It was the most depressing-looking house Jack had ever entered. Along with the two patrolmen, Jack and Kate searched every room and every cupboard, even searching the roof. There was no sign of Stuart or anyone else for that matter. In desperation, they knocked on walls, checking for perhaps a false wall, but there was nothing—no clothes, no personal items, not even a fucking roll of toilet paper. Jack's fists clenched in frustration. Two steps forward...one step back.

Kate called Pete, who advised that crime scene techs were en route and a press release with the Identikit image had been released. It would no doubt lead the news tonight. Pete said he had arranged regular drive-bys over the weekend by uniformed officers. And they should both take tomorrow off to recharge. He advised them both to go home...start with fresh eyes next week. Kate had a party to set up, and Jack had Will to get home to. Before heading back to the station, they left instructions for the uniforms to wait for crime scene techs and stay vigilant in case their suspect made his way home. Jack, for one, couldn't wait to get home.

ELEVEN

WILL HAD BEEN thinking about tonight all day. As incredible as the previous night had been and as enthusiastic as he was about exploring his newly discovered sex life, Will yearned for more. After a lifetime of solitude, he wanted a friendship—a partnership rather than just a casual hook-up. And he wanted it with Jack. Jack, who made him feel alive and safe and who treated Will as if he was a normal person. It may have been a pipe dream, and he may have been setting himself up for a huge disappointment, but he wanted to try. Now he just had to find out where Jack's head was and see if he could get him on board. Obviously, Jack was attracted to him, but would Jack want someone like him? *Really* want a relationship with someone who could barely leave the house? Would he want to be with someone with so much baggage? After all, that's what Will was after—a real relationship. That's why he now found himself pacing Jack's small living room, waiting and struggling desperately not to lose his nerve.

Will tried to convince himself that it was a simple, normal thing to ask a lover out to dinner, but he knew it was anything but for him. For him, it was a giant leap, not least because of the fear of rejection, but he was also committing to going out at night. He wanted to do it though, for himself and for Jack. He had spent a good hour earlier that morning hashing things out with Dr Granger: how he felt, what he needed to do to make the evening successful. He had felt ready, prepared, but as the time drew near for Jack to return, he felt himself losing confidence and his nerves rising.

"You okay?" Mosley asked, pulling Will from his thoughts.

"Good, yes. I'm good, thanks." Nathan Mosley looked less than convinced about Will's state of mind. They were roughly the same age, Mosley maybe two or three years younger, and Will thought maybe Mosley could offer him some advice. Gathering his courage, he ploughed on. "Actually, maybe you can give me some advice"—deep breath in—

"There's someone I am interested in, and I'd like to ask them on...on a date."

"Great. So what's the problem?"

"I don't know how?" Will replied honestly.

"Shit... I mean okay. Well, I don't know how else to say it, but you just ask. You know, like 'Hey Mindy, would you like to have dinner with me?' and then Mindy will say yes and off you go. You've done it before, right?" The confusion on Mosley's face was priceless. Obviously, it never occurred to him that someone of Will's age had never asked anyone out before.

It was Will's turn to be embarrassed. "Ah, no, actually, never. I've never been on a date."

Mosley's eyes were so wide Will worried they may actually pop right out of his head. "Hoooly shit. Are you the big V, man?" Mosley commenced pacing, plainly distressed by the news, whatever the hell the big V was. "Course you are. Okay listen. Here's the goods, my friend. You want to wine her and dine her, treat her like a fucking queen. You need to be a gentleman, which *you* won't have any problems with. Don't rush it, but just in case things head that way, let me give you some tips..." Nathan was talking so fast Will wasn't quite sure what the hell he was saying. He hadn't picked up on the fact Will was gay, but there was no chance to correct him as words were pouring out of the man's mouth. Evidently this was a subject Nathan was enthusiastic about. Will tuned back in, to his eternal regret. "So you want to make sure she's nice and wet, and"—oh God, Will thought his ears may be bleeding—"now once you're in you want to move your hips—"

"Stop! Oh, God, please stop." Will couldn't listen to another minute. His face burnt with embarrassment. "That's ah...great, Nathan. I really appreciate your help, but um, actually I'm interested in a man."

"Fuck. Sorry, man, I can't help you there. Never had the um...pleasure. My mate Josh is gay though. We could give him a call..."

"That's very kind of you, but I think I'll be okay." Will liked Nathan Mosley and not just because he had saved his life. Nathan was open and honest, a little too open and honest perhaps, but he genuinely wanted to help.

"No worries. If you need any help with...um...you know...I—"

"Yes, sure. Sorry, I'm just getting a little restless about it, but if I need any help, I'll let you know, I guess," Will replied. Awkwardness was a heavy fog in the room as the front door opened. Will jumped a little and gasped when Jack strode into the room.

In his periphery, he could see Mosley moving to get his jacket and keys and start to make his way towards the door. Will's gaze remained fixed only on Jack moving towards him. Mosley patted Will on the shoulder as he passed and leaned in so he could whisper to Will, "Relax, Will. He's gonna say yes." He chuckled as he continued out the door with a brief greeting to Jack. How the fuck did he know? Guess cops truly did notice everything.

Jack was watching the exchange with an expression Will couldn't quite decipher.

"Mosley seemed happy tonight," Jack said.

"Um...yeah." Will hated his rather bland reply. He couldn't think straight—Mosley's little advice speech had his head spinning, and he didn't know how he should act with Jack. Should he give Jack a welcome-home kiss or hug? What were they to each other now? God, he just had no idea what he was doing. Jack walked up to him so they were only inches apart and placed a soft kiss on the tip of his nose. Jack had done that a couple of times now, and ridiculous as it may be, Will just adored it.

"You okay, Will?"

"Sure, I mean yes, yes I am." *Well here goes.* He launched into his practiced speech. "Actually, I was wondering if you would like to go out for dinner tonight—" The practiced speech flew from his mind, so foolishly, he decided to ad-lib. "—Of course if you don't want to, that's okay. I just thought that maybe it might be nice to get out for a while, and I could treat you like a queen... I mean, shit...we could have a decent meal, but it wouldn't have to mean anything. I mean, it's just dinner, but of course, there's some nutjob after me, so maybe it's not such a good idea, and we have cheese and vegemite. In the fridge I mean...so we could have toasted sandwiches, and let's just forget I said anything. So how was your day?" Well, the first sentence was just as he had practiced it. After that it just went to shit. What the hell had he even said? Was he talking about cheese and vegemite? And Jack was looking at him with a grin on his face; no doubt, he thought Will might actually be a simpleton. He had to get out of there; he was too hot; he couldn't think. And now he was going to hyperventilate. *Jesus, what a screw-up.*

"Will, look at me," Jack commanded as he took ahold of Will's trembling shoulders. Will didn't want to, but he complied and looked up into Jack's eyes. "I would love to go out to dinner with you. It's not a stupid idea, and I don't want toasted sandwiches tonight. So let me have a quick shower and we'll go." Jack moved past him and went towards the bathroom. He turned back to look at Will just as he reached the bathroom door. "Ah...and Will? Did you just offer to treat me like a queen?" Will flushed so red and hot he thought he may burn the clothes right off his body, but Jack just laughed and continued into the bathroom.

Will could hear Jack moving around, and he could hear the water running, but he didn't move from his spot. He couldn't believe he had actually done it. He had asked someone out on a date. He hadn't done it well, but still... A few minutes later Jack returned, freshly showered, with Will's jacket in his hand.

"Oh and, Will, this does mean something," Jack whispered before pressing his lips to Will's for a brief, tender kiss. Will thought about all the books he had read describing people glowing with happiness. He wondered just how bright he was glowing now, incandescent enough to outshine the stars, he thought.

Will never went out to eat. So he let Jack suggest a little Chinese restaurant just a block from Jack's place that served, according to Jack, the best Chinese ever. Jack's enthusiasm was contagious, and Will started to relax into what was essentially his first adult date ever. The short walk to the restaurant was easier than Will had expected. He still sweated and flinched at every sound and movement, but he felt safe with Jack there, his physical presence soothing. And thankfully, Jack had the decency not to remark on Will's conduct earlier.

The staff warmly greeted Jack; obviously, he was a regular. It was unquestionably a *little* Chinese restaurant. Will estimated no more than twenty people could fit in the dining area at any one time, but it was pleasantly and authentically decorated. The lighting was low, and the whole room felt warm and comfortable. The waiter showed them to a small table towards the back of the restaurant. Jack took the seat with his back to the wall facing the rest of the room. Will had seen enough movies to know Jack was keeping watch on who was coming and going, making sure Will would be safe. Their waiter took their drink order and left to give them time to peruse the menu.

"Anything here is great, Will, but the sweet and sour pork is to die for. We could get a few dishes to share if you like," Jack suggested.

"That'd be great. How about the pork? And I love beef and black beans and maybe something with chicken?"

Jack seemed amused with Will's growing enthusiasm. "Great, and we'll get a Mongolian lamb and some fried rice to go with it."

"And prawn crackers," both men said together. They shared a look and burst out laughing. God it felt good. Not since before his abduction, with his mother and brother, had Will felt so comfortable with another person. He couldn't help but be surprised at the turn his life had taken. Oddly, it seemed to Will there were times when Jack, too, was marvelling at the turn in their relationship just as much as Will.

At some point during his musing, the waiter had returned with their drinks and Jack was finishing up ordering their meal. The man reached for their menus and left them to their drinks and conversation.

"So, um, how is the case going, Jack?" Will ventured.

"It's progressing, actually. It's slow-going as these kinds of investigations are, but I think we are close." Jack took a sip of his Corona. "These types of cases are often slow, slow, and slow, and then all of a sudden, everything just heats up, and it's pedal to the metal."

"Do you think—I mean, what about Stuart Bates?" Will's question seemed to leave Jack somewhat tongue-tied. Just as Will considered moving the conversation on, Jack answered.

"Honestly, Will, I'm worried. The time frame is almost up, plus the perp must know we're closing in so that may spook him, and I'm afraid that...you know." Jack trailed off.

"Yeah I know, Jack. God, I'm sorry. I shouldn't have mentioned it. I wanted this to be a relaxing dinner for us."

Jack reached over and covered Will's hands with his own before squeezing gently. "It's okay, Will. I know this is a huge deal for you, not just the case, but coming out to dinner with me, and I'm just really happy that we are here...together." Will might have melted into a sappy puddle of goo right there if he didn't think he'd die of shame for being so pathetic. It was time for a change in conversation.

"Favourite animal and why?" Will knew his conversation style was unusual, but it was all he knew, and Jack didn't seem to mind.

"Ah...otters actually," Jack responded, "and don't look so surprised. Those little creatures are awesome, and their antics are hilarious. Those mother otters when they float on their back so the babies can sleep on their tummies...adorable." He may be mistaken, with this lighting, but Will suspected Jack may have actually been flushing a little.

"And you?" Jack eventually asked.

"Easy. Sharks," Will stated.

"Sharks," Jack gasped.

"Yep, sharks. They are amazing. So sleek in the water, they're perfect predators, top of the food chain. They are magnificent."

"Now I'm even more embarrassed about the whole otter thing."

"Well, given that they would be a light snack for my shark..." Will let the insinuation hang, both men smiling at each other.

"Least favourite animal?" Jack asked, appropriating Will's conversation style.

"Oh God, spiders. Nothing needs eight legs. It's unnatural." Will winced.

"Let me get this straight: man-eating killing machines that are at least two or three times your size you love and admire, but teeny, little spiders are scary?" Jack seemed incredulous.

"Eight legs, Jack. Eight. It's not natural."

"Wow, okay then."

"Well how about you, Jack? What animals creep you out?"

Jack seemed reluctant to answer, and Will wondered how bad it could be. "I don't...like giraffes... They scare me," Jack mumbled.

"Giraffes scare you?"

"Their necks are freakishly long, and how do those things stay up anyway? And what if the neck collapsed, and you were under it when it did? What then, Will? Talk about unnatural." Jack shuddered, and Will couldn't help the laughter that bubbled out of him.

The waiter reappeared just then with their food, and they settled into what turned out to be a comfortable dinner with excellent food and company. They talked about their childhoods and families. By the time dessert arrived, they had begun to tiptoe through the minefield of their futures. Will decided to leap right in; nothing ventured, nothing gained and all that.

"I want a simple life," Will responded when Jack asked what he wanted for himself in the future. "I don't have dreams of grandeur. I love my house, and I just want a quiet life there, hopefully, maybe one day, with a partner to share it. A job I enjoy and, who knows, maybe even some kids one day." Will looked up at Jack, not knowing what sort of reaction to expect to his little speech. Jack held Will's gaze as he quietly replied.

"That sounds real nice, Will. Really nice."

"What about you, Jack?"

Jack remained quiet for a short while, and Will was starting to wonder if this had gotten too serious for him, when Jack began speaking.

"You know, Will, I always used to think my life would pretty much continue as is, maybe a promotion at work down the track, but I always imagined I'd be alone." Will felt utter disappointment at Jack's words. He opened his mouth to try to change to a less serious and discouraging topic before Jack could let him down easy. But Jack continued before he got the chance. "I've always thought that people who do the work I do shouldn't have partners, for various reasons. It's not an easy road being married to a cop. Now, I kind of wonder if I was wrong. If maybe I was just using that as an excuse because I hadn't found anyone. Maybe there is someone out there for me." Jack winked at Will and took ahold of Will's hand again, this time interlocking their fingers. Will knew he was blushing to the tips of his ears, but the disappointment of a moment ago had turned into another fragile hope.

A comfortable silence settled over the table, both men seeming to be lost in their own thoughts. Jack roused himself first. Standing, he reached for Will and helped him to his feet.

"Ready for the walk home?"

"I think I need the walk home. That meal was delicious, Jack, but I ate way too much. Thank you. Oh, and by the way, I can't wait for the birthday party tomorrow."

"Dinner was your idea, remember? So, thank you." Jack took his wallet out, and a small battle of wills ensued over who was paying. A truce was negotiated when Will suggested that Jack could take him out for lunch another time. Halfway through paying the bill, something seemed to occur to Jack, and he turned to face Will.

"Wait...what did you say about a birthday party?"

"Kate invited me to go to her son's birthday party. She said you were going, and you'd be happy to take me." Will smiled broadly as he spoke.

"Jesus, I am going to kill her."

"She said you'd say that."

"Are you two ganging up on me?"

"She said you'd say that too." The look on Will's face was pure smugness now. "She told me to tell you that no one is ganging up on you, and perhaps you should see someone about your persecution complex." As he turned to walk out, Will thought he caught a muffled curse coming from Jack.

Stepping out of the restaurant, Will noticed it had been raining while they'd been inside having their meal. Will should have expected it. It had been a stiflingly hot and humid February day. On days like those, you could almost guarantee Sydney would be lit up by a thunderstorm rolling in over the harbour to cool things off, however temporarily. There was still a light drizzle falling. Will could see, by the puddles that still littered the road and footpath, that quite a bit of rain must have fallen earlier. Without giving it much thought, Will stomped down into a puddle just to his left, angling his leg just so and giving a little kick at the end so that the bulk of the splash caught almost the entire right side of Jack. Jack stopped walking. His stunned expression fixed on Will, who now stood there immobile, wondering where that great idea had come from. He watched as a small smirk started to form on Jack's lips, and then Will took off. Will knew Jack was right behind him, and he knew he would catch him any second. Will was fit but nothing compared to Jack. He was horrified to realise he had actually started giggling. But stopped caring when he could hear Jack similarly giggling behind him.

"You better run, boy," Jack called out. "When I get ahold of you..."

"What, Jack? What will you do? And you have to catch me first, old man," Will called back. It was hard to talk while running and trying to suppress his laughter, but Will thought he got the message across.

Jack's arms winding around his waist came even quicker than Will had expected. They almost fell in a tangle of limbs, but Jack managed to keep them on their feet. They were breathing heavily, and Jack did not take his arms from around Will.

"So you caught me." Will turned to face Jack.

"Yeah I caught you." Their eyes hadn't left each other, and rather than easing up, their breathing seemed to be getting heavier. Jack had also closed the distance between them, so much so that Will couldn't look into Jack's eyes without his vision blurring. One of Jack's hands moved up to cup the back of Will's head, and then Jack's mouth slid over his. Jack's lips were warm and soft, but his kiss was fierce, his tongue demanding entry, and Will could do nothing but comply. By the time

Jack had finished ravishing his mouth, Will wasn't sure he would be standing if Jack's arm wasn't still around his waist, holding his body tightly to Jack's.

"Not much of a punishment," Will finally managed to splutter.

"Let's get home, Mr Blaikie, and I will show you punishment." Jack kissed the tip of Will's nose, let go of Will's waist, and set out for home. Will felt a shiver rip through his body, and it had nothing to do with being cold.

JACK'S DATING LIFE had, to date, been virtually nonexistent. If he was honest with himself, he hadn't been on what could loosely be described as a date since movie dates in high school. After tonight, Jack finally knew what he had been missing out on. Though he doubted he would have had such a great time if he had dated in the past because it wouldn't have been with Will. He was positively giddy, and if he wasn't so damn happy, he would have been disgusted with himself. Will was extraordinary. Despite his complete lack of experience with love and romance, Jack thought he may just be on his way to being head over heels with Will Blaikie. He remembered Kate once telling him that Cupid gets everyone eventually. He had laughed and smugly told her that he, Jack Mitchell, would never feel the pierce of Cupid's arrow. Perhaps he should start considering the likelihood of requesting a new partner. He knew there would be no living with Kate once she found out how he was beginning to feel about Will.

"Back at dinner, Jack, you said you always thought you'd be alone. Why would you think that?" Will's question startled Jack after the silliness they had engaged in outside of the restaurant. Was Will deciding whether or not to risk himself with Jack? Was he wondering if there was any hope of a future for them? Will had suffered during his life and taking any kind of risk would not be easy for him. It was up to Jack to inspire some confidence in the idea of them together.

Will's was a question that used to have a simple answer for Jack. But like many of his previously held notions, the idea that he would or should always be alone had been challenged by the arrival of Will in his life. "I've seen what happens to relationships when you're a cop. It's nobody's fault, but there's a lot of stress and relationships just seem to break under it. Most of my colleagues have lost a relationship because of the job. I always told myself that perhaps cops should be single." Jack watched the earnestness in Will's face crumble, genuine sadness taking its place. His natural instinct was to protect Will, take away the sadness. It almost felt as though that was his job now. "Hey, I'm starting to think I was very wrong."

"Good." It was the only response Jack got.

It only took them ten minutes to walk back to Jack's unit. They walked mostly in silence, and as they approached the unit block, Jack was kicking himself for not holding Will's hand during the walk. He promised himself that next time he would. Will was much calmer than he had been on the walk to the restaurant. Jack hoped it would get easier for him every time he went out.

Now that they were almost home, Jack started feeling unusually nervous. He wasn't sure what Will expected of the rest of the evening, but he knew it wouldn't be his usual quick fuck or blowjob against the wall, nor did he want it to be. Will was a virgin, and if he was going to trust Jack enough to have sex with him, then Jack sure as shit didn't want to fuck it up.

As if reading his mind, Will turned to Jack just as they came to the elevators, his expression solemn, and he was nervous. "Jack, I...um... I'm not sure what you're expecting, but I figure we've been pretty honest with each other so far, so I see no reason to change that." Will paused and took a deep breath before plunging on. "I want to be with you tonight, Jack, and well, I hope you don't think I'm easy or anything. I mean I'm a virgin, right? So I can't be a slut, but it's just that I want you so much, and I think I'm ready, and I hope you want it too, otherwise I'm just making a colossal fool of myself in which case—" Jack silenced Will with a kiss to the tip of his nose, even though he adored his rambling. He was quickly becoming addicted to giving those little kisses. Given the way Will's eyes softened and the small smiles that tugged at his lips after each one, he figured Will enjoyed them too. God, he was gorgeous.

"Will, if all you wanted was to cuddle, that would be fine with me. Don't get me wrong—if you want more, I am more than happy to oblige you, but as long as I can hold you all night, I am happy."

"Jesus, Jack, you wipe me out when you talk like that."

"Yeah...really? You wanna know something? I have never talked like this to anyone before. I guess you wipe me out too, Will." Jack watched the smile widen on Will's face and the blush bloom on his cheeks. "Fucking adorable," he exclaimed before leaning in for a soft kiss.

The elevator pinged and the doors opened. Will stood back and motioned for Jack to enter. He moved to the back of the car. When Will entered, he walked right up to Jack, turned so his back was to Jack's front, grabbed Jack's arms and tugged them around his waist, and leant back to rest against Jack's body. Jack heard a contented sigh, but he felt so serene and blissed out he couldn't be sure if it had come from Will or himself.

Despite the barely suppressed lust coursing through his body, Jack was determined to take it slow with Will, but when they walked through the front door and Jack found himself pinned up against the nearest wall, Will's body plastered to his, and Will's tongue down his throat, all thoughts of slow and sweet fled his lust-addled mind. Jesus, it was always the quiet ones. He could feel Will's hands push between their bodies and fumble with the zipper of Jack's pants. Jack pulled his lips from Will's mouth and rested his forehead against Will's so he could look down at his and Will's hands trying desperately to get each other's pants open and off. They fumbled and pressed against each other for support and finally got their zippers open. When Jack reached into Will's jeans to touch his cock, he realised he was touching bare flesh.

"Jesus, Will, commando? Are you trying to fucking kill me?" Jack grabbed hold of Will's hand and then dragged him, almost caveman-like, to his bedroom. "Lie down. On your back." His control was gone; patience snapped, he needed to be inside Will. Now.

Jack shucked his clothes in record time, his eyes never leaving Will, who was openly, and rather lecherously, watching Jack strip off. His cock was hardening and shamelessly pointing to where it wanted to be. Jack leant over and lifted each of Will's legs one at a time to remove his shoes before dragging his pants down and off. Will had been trying to take his T-shirt off at the same time but was having a hard time of it. Jack pulled him to a sitting position and ripped the shirt over his head before pressing Will back down to the bed. He stood over Will, looking his fill before crawling over him to reach his mouth. Jack had always enjoyed kissing, but he fucking loved it with Will. The way Will searched out his tongue and tangled it with his own, the feel of Will's body under his own, their cocks rubbing together. He was pretty sure he could get off from this alone but not tonight. Tonight, he wanted all of Will.

Jack reluctantly left Will's lips to reach across for lube and condoms in the side table drawer. He put them within easy reach and looked back at Will. For a moment, he marvelled at how relaxed Will seemed. The trust he could see in Will's eyes was a burden of responsibility he was more than willing to shoulder. He watched as Will's eyes travelled the length of Jack's body, his tongue licking at his lips as his gaze reached Jack's erection. As Will's focus lingered, Jack reached for his own cock, stroking the length of his shaft. He watched in fascination as Will's eyes boggled and his breath hitched.

"Fuck, Jack, come on," Will exclaimed, surprising Jack as always. There was no sign of his timid, shy Will.

"Will, are you sure?"

Will answered Jack's question by leaning over and licking the underside of Jack's shaft, grinning up at him when he reached the tip. Jack pushed him back down and took Will's cock into his mouth as his own reply. He reached for the lube, while his mouth worked steadily up and down, his tongue circling the head on each downstroke. He drizzled some lube onto his fingers and reached below Will's balls, giving them a gentle tug as he passed on the way to find Will's hole. He gently rolled his fingers over it, and Will's entire body jerked in response. He kept using his mouth as a distraction as he eased a finger inside.

Will was tight but Jack went in up to the knuckle and circled his finger around to stretch the muscle. He slowly added another finger before crooking them to search for the little gland he knew would blow the top of Will's head off. He rubbed over it when he found it, and again Will's body jerked, and Jack could hear him cursing and muttering nonsense. Will was coming apart, and Jack fucking loved that he was responsible for it. He eased off Will's prostate, not wanting him to come until Jack was inside him. He added another finger. He needed to watch his fingers moving in and out of Will's body, so Jack pulled his mouth from Will's cock, but he missed his taste immediately.

He knew Will was ready when he was writhing uncontrollably on the bed. He eased his fingers out and reached for the condom. Will propped himself on his elbows and was now watching Jack, his pupils blown, his eyes almost black, his breath panting. Jack drizzled more lube onto his now-covered cock and some more onto Will's hole before pushing at Will's knees to more fully open Will up for him. Will caught on and took ahold of his own legs, dragging his knees almost back to his ears. He looked fucking perfect. Jack lined up the tip of his cock to Will's entrance before he started to push in, watching Will's face the entire time. It was so damn tight, but the muscle eventually gave, the tip of Jack's cock entering Will's body. He heard Will whimper and he stopped.

"Don't you dare stop," Will encouraged, and Jack started slowly pushing in again. With a last little thrust, Jack's entire length was in Will's body, his balls touching Will's arse.

Jack had to stop and take a calming breath. It felt too good, and he was worried he might humiliate himself and come right then. He leant down to kiss Will and felt Will's hands grab ahold of the back of his head, slamming him down for an almost-frenzied kiss. In that moment, Jack wasn't sure he could have stopped himself from moving even if he wanted to. He thrust into Will over and over with long, deep strokes. Will was panting hard but kept ahold of Jack's head, kissing him through the moans that were ripping from each of them.

"Fuck, oh fuck, Jack, I'm gonna come," Will managed to pant out. Jack reached for Will's cock, which was rock-hard again after briefly flagging. A handful of strokes were all it took before Jack felt Will's dick harden even more and begin pulsing out stream after stream of come between their bodies. Will kept up a litany of "Oh, fuck" while his orgasm took him over. Jack couldn't look away. Will coming was the sexiest thing Jack had ever seen, and Jack could feel his own orgasm building. In moments, it was ripping through him, his strokes faltering, his balls drawing up tight against his body. Then he was coming inside Will's snug heat with a roar.

When his body finally stopped trembling, Jack carefully withdrew from Will. He removed the condom and tossed it in the bin beside the bed. He collapsed onto his back, and reaching over, pulled a thoroughly debauched Will to him. Grabbing onto Jack as if he were a lifesaver, Will rested his head on Jack's chest. Letting go of him would cast Jack adrift in a stormy ocean filled with feelings and emotions Jack had never experienced and didn't understand. Jack carded his fingers through Will's hair as they both tried to settle.

"I've never... That was...and I..." Will struggled with his words. "Jesus, when you hear people say sex rocks their world you think it's just hyperbole, but I swear to God, my world was shaking, Jack. Can we do that again?" He finally managed to get a coherent thought out.

Jack chuckled, turning Will's head up to face him before planting a kiss on the tip of Will's nose.

"Fuck yeah, we can do that again...maybe not right now though."

Will snuggled back into Jack, seemingly content with that answer.

TWELVE

KATE AND HER husband, Phil, lived about twenty minutes from Jack in a split level that still had its original seventies bathroom and kitchen. The kitchen was an assault to the eyes, with dark wood cupboards and an astoundingly bright-orange countertop, while the bathroom had an unfortunate blend of mint-green tiles and an insipidly pink bathtub and sink. Jack had a hard time believing that even in the seventies these colour schemes were considered good taste. Kate desperately wanted to renovate, but Phil was unaccountably taken with the hideous decor. As far as Jack was aware, negotiations were ongoing. The rest of the house was not modern, but pleasantly, if somewhat messily, decorated. Jack assumed it was probably how a typical home with two young children looked. Toys seemed to take up every available bit of floor space, even creeping out into those areas that had been deemed 'for adults only'.

Standing on the patio, beer in hand, barbecuing with Phil, Jack watched as five six-year-olds were scampering to and fro in the yard playing with—or from what Jack could see—tormenting the new puppy Alijah had received from his nan and pop for his birthday. Jack hadn't had a chance to speak to Kate alone yet, but he suspected she was none-too-pleased with the gift. She was currently standing, stiff as a post, at the bottom of the patio stairs with her mother-in-law, supervising the screaming horde.

It had taken Jack and Will close to fifteen minutes to make it this far into the house. Alijah had gleefully welcomed them inside before promptly disappearing once he had his gift in hand. Little Bailey, though, had taken a shine to Will immediately and had insisted on showing them, in detail, every single toy they came across from the front door to the rear patio. He was currently ensconced on Will's lap, matchbox car in hand, using Will's body as a racetrack. It appeared Will was equally besotted with the two-year-old, not even flinching when the little car was driven all over his face.

Jack was half listening to Phil and his father lamenting the unfortunate turnaround in form of the Parramatta Eels. Top-of-the-table grand finalists to wooden-spooners in last place, all in the space of one season had even the most diehard of fans questioning what was going wrong with their team and if they could get their form back this year. The Eels weren't Jack's team, but he had fond memories of watching the grand final with Kate and Phil one year when the Eels had played his home team of the Penrith Panthers. Of course, his fondest memory was the Panthers' victory and the relentless gloating he had dished out for the rest of the day.

Most of his attention now, though, was on Will. He couldn't take his eyes off him. Jack had experienced a lot of good sex in his life, a little bad sex too, but last night with Will had blown his mind. He couldn't remember ever feeling so damn good. Was the sex with Will better because Jack cared about him? Quite possibly.

"You with me, Jack?" Phil's tone suggested he knew Jack had not been paying one bit of attention to the conversation.

"Huh. Yeah, yeah I'm with you." It was a safe bet—Phil and Jack usually agreed on most things. He could tell by the looks on the faces of both men that he had chosen poorly.

"*You* are going to join Phil in shaving your head if the Eels finish last again this year?" Phil's father, Doug, looked incredulous.

Jack could tell from Phil's smirk that he had set Jack up for this. *Nicely played, Phelps.* "No, no. I meant I was with you in spirit only. No one touches this beautiful head of hair, my friend."

"Ack...you're both as mad as a cut snake. Another beer?" Doug was already walking towards the cooler as he spoke. Both Phil and Jack nodded in answer.

"So Will seems nice, Jack." *Oh fuck, here we go.* Jack considered that Kate may have put Phil up to this, but he wasn't sure if he was ready for the 'boyfriend' talk.

"He's a great guy. He's had a tough road, but he's...he's very brave." He was keeping it casual, impersonal.

"Listen, Jack, before Kate gets over here. She wanted me to pump you for info but...well, your shit is your shit, mate. I just wanted to give you one piece of advice and maybe ask one question. First, the advice—being with a cop is hard, so go easy on him, okay? He'll worry...a lot, so just keep in contact with him." Phil's eyes were fixed on his wife as he spoke to Jack, no doubt thinking about his own fears for his wife. "And my question is—"

"I swear to God, Phelps, if you ask me if I pitch or catch..." Jack chuckled.

"Dammit, Jack." Phil stormed off in mock anger. It was a running joke between them that had helped break the ice when he and Kate had first been partnered up. There had been some initial jealousy, which had cooled off when Phil caught him with his tongue down some bloke's throat at the staff Christmas party—actually, at the pub after the party— Jack knew not to get your meat at the same place you get your bread. Jack had never felt the need to explicitly tell Phil he was bi, but he sure as hell didn't hide it either. Phil was right about Will though—dating a cop was tough. Would Will want that? The man in question had lost his little shadow and was making his way towards him now. There was a grin on his face, and his eyes were alight. He was having a good time, and Jack couldn't be happier.

"So...ah anything you want to tell me, Tony?"

Pulling himself up to his full height, fake indignation written all over him, Jack stared at Will. "I don't know what you mean."

"I have it on very good authority from a certain two-year-old that 'Uncle Tony is the best' and something about Thor that frankly I just don't want to know anything about." Will's smile was wide and, like all of Will's genuine and far-too-rare smiles, it was dazzling.

"I am embarrassed for you, Jack. Claiming to be Tony Stark when you could have picked Steve Rogers..."

"Hold up. Are you telling me that you are team Captain America? Because that could be a deal-breaker right there." Jack grinned broadly to ensure Will knew he was joking.

"It's just that Iron Man is all covered up, but the Captain gets his muscles out and just damn..."

Jack's entire demeanour softened. "You are so gorgeous. I just want to—" Jack didn't get to finish, Kate choosing that moment to come up behind him and pinch his ear, not gently.

"If you finish that sentence at my six-year-old's birthday party, Jack, I will take you down," she hissed.

"What? Come on, Lucille, I was just going to tell Will I want to get another beer—oh look, here's one now." Doug saved the day. Will's raised eyebrows suggested that they would be finishing that conversation later. Kate's glare sensibly suggested she didn't believe him, not for a second. And Doug's genial manner allowed Jack to slither out of another minor mess.

It turned out to be one of the best days Jack had in quite a while. It was also one of the most exhausting... Who knew tiny humans could be so tiring? The best part turned out to be sharing it with Will. Though they were not openly there as a couple, it had felt like it to Jack, and it had been good. It had also been surprisingly easy. He was comfortable with Will: unlike the way he was with the majority of the human race. He felt peaceful around Will. If this was a sneak peek into what a relationship was, it was nothing like he had expected.

AFTER THE BIRTHDAY party yesterday, Will and Jack had enjoyed a quiet dinner together before engaging in a slow sensuous exploration of each other's mouths and bodies in a marathon kissing session that had left them gaping at each other, absolute incredulity in their eyes. Was it always like this? Will's arse had been a little too tender for him to take Jack again, so they had swapped blow jobs for dessert before falling into bed. Both men had been tired from the party and the kissing, but Will had loved every minute of it. Kate and Phil were great, and the kids were entertaining. It had been many years since Will had been to a social gathering; in fact, it was before his monster, but Jack and the others present had made it not just tolerable but enjoyable.

Will had been loved by his family while growing up, and he'd had a few friends in the past, but the friends had fallen away after—the awkwardness of being around someone who had been through what he had made it too uncomfortable for them. His mother was gone, and Sean, well, Sean was absent from his life. But the party had been almost like having family and friends again. And he felt safe—anywhere with Jack he felt safe. But, of course, Will knew better than most that safety was an illusion, and there were always horrors out there waiting for him.

Will had never shared a bed with anyone before, aside from the nights he and Sean had endured cramped together in their grandparents' single guest bed when they were growing up. And now, for the third morning in a row, he had awoken wrapped securely in Jack's arms. As wonderful as yesterday had been, nothing he experienced before compared to how he felt when the morning slowly pulled him from sleep, and Jack's arm tightened around his waist, his arse pushed back against Jack's crotch, and the tickle of Jack's breath ghosted over the back of his neck. Jack's erection pushed against his buttocks, and he wriggled and squirmed until it was nestled between his arse cheeks. The intimacy overwhelmed Will almost more so than the physical pleasure he had experienced with Jack in the last couple of days. Never had he thought he would feel so close, so intimate with another person. It was a heady feeling.

Knowing he could share anything with Jack without fear of mockery or rejection, feeling absolutely safe with another human being both physically and emotionally was something to be treasured. Will suspected he was the luckiest man in the world, and though he wasn't yet sure it was the big L, he for damn sure wasn't going to leave Jack wondering how he felt. He had read too many books where lack of communication led to unnecessary angst. Sure they got their HEA in the end, but Will didn't think he could be bothered with the whoo-ha and trouble. He wanted Jack for keeps, and he was going to let him know it.

Unexpectedly, Jack's lips pressed to the back of Will's neck, and his hand reached down to encircle Will's growing erection. Will began rocking, feeling Jack's erection sliding between his cheeks.

"Hold that thought," Jack murmured into his ear, and when Jack's body moved away from Will's, he almost cried out at the loss. He felt Jack moving about behind him, and then he heard the snick of a lid opening, and moments later, closing. Then Jack was back, just where he had been before. Jack's lubed-up cock slid easily between his thighs now, and with Jack's hand back on his cock, the friction was easier with the lube. It was slow, it was languorous, and it was fucking extraordinary.

"Fuck, Will, you have no idea how much I want to be inside you right now, pounding your sweet little hole."

Will's entire body shuddered at Jack's words. Jack licked a trail up the length of Will's neck and then nibbled on his ear lobe. Will tried to reply to Jack, to tell him to take him just like he, like they both, wanted, but Jack's hand on his cock and tongue in his ear left him dumbstruck.

"Let me get you off like this now...but, Will, tonight your arse is mine." With those words, Will shot all over Jack's hand, his orgasm taking him by surprise and leaving him boneless. Will was still twitching through aftershocks when Jack stiffened and jerked behind him, shooting his seed between Will's thighs.

They lay together panting for some time before Jack turned Will to him and kissed the tip of his nose. "Good morning, sweetheart." Jack smirked at Will, quite pleased with himself for good reason.

"It is a good morning, Jack, and I see you are feeling quite proud of yourself," Will responded.

"Well, you know I don't mean to brag, but that was some pretty damn good loving I gave you if that orgasm was anything to go by." Will knew Jack was just fooling around, but there was no way he was letting him get away with it. Before he could second-guess himself, he reached over and slapped Jack on his bare arse...hard. By the startled look on Jack's face, Will could tell he had shocked the shit out of him.

"What the... Did you just...? Oh, you are going down, Will Blaikie," Jack spluttered.

"Not sure you could get it up again right now, but I would be happy to go down later, Jack." If possible, Jack's eyes widened even further at Will's words.

"You cheeky shit." Jack laughed, trying to pull Will into a hug. Will fought him and it soon turned into a playful tussle that left both men breathless, with Will pinned securely under Jack's larger frame. For a long moment, they stared at each other until Jack leant down to kiss Will softly on the lips, breaking the spell. In a way he had never anticipated, Will adored how Jack couldn't seem to keep his hands off him now. Every touch to his skin, regardless of how chaste or where on his body, was a little zap of pure ecstasy, reminding Will of the incredible direction his life had taken.

"How about we shower, and I take you out for some brunch?" Jack asked. Will couldn't think of a single thing he'd rather do. Well, maybe he could think of a couple of things, but that could wait till later.

IT FELT DAMN good to hold Will's hand out here on the street in front of God and everyone. It felt right. How anyone could look at them with disgust was beyond Jack. This was right. This was beautiful. This was natural. And to hell with anyone who thought otherwise. It was a warm morning, the sun already high in the sky ready to bake anyone who stepped outdoors. The Sunday morning crowd was out in force, holed up in their café retreats, their skinny-flat-white-half-caf-decaf cappuccino, or whatever concoction they drank, in hand. Sunday newspapers for the diehards spread across the table. For the less old-school, they stuck to their tablets or iPhones. A few tables of patrons would actually engage in conversation.

Usually Jack would walk this road, pick up his paper from the newsagent, and head back to his unit—alone. Not today. He felt so good, not just from the amazing sex, but because of Will. That little slap on the arse before had surprised the hell out of Jack, but it had also made something click inside him. At that moment, he knew without a shadow of a doubt that he could love Will, and he admitted he was already more than halfway there. Will just blew him away, plain and simple. He was hot as fuck, he was fun to be around, and Jack respected how he chose to live his life after what had happened to him. Will was not bitter; he had accepted what had happened and got on with things. He was a fighter, a survivor.

As he started to turn his head, overcome with the absolute need to look at Will, something—some feeling or sixth sense—made him, instead, look in the opposite direction at the last moment so that he glimpsed the muzzle flash a fraction of a second before he heard the shot. He only needed to move just a fraction, and he was between Will and danger. He felt the impact in his left shoulder, as he was propelled backwards from the force of the shot. He knew Will was falling back with him because he was still holding his hand. He felt the impact of the second shot in his left leg, mid-thigh he thought. It shocked him to discover that people were right about time actually seeming to slow down. He could feel the pain, and he could feel Will's body as it covered his own. Jack was squirming, trying to flip their positions to get Will underneath the shelter of his body instead. But Will's body lifted from his, and he knew Will was screaming at him because he could see his lips moving frantically, eyes bulging, and veins in his neck protruding, while he peered down at Jack. Jack couldn't make out what Will was trying to yell to him. He was desperately clutching at Will, still trying to pull him down and underneath the protection of Jack's own body. He needed to get Will out of danger.

Will moved his hand over Jack's face wildly, his other hand pressing down onto Jack's shoulder. He could hear Will now, trying to comfort him, assure him he was okay, and tell him the gunman was gone. Jack clutched at the hand that had come to rest on his cheek, trying to anchor himself to the comfort Will provided. He could hear the wailing of approaching sirens. There were several more concerned faces above him now, but he paid them no attention. There was only one face he focused on, only one voice he listened to. It seemed as though it was getting dark, though, and that made no sense as Jack was sure they had left his unit only a short time ago for brunch. His body began trembling uncontrollably, and the darkness kept creeping in. It occurred to Jack that he was passing out just before everything went black.

THIRTEEN

THE SOUND OF gunshots stopped as abruptly as they had started. He could feel Jack squirming beneath him. It was proof that he still had Jack, proof that he hadn't lost him to meaningless violence. His own body felt paralysed, unable to get off Jack's heaving chest. He concentrated and forced his fingers to move, tentatively wiggling them, assessing his fragile control over his body. They sluggishly responded. Regaining some power over his arms, he shifted his focus to his legs. His toes wiggled but his legs were fighting his influence; they felt too weak, too frozen in shock. He would never be able to move. He had to get off Jack, had to see how hurt he was, had to help him. Like a puppeteer, he metaphorically snatched the strings of control for his body and hefted himself away from Jack.

Will kneeled, as if in prayer, beside Jack's body, instantly spotting a gush of blood from Jack's shoulder. There was also blood on his leg but not as much. Will was screaming words of gibberish, the indecipherable mutterings of the truly terrified. With one hand he pushed down hard on Jack's shoulder, the blood seeping between his fingers. His other hand frantically brushing over Jack's face, too rough for a caress; it was instead a frantic reassurance that Jack was still with him.

"It's okay, Jack. You're okay." His words were a constant loop. Jack's eyes were drifting shut, and Will suspected he was passing out, but he could still see the comforting rise and fall of Jack's chest.

The initial chaos of the shooting was easing. People were poking their heads up to calculate the danger, resembling little periscopes cautiously protruding from whatever safety they had found. Several police cars were pulling up, and minutes later, an ambulance maneuvered in behind them. Bystanders were starting to mill about, some of them with their phones out, gleefully capturing the shocking moments of Will and Jack's life to broadcast on YouTube. Will thought it to be disgustingly ghoulish. Others were overcome with shock, wailing and shrieking out their emotional reaction to what they had witnessed.

Several witnesses told police that the gunman had fled down the street to the south, and officers on foot and in cars were drifting off in that direction, ostensibly to give chase. Will doubted they would have much luck, though he dared to hope. He remained at Jack's side, one hand caressing his cheek, the other desperately trying to stop the flow of Jack's blood from his shoulder. Similar to a song skipping in the one place, he kept reassuring Jack over and over that he was okay. Paramedics were talking to him, trying to ascertain the seriousness of the situation. Their words were jumbled; he couldn't decipher what they were asking him; he didn't know what they wanted. Two police officers joined the group that had formed around Jack's prone body. What did they want? He couldn't focus. They grabbed at Will's arms, lifting him to his feet and dragging him away from Jack. He wasn't being purposefully belligerent—he just couldn't get his mind to function properly. He was on high alert, ready to stand between Jack and harm again if needed.

The two men who had dragged him from Jack eased him down to the footpath only a few feet from him. He could see the paramedics working, unhindered now, on Jack. Another tentatively approached Will. He mumbled barely comprehensible replies to the paramedic's questions and was eventually left alone.

More and more police officers were arriving at the scene, one of them ultimately recognising Jack. Word went out that the victim was a police detective, the demeanour amongst the emergency services noticeably changing. They seemed even more vigilant, even more alert, even more determined. This was one of their own. Will had always admired those in the police force, not only for the part they played in rescuing him all those years ago, but he also admired how they continued to serve despite the danger and despite the frustration of seeing criminals freed by a failing and often unfair legal system. The criticism they sometimes received from the media and others, who *had* never and probably *would* never put their lives on the line for someone else, galled Will. The camaraderie he observed now only increased his admiration.

The paramedics advised Will they were leaving to take Jack to the hospital and assured him that Jack would be okay. Will remained seated on the ground. The police were setting up perimeters, speaking to other witnesses, and going about the business of serving and protecting.

They wouldn't let him go in the ambulance with Jack. Though the paramedics had assured him that Jack would be fine, Will didn't want to leave his side. Never had he been so afraid in his whole life as when he had realised Jack had been shot—beside him, their hands still intertwined. Fearing for yourself was one thing, but fearing for someone you cared about was another beast entirely. It came at you from a whole other angle, clawed up from the pit of your stomach and grabbed your throat so tight that a single breath could barely slip by. Will had felt it in the seconds after the first shot. Adrenaline had quickly kicked in, impelling him to act. The adrenaline was deserting him now, and he collapsed with exhaustion, his body crumpling onto the footpath.

It was here that Kate found Will, still staring at Jack's blood on the ground and the leftover gauze and other detritus from where Jack had fallen and been treated.

"Will? Honey, it's Kate Phelps." Kate reached out to pat his arm. Perhaps she was being so gentle because she feared he may startle like one of those fainting goats and end up flat on his back with his legs in the air. The image almost brought on an untimely giggle.

"Hey, Kate." He managed in response.

"How about I take you to the hospital, Will, and we can see how Jack is?"

"Sure, Kate." Will felt as though he was on some sort of autopilot, his body coasting through the whole situation, but he was not fully engaging in the reality of it. He couldn't work out how he was feeling or what he was thinking. All he could see, all he could focus on was Jack's face as he had lain there on the ground, deathly pale, blood pooling around his body. He couldn't lose the man he had come to care so much about.

Will wasn't sure if he had docilely followed Kate, or if she had manhandled him, but he suddenly found himself in her car. Mercifully, Kate remained silent during the short trip to the hospital. Will didn't think he'd be able to hold a reasonable conversation just now. His legs still felt gelatinous, stepping out of Kate's car, and he gladly took her arm when she offered it. Together they walked into the harsh light of the hospital emergency room. A quick flash of Kate's badge, and they were taken through to a small waiting area much faster than usual.

Will could see another older man already pacing the waiting room floor, and when the gentleman turned to face them, Will recognised him as Jack's boss. Kate walked straight to him, and they shared an uncomfortably awkward embrace. Will speculated on which of the two was the hugger—he suspected it was Kate, and she was forcing the consoling gesture on her boss.

"Heard anything, Pete?" Kate asked.

"All I know is he's in surgery now, but they'll let us know as soon as they're done," Pete almost barked in response.

"Sorry." Kate remembered Will's presence. "Pete, you remember Will Blaikie? And, Will, our boss Pete?"

"Sure, I remember." Pete took on a slightly gentler tone as he reached out to shake Will's hand. "I heard you were there, Will. Don't have the details yet, but I'm glad to see you're okay."

Will wasn't sure who, if anyone, knew about his intimate relationship with Jack, but he figured there surely wouldn't be a problem with them being out as friends. "Thank you, sir. I'm...not okay but coping. I'm out of my mind with worry about Jack." Was that too much for a friend? If he was honest with himself, he just couldn't care right now.

"I am too, Will." Pete squeezed Will's shoulder, surprisingly gentle and comforting. Jack had spoken fondly to Will about his boss, what kind of man he was, and how his wife had left him because of the job. Will liked him a lot just from those stories, and his behaviour now further recommended him. He was absolutely one of the good guys. "Jack's a tough son of a bitch. I know he'll be okay." Another squeeze to his shoulder, this time a little harder, as though that would help guarantee everything would be okay.

Several more men and women entered the waiting area, and Kate introduced Will to more of Jack's colleagues. For all his talk about not having many friends and people generally not liking him, Will wished Jack were here right now to see how wrong he was, how many people cared. Will promised himself he would tell Jack about them as soon as he got the chance. Jack would be pretty chuffed by it.

The officers either sat silently or joined Pete in pacing a hole in the carpet. Will sat in one of the single armchairs, leaving the couch for some of the others to use. He was still shaking slightly, the adrenaline almost emptied from his body, but he was determined to keep it together.

The man Kate had introduced as Ivan Kassel approached him, and he was without question the tallest man Will had ever seen. His height easily towered over Will, and probably even Jack's considerable height. His size was emphasised by the fact that Will was seated while Ivan loomed over him. Will even caught himself doing a clichéd gaze, starting at Ivan's feet and drifting up and up and up until he finally reached the man's face. He charted massive muscles and easily the broadest chest he had ever seen on the way up. Thankfully, the man had a wholly pleasant rather than menacing face, or Will was fairly certain he would have fled in fear.

"I spoke to some of the officers at the scene, and they told me what you did for Jack, trying to cover him with your body." Ivan took in an audible breath. "Jack doesn't have any family, well, except for us here on the force, so I just wanted to say thank you...on behalf of us." Ivan extended his massive hand to engulf Will's much smaller one. "They also think he was the target. Witnesses said he tried to move in front of you, so he got hit in the shoulder, not the chest."

Will was just about speechless, nodding his head before he managed to choke out a simple "You're welcome" before Ivan moved away to rejoin his colleagues.

Kate leaned over from the chair next to Will as Ivan walked away and took Will's hand. "I don't know exactly what happened—yet—but if Ivan thinks you should be thanked, then I thank you too. For Jack. He's not perfect, but he is a damn good partner."

"I couldn't agree more, Kate," Will replied and didn't miss the knowing look Kate gave him.

Silence and the frustrating drudgery of waiting returned to the room. It was conceivable that Will would lose his ever-loving mind if he didn't get some news on Jack soon. Kate had taken several calls from her family, obviously concerned about not just Jack but her too. Will listened wistfully as she assured each member of her family that she was fine, and yes, 'Uncle Tony' was going to be fine too. His heart skipped a beat when she assured little Bailey that Will was safe too. Family. He missed it, and he wanted it, in whatever shape it may take for him.

It must have been several hours later when a doctor, who barely looked old enough to drive, entered the room. Several of the officers present had fallen asleep in whatever pose they could get remotely comfortable in. Ivan Kassel was asleep with his massive head resting on the top of Kate's much smaller one, but she appeared completely unfazed by it. Another officer had curled into a ball in the corner, snoring contentedly. Pete was still pacing, and Will was fairly certain he had not sat the entire time.

"Well I guess you're all here to hear news about Detective Jack Mitchell. I know he has no family, and he has a Captain Peter Delany named as next of kin. Is he here?" The doctor spoke succinctly and professionally to the entire room, belying his age.

"I'm him, and you can speak to the whole room, Doctor."

"Okay. Well, I'm Dr Rashan, and I can tell you that Jack is out of surgery and in recovery. He should be taken up to the ward shortly. His leg wound was a nick to the upper left thigh requiring twelve stitches. His left shoulder wound was more serious and required surgery to remove the bullet. He lost a fair amount of blood but nothing life-threatening. He will be out of work for several weeks, I would imagine, but we can discuss that more as things progress. He also sustained a bit of a knock to the head, but we don't think it's an actual concussion, though we will continue to monitor things."

"Can we see him?" Will's boldness in speaking out in front of a room full of people was unprecedented, but he needed to see Jack. He would do anything for Jack.

"Well, not all at once," Dr Rashan dead-panned. "No more than two at a time to start with, and keep things calm." With the doctor bringing a reprieve from the anxiety into the room, Will could finally start to relax. He wasn't sure of the etiquette for the situation he found himself in, but he would damn well fight if necessary to get into that room to see Jack with his own eyes. Fortunately, thanks to Pete, it didn't come to a fight.

"Will, Kate, how about you two go in first?" Pete glanced at Will as he spoke, and it was clear that he at least suspected he and Jack had become closer than what was typical in these situations.

Will and Kate stepped forward, and Dr Rashan led them through a maze of corridors and up two floors. Will began shaking again, his nerves stretched tight as he was ushered into a small room.

There was absolutely nothing in the room save for a too-small bed with a too-large and too-still man on it. There were also various pieces of medical equipment, which unfortunately, Will was all too familiar with. Jack lay in the bed hooked up to several of the machines that beeped the evidence of Jack's still-beating heart. It was music...the music of Jack's continued life, and Will could have listened to it forever. He approached the bed and, without any forethought, reached for Jack's hand. The gesture came as naturally as breathing. Kate moved to the other side of the bed and held Jack's other hand. Jack's eyes remained closed, though Will had been told that he had woken safely after surgery. Will had the strangest urge to wrap Jack in the biggest cotton-wool ball he could find to ensure that he could never be hurt again. Such feelings of tenderness for Jack overcame him that it literally knocked the air out of his lungs with a giant whoosh, and Will had to bend forward to rest his forehead on their joined hands to prevent himself from landing on his arse.

"Shh, baby. It's okay. I'm okay." Jack's voice was so quiet and husky Will barely heard him.

"Oh fuck, Jack, thank God." Will popped up and kissed Jack square on the lips, none too gently. He could hear Kate doing something between a giggle and throat clearing beside them as the beeping in the monitors picked up the pace. Jack pulled away from Will's lips, much to Will's displeasure.

"I hear you there, Katie Bear." Jack smirked. To Will's utter shock Kate reached over and smacked Jack on his good arm.

"Jack, you arsehole. What the hell were you thinking getting shot like that?" Will didn't quite know whether to laugh or reach over and smack Kate himself. A glance at the grin on Jack's face told him they shared one of those close relationships where teasing showed that you cared, even in highly stressful situations.

"Oh Kate, you were worried about poor little old me, hey? You know it would take more than a couple of bullets to bring Iron Man down."

The joke clearly eased Kate's anxiety. She and Jack were now smiling warmly at each other. Kate released her hold on Jack's hand and carded her fingers tenderly through his rich, amber-brown hair. "Now that I've seen for myself that you're still around to give me more grief, I think I'll leave you two alone."

Will wanted to do the right thing and tell her that it wasn't necessary for her to leave, but the less noble, more selfish part of him wouldn't let him open his mouth. He wanted Jack all to himself.

"Thanks, Kate." Jack patted her hand as she turned to leave. She winked before turning her gaze to Will.

"Will, I'll wait downstairs with the others. When you're ready, I'll give you a lift home." Possibly in reaction to the look Jack gave her, she added, "We won't let you out of our sight for a second, Will. I promise." She looked straight at Jack as she uttered her oath, despite addressing Will.

Will hadn't spent as much time with Kate as he had with Jack and the other officers who protected him, but he liked her a lot and was beyond grateful for her thoughtfulness. "Thanks, Kate. I won't be too long. I'm sure Jack's tired."

JACK COULD HARDLY take his gaze off Will long enough to wave goodbye to Kate as she walked out the door. When he had opened his eyes a few moments ago to see Will slumped over him and so openly upset, he had wanted nothing more than to scoop Will up into his arms, hold on tight, and never let go. The relief he felt watching Will as he stood beside his bed obviously unharmed was overwhelming. Jack's memory of the shooting was muddled, but he could remember the fear, for himself, yes, but more so for Will. He hadn't got a good look at the shooter, so he wasn't sure if it was Andrews or if they had just been the unfortunate victim of some random violence. He did remember moving to place himself in front of Will, knowing he would take the bullet but still feeling helpless, so desperately helpless.

Jack patted the bed to indicate for Will to sit beside him. He was sore, but it was bearable, and he wanted Will close. He could feel that same need to touch Will, to ensure he was safe, that he had felt the day Jim Moore was shot. Will sat and immediately grabbed Jack's hand again. Jack loved it.

"Hey," Jack whispered.

"Hey," Will answered.

Jack could feel Will's thumb rubbing the back of his hand as he held it, and they remained silent for a while. Both of them unsure what to say, what needed to be said at a time like this. They were as fragile as two newborn fawns with this relationship stuff, shaky and awkward and neither with any real clue of what they were doing. Jack was more than happy to muddle through it together.

"Jack." His name was merely a breath coming from Will's lips.

"I know, baby. I was so scared too, and I couldn't—I wanted to—but I couldn't do anything to help you." Jack stopped, closing his eyes and breathing deeply as the thoughts of what might have been teased his mind. They were both safe. He had to remember that. "I'm sorry, Will. I tried."

"Don't you fucking dare," Will thundered at him. "Don't you fucking apologise for what that bastard did or for not saving me or whatever other bullshit you have no business apologising for, Jack. I'm okay. You got shot. You got shot for me. And the blame is only his. Not yours, and not mine, but his. Do you understand me, Jack?"

Jack had never seen Will so fierce, and even if he hadn't just been shot—twice—there was no way in hell he was arguing with him. "Yeah...yeah I know. I do. I just...it's what I do. I protect...especially you."

"I know, Jack, and you did—you did protect me." Jack tried hard to believe him, but he wasn't so sure. Will beamed at him though, as if he thought Jack had hung the moon, the stars, and the whole damn galaxy. "And just so you know, I call bullshit on your whole 'I have few friends and nobody likes me' pity party." Jack didn't know what the hell Will was talking about, but he could happily listen to him talk all day. "There is a room of about fifteen very worried people downstairs waiting to see you and make sure you're okay. Though I guess some may be waiting to see how long they'll keep you here—you do tend to rankle some folks—if some of the stories I heard downstairs are to be believed."

Jack felt humbled when Will informed him of this, and unable to find words, he squeezed Will's hand in thanks. The prick of tears at his eyes neither embarrassed nor disgusted him. "Wait a minute...what stories?" Jack racked his brain for any stories he absolutely would not want Will to hear. There were...a few. "If Jenkins told you the story of the biker with the chains and the four-kilo rabbit...it is unequivocally not true."

"No, I definitely didn't hear that one, but I think I should." There was another genuine smile from Will. One day Will's smiles would be so commonplace that Jack wouldn't have to take special note of each one, and Jack would do his best to make sure of it.

"Jack, I think I'd better get Kate to take me home so I can shower and get rid of these clothes. I'll let you sleep, but if it's okay with you, I'd like to come back afterwards and stay with you for as long as they'll let me." Jack hated the thought of Will leaving, but he hated seeing Will in those bloody clothes more. He tugged on Will's hand till he got the message and came down for a sweet, sweet kiss. Jesus, how had Jack never known it could be like this?

"Alright, but hurry back, and, Will, you make sure you stay with protection. They'll be even more vigilant now, so you stay with them. Promise me?" Jack demanded.

"Of course. I promise, Jack." Will leant down for Jack to kiss the tip of his nose, and then he was gone.

IT FELT LIKE several minutes later when Jack fully woke up. Yet Jack soon discovered that it was actually many hours. In fact, he had slept, albeit brokenly, through the night, and it was midmorning of the following day. Hospital drugs were good shit. He had been interrupted a few times by Pete and some of the other well-wishers from the station. There were several get-well-soon balloons in the room including a Superman-shaped one and another that Jack thought looked suspiciously phallic. Where did you even get something like that? Pete had told Jack, at some point, that Will would be gone for a while as the police wanted to get a preliminary statement from him about the shooting, but he assured Jack they would go easy on him. Pete had organised a small army of officers to stay with Will. Not for the first time, Jack wished he was here with him.

A bear of a man wearing nursing scrubs entered his room with a phone outstretched in his oversized hand. Jack could easily imagine him as a hairy-man-lover's wet dream. The abundance of chest hair poking out of the collar of his scrubs was enough to have any bear-loving twink worth their salt swooning. He passed the phone to Jack with a wink before leaving Jack to his phone call.

"Hello," Jack croaked into the phone.

"Jack. It's Pete. How're you feeling?" Pete sounded tired, even over the phone, and Jack knew he probably hadn't slept at all.

"A bit stiff and sore, but it's nothing. How's Will?" He tried not to sound too desperate.

"He's good, Jack. He's given his statement and has slept a bit. There are just a few more things to go over with him this morning, and then he plans to be back at the hospital for dinner." Pete cleared his throat from what sounded like the beginning of a chuckle. "Apparently he enjoys hospital food and your company. No accounting for taste I guess."

"Hey!" exclaimed Jack, slightly offended.

Pete was actually laughing now, and it was damn good to hear. "Don't strain yourself, Mitchell. Put your feet up, enjoy your sponge baths, and the rest of us will do the hard yards, hey."

"I got shot, Pete. Shot." Jack was outraged.

"Scratches, Iron Man. I gotta go. Seriously, Jack, take it easy. I'll be in to see you as soon as I can." He clicked off before Jack could respond.

The phone call had eased his mind about Will, so Jack was able to doze on and off for the rest of the afternoon. He had never slept so much in all his life.

One of the nurses—Angie, Jack thought—came in with his dinner around sixish. Jack couldn't help but laugh when he noticed there were two meals on the tray. Angie cocked her eyebrow at him and rolled her eyes. "Apparently you have some sway here, Detective Mitchell. I believe you have a dinner date on his way up. Must be the perks of being a hero cop, I guess." Several weeks ago, Jack would have flirted the hell out of nurse Angie but now he felt nothing. He felt nothing at all except for professional respect and gratitude. Fuck, could that be Jack Mitchell maturing?

"I'll be back around seven with your medication. It's a fairly strong painkiller, so you'll sleep very well again tonight." As she walked out the door, she turned back to Jack with what could only be described as a mischievous grin on her face. "Well, speak of the devil. It seems your date has arrived, Detective." And with a wink, she was out the door, replaced by the infinitely hotter—to Jack anyway—Will Blaikie. Will pushed right into the room and straight to Jack's bedside. With no hesitation or hint of shyness, Will leant down and took Jack's mouth in a thorough and far-from-innocent kiss. Jack loved this side of Will; there was a confidence to him now that Jack found incredibly sexy.

"Hey, Jack. How are you feeling— Oh, dinner." Will reached for the covers hiding whatever frightful creation passed for food in this place. Jack chuckled at Will's obvious delight in whatever he found under them. Will did have some weird liking for hospital food despite the consensus of most of the population that hospital food was pigswill.

"I'm feeling good. Thanks, Will. Now if you can drag yourself away from that slop for just a little bit longer, I wouldn't mind some more of that welcome-back gift you had for me." If he wasn't sure it would hurt like a bitch, Jack would have reached out and pulled Will right down on top of him, kissed the hell out of him, and be damned if someone walked in on them. As it was, he would just have to get Will where he wanted him with smooth words, though from the look on Will's face, Jack didn't think he had been terribly smooth at all.

"Really, Jack, that's the best you've got? I mean, you could have gone with the whole 'I got shot yesterday and nearly died' line. It's a good thing you're pretty, or I don't think you would ever get laid."

"What the fuck? Pretty? I am not pretty. Devilishly handsome—yes. Ruggedly sexy—yes. But not pretty. Hot as fuck, sexy as all get-out, drop-dead gorgeous, sex on legs... Shall I go on, sir, or do you understand the error of your ways?"

"Sir...eh? I'm up for that when you get out of here. You could use a good spanking, boy." Will barely got the last word out before falling into fits of laughter. Jack wasn't sure if Will was laughing at their conversation or the look on Jack's face, which he knew had to be beet-red, eyes wide, and mouth hanging open in shock. Jack could also feel his dick harden at Will's words, and fuck, if he didn't want to try a bit of D/s for the first time in his life. Hell, at this point, he thought he'd try anything where Will was concerned.

Seemingly oblivious to the cat he had just let out of the bag, Will continued to investigate dinner, removing covers and setting Jack's out for him. Will pulled a chair over and sat himself in it with his tray on his lap, humming the entire time, a smug look on his face. Clearly he was not as oblivious to the effect he had on Jack as Jack had thought.

Ten minutes later, neither man had uttered a word. For his part, Jack was still in a little shock at the turn in their previous conversation. He was very quickly learning that he did not always hold the reins in this relationship. His dinner sat largely untouched in front of him, and his eyes constantly turned to Will, waiting for what? Angels to sing, rainbows to appear? He knew without a doubt he was falling in love with Will, and he had stopped questioning it the moment Will had told him he needed a spanking. Oh, it wasn't that he was overly interested in BDSM—hot vanilla sex was perfectly okay with him. It dawned on him, at that moment, that he loved being around Will, loved how he felt about himself when they were together, and he suspected it was just a short hop, skip, and a jump to being irrevocably in love with him. He felt so damn incredible with Will, and it was beautiful and wonderful and terrifying, and Jack couldn't remember a time he had ever been so happy.

"Um, Jack, are you okay? Did you have your meds already?" Will interrupted.

"No, not yet. I'm fine. Why?"

"Well, you just got this dopey sort of grin on your face like maybe you're high. I thought maybe I should go and let you sleep." Will seemed a little concerned, but Jack didn't want him to leave, so he reached out and took his hand. He loved the way their hands fit together, fingers entwined. Jesus Christ, he was turning into the biggest fucking sap ever.

"Don't go, Will. Please. Stay with me for just a little while. Please." Jack was practically begging.

"I'll stay, Jack. Promise." Will brushed his fingers through Jack's hair before tugging his hands back and wheeling the table out of the way. He retook his seat next to Jack, and to Jack's absolute delight Will reached for his hand once more before Jack even had a chance to. Will leaned forward in his chair and kissed Jack's knuckles. Will rested his head on the bed and closed his eyes. Jack realised at that moment how tired Will had looked before. Of course he would be tired after the events of yesterday. Jack lay quietly watching him as Will seemed to drift off. Will didn't even stir when Angie came in a short time later with Jack's pills.

JACK WASN'T SURE what time it was when he next opened his eyes, but he knew immediately something was wrong. His mind was *too* foggy from the pills, and his body felt *too* heavy as though he was filled with lead. It was dark in the room but not pitch-black because it was a hospital, after all. He could hear a noise to his left that reminded him vaguely of the scuffling sounds from some of the few fights he had been in. He felt so heavy and disconnected from his body that he could barely get his head to turn towards the sound. When he finally did, the picture he was confronted with was enough to clear the fog from his brain though his body was still beyond his control.

A man stood behind a struggling Will, one of his arms around Will's waist, the other covering Will's mouth. Jack could see the terror in Will's eyes though he was fighting hard to free himself.

Jack tried to leap up from the bed, but his body was just not cooperating. Where normally he could move without conscious thought, it now felt as though Jack had to give each limb specific instructions before his body would even consider moving in the way Jack wanted. He was also trying to yell, hoping to attract the attention of the cop he assumed stood guard outside the door, but even his voice was uncooperative.

He looked at Will as he tried to get his body to obey him, and he could see that the fight was ebbing from Will; his eyes were heavy, almost closed. With enormous effort, Jack threw himself off the bed. Without the cooperation of his body though, he landed in a heap on the floor. He felt no pain—drugs or adrenaline took care of that. He scrabbled on the floor like a turtle on its back trying to get his legs under him, but nothing was cooperating.

The man had dragged Will's now limp body to the other side of the room, their legs clearly visible under the bed. He could see the man was putting Will in a wheelchair. Still, Jack struggled for control of his obstinate body. He watched the wheels of the wheelchair turning and the door open. They stopped, and the man walked back to his side of the bed. He looked up into the man's smiling face and watched as Russell Andrews smirked at Jack, giving him an arrogant salute. And still Jack struggled. All he could do was watch helplessly from the floor as both the wheels and the man's legs exited through the door, and it shut behind them, taking Will away from him. And Jack couldn't even get his fucking body to punch the wall in anger and fear.

FOURTEEN

IT SMELT FAMILIAR in the cold dark. It was an odour he had smelt before and had never wanted to experience again. Everything about this seemed horrifyingly familiar: the smell, the achy feeling in his entire body, the inability to freely move either his hands or his feet. He was bound, in the dark—again. Much as he had done the first time, he thrashed wildly in his bonds. Desperate to escape. He couldn't do this again. Not again. This time he wouldn't get out; this time he would die here.

He remembered the look on Jack's face when he was being taken, his anguish and his pain. He had to get back to him. Will fought his bonds, fought for himself and fought for Jack. He convulsed on the ground, vomiting up bile from either fear or whatever drug had been used to knock him out. He slithered away from the mess. He tried to calm himself. He needed to think, rather than thrash uselessly—that would only exhaust him, and he needed to be ready. He knew this. He knew how to survive. He knew from last time. Will closed his eyes, willing away the panic, calming his breathing, preparing himself for the real fight that was yet to come. It would be a mental battle as much as a physical one when it came. And he would be ready.

Once he was calm, Will opened his eyes. He tried to see where he was, but it was so dark he couldn't even make out shadows. The space he was in felt small, maybe the size of a small bedroom or study, but the floor beneath him was dirt. Perhaps it was a shed? He dragged himself along the ground trying to reach a wall. He could sense it drawing near, but he still smacked into it head first. He turned and backed up to the wall so that he could feel it with his bound hands. Wood? Wooden slats perhaps? Maybe some sort of wooden shed or barn? He didn't know how long he had been out of it, though it didn't feel an extremely lengthy period of time, so he had no way of knowing how far they had travelled. Was he in the country, somewhere remote, or were they still in the city suburbs?

He slid his body along the wall, keeping his hands connected to it so he could search for an opening. He could feel splinters going into his palms, but they were nothing—immaterial compared to what he'd suffered before and to what, he dreaded, was sure to come. On the third wall, he found a door. He felt along the edges, standing as much as he could with his feet loosely bound, leaning against the wall to reach the top of the door. It was small; he would need to stoop to fit through it. There was no handle on this side, and it didn't budge when Will pushed on it. He was making plenty of noise, but he didn't care. Let the monster come, let this be finished one way or another. He banged on the door. He yelled for help but heard only silence in return. He completed his circuit of the room and found no other doors or way out. He came back to the door and sat to the side of it. He closed his eyes and thought, trying to plan some way out. His breathing slowed, and he concentrated just as he'd been taught.

Will was so lost in chaotic thoughts that he almost missed the faint knocking coming from the wall to his left. He hugged the perimeter of the wall as he made his way over to where he thought the knocking had come from and waited. Several minutes passed in silence, so he wondered if perhaps he had imagined it. Then he heard it again—louder this time, though, the still almost imperceptible sound of knocking was coming from the wall not far from his head.

"Hello," Will whisper-shouted. More knocking was the only reply he got. For a moment he flashed to an old movie he had seen when he was young. The very dashing James Mason had been captured and had heard knocking through the wall. Mason's character had spoken to the knocker, asking for help to get him out of there only to discover that the knocker was a duck pecking at the other side of the wall. "Hello." He tried again. More knocking, and his hopes were beginning to fade. Was he talking to a fucking duck too?

He needed to know. "Knock once for yes and twice for no," he tried.

"Do you understand?" One knock. Thank fuck.

"Have you been kidnapped too?" One knock.

"Are you hurt?" One knock. Shit.

"Is your name Stuart Bates?" One knock.

Will's relief upon hearing the single knock was palpable, and he released the breath he hadn't quite realised he'd been holding. For some reason, Will always felt somehow responsible for these copycat murders.

Logically he knew that was foolish, but logic had a habit of deserting him in moments of crisis, and he hadn't been able to fully divest himself of the guilt. To discover Stuart Bates was still alive was an enormous comfort, though neither of them was safe yet by any means. He could offer some hope to Stuart now, though. "Stuart, thank God. People are looking for you, and the police are close. I know they are. Hang in there. We can get out of this. I promise you." One knock.

They sat in silence for a time. The unreality of the situation made it difficult to come to terms with what was happening. However, Will imagined that Stuart was getting as much comfort simply from knowing Will was there as Will was getting from Stuart being alive.

Last time, his monster had kept him away from any others. He could hear them screaming, but he could never talk to them. They had never been able to give each other comfort through words. Even at the end, when he had been forced to watch, he had been gagged, unable to offer words of support, not that any words would have been a comfort at that time. Will knew that just knowing you weren't alone in these situations helped, as selfish as that may seem.

His mind wandered back to Jack, always to Jack. What would he be doing now? He was going out of his mind, but he trusted Jack. He trusted that he would be doing everything he could to get to Will. He wouldn't allow himself to consider the possibility that the monster may have hurt him after Will had fallen unconscious. Jack was alive, and he was coming for him—that was the only possibility. Nothing else was an option.

JACK WANTED TO tear the world apart. He wanted to be out there searching every damn house, unit, office block, or building he came across until he had Will safely back with him. He felt as though he couldn't breathe whenever he thought of Will. A physical pain, a blow to his body worse than anything he had ever felt, stabbed him whenever he thought of Will in the hands of that monster. Jack had failed him twice now, and being confronted with his own helplessness was a terrible thing. The guilt, the fear, and the anger all threatened to crush him, but he wouldn't let it break him—at least not until Will was safe. Then he would break, and he could let go and let his failure rip him apart.

He held himself still while the doctor restitched his leg where the stitches had popped when he had tried uselessly to save Will. He had refused a local anaesthetic, wanting to feel the physical pain of his failure. They had taken blood from him too. It had been clear Jack had been drugged, for as strong as his painkillers were, they still should not have rendered his body so utterly unresponsive.

The police guard at his door had been found in the tea room, drugged to unconsciousness, and as far as Jack was aware, he was still out cold. When Angie had found Jack on the floor of his room, he had been inconsolable, *crazed* he thought he heard Angie say to the doctors, and he wouldn't let any of them near him until they had given him a phone so he could contact Pete. Moments after Pete had been called, he and Kate were on their way. Pete promised he'd get people out looking for Will immediately. Hospital security had also been called, and though they were currently still searching the hospital, Jack knew Will would be long gone.

He could see the pity in Angie's eyes now as she stood helping the doctor stitch him back up. He didn't want the pity; he didn't need it or deserve it. He had failed, oh God, how he had failed, and now Will, oh Will, he couldn't—he just—couldn't. Fuck, he could feel the tears welling up again. Fuck that. No, he didn't have time for tears. He ferociously reined in his emotions. He was no fucking use to Will if he couldn't get himself under control.

Jack could feel the pinch and pull of the stitches, but the pain was negligible. He watched the needle piercing his skin, threading the suture into him. He needed the distraction; he needed something besides his own weakness and failures to focus on.

It was quiet in the room, but outside he could hear a commotion starting up. He recognised the booming voice of his boss and the softer yet no less fierce sound of his partner. Jack pitied the poor fool who was trying to get in their way. The heavy treatment room door burst open, and Pete and Kate stood there shoulder to shoulder, the muffled objections of hospital staff coming from behind them. Like the absolute professionals they were, Angie and the doctor continued on with their business, ignoring the intruders who were now making their way into the room, twin looks of concern on their faces.

Jack was so choked up he didn't trust himself to speak. Pete seemed to have no such trouble.

"Jesus fucking Christ, Jack, what happened? Where was that fucking idiot at your door?"—he was shaking his head in disgust—"Half the force is already out looking, and we have teams scouring CCTV around the hospital. Goddammit, *how* did this happen?" Jack actually worried that Pete might pop a blood vessel the way he was going. Before he could even open his mouth, Pete went on. "Are you okay? What happened? Fuck, when I..." Pete ran out of steam, his body hunching over on itself. Kate patted his arm and guided him to one of the chairs along the wall.

Returning to Jack, she looked at him with such sorrow that Jack wasn't sure he could bear it. "He'll be okay, Katie. We'll find him, and he'll be okay." No other outcome was an option.

She smiled sadly at him and then seemed to gather herself together. "Damn right we will, Jack. He's tougher than you or me, that's for sure, and he's going to be okay. That fucker can't have planned this one. He's panicked and that means he will have made a mistake, so we're going to get him." Kate drew in a deep breath, let out a sigh, and rested her hand on Jack's shoulder. "How are you doing, Jack? Honestly?"

"Fucker drugged me, Kate." He bowed his head. "I couldn't move, couldn't get to him. I just lay on the fucking ground like a useless dick and watched him drag Will out of there. I couldn't..." Jack shook his head, choking up, disgusted with himself all over again.

Kate nodded at Jack, and he could see the fire in her eyes, the determination that they were all going to need if they had any chance of getting Will back. "You were drugged, Jack, on top of already being injured." Kate squeezed his shoulder in gentle support. "Right, enough of that. I'm going to security. They're already checking cameras for us, so I'm going to see what they might have found, and then I'll be back. You get yourself fixed up because Will's going to need you, Jack. Understand?" Jack nodded in response but couldn't help thinking Will needed better than what Jack had given him so far. He watched Kate walk out of the room and then turned to the doctor who had just finished patching him up.

"I can already tell this is going to fall on deaf ears, but here goes. Bed rest for you, Detective Mitchell. No undue pressure on your leg, and certainly, keep your left shoulder as immobile as possible. You're lucky you didn't pop those stitches too. Not to mention your body will be expelling the drugs you were given for a while so I recommend you stay right here for at least the next few days. What are my chances?"

The way the doctor spoke, Jack suspected he already knew what Jack's response would be. "Sorry, Doc, I can't."

"Thought as much. At least make sure you keep the dressings on, and take the antibiotics. You don't want an infection on top of everything else."

"I promise, Doc." As the doctor left the room, Jack turned to Pete who had sat quietly since his outburst earlier. Pete's next words shocked the hell out of Jack.

"I am so fucking sorry, Jack. I suspected about you and Will, but Kate told me on the way over." Swallowing thickly, Pete seemed to collect himself and continued on in a manner far more familiar and comforting to Jack. "Look, we aren't the secret service, so there's no rule against it, but I'll still ream you out about the ethics of fraternising with someone you're supposed to be protecting once we get Will back. Until then, get your lazy arse out of that bed, and do some actual fucking work, huh?"

Both men smirked at each other, and Jack suspected they each looked just as feral in their determination.

They met Kate in the hospital security office. She seemed settled in with a coffee and half-eaten muffin. A petite lady Jack guessed to be somewhere around fifty sat beside her. They were focused on the screen before them that appeared to be showing CCTV footage. But from where Jack stood, all he could see were hazy moving patterns.

"Found anything?" Pete asked.

"Oh, we got them. Your Mr Blaikie was captured being pushed in a wheelchair straight out the front door and being loaded into a dark SUV. We even got a good image of the license plate," the older lady answered.

"I've already called it in, and the BOLO has been put out," Kate interjected. "Oh, and this is Kathy Leonard, head of security. Kathy, this is my boss, Captain Pete Delaney. And my partner, Detective Jack Mitchell." Both men leant forward and shook hands with the still-sitting lady. Kathy barely took her eyes off the screen long enough to shake their hands, and Jack considered it was likely that she took it personally that Will had been taken during her watch.

"We lose them just as they turn right onto Fielding Street. That's as far as our cameras go, but the council cameras should pick him up from there."

Jack was still feeling a bit fuzzy and out of the game, but thankfully, Kate seemed to be on hers. He could barely think clearly enough to consider their next move.

"I've already spoken to council, and they're checking the cameras on Fielding Street for us. We can head over there as soon as you're ready."

"Good work, Kate. You head over to council and Jack—"

"I'm going with her, Pete."

"Didn't really doubt if for a minute, but a man can hope." Pete sighed one of his exasperated sighs he had perfected over the years working with Jack. "I'm going to head back to the station and coordinate from there. Regular check-in please, and I'll let you know if anything turns up." Pete was all business again, and Jack couldn't be happier. "For God's sake be careful, and, Jack...stay out of trouble, hey," he finished with a smile. Time to get down to business, and get Will back.

FIFTEEN

WILL COULDN'T BE sure what time it was. He had nodded off for a short time after discovering Stuart Bates was alive in a room next to his. Exhaustion infused every part of his body, tired from the drugs and aching from being bound in an uncomfortable way. He still couldn't quite believe he was here again—didn't they always say lightning never struck in the same place twice? How could this be happening again?

For the first time in his life, though, he was seething at the unfairness. The first time he'd been kidnapped he'd been too scared to be angry, and afterwards, just too messed up to really think about anger. But he was pissed now. He had been just starting to feel safe again, for the first time in years, and he had been so...so happy. Everything changed when he had met Jack. He would give anything to be back with him right now, to feel Jack's strong arms around him, to feel one of Jack's tender kisses on the tip of his nose. Will was going to use his anger. He was going to use it to fight and make it back to Jack.

He couldn't hear any sound coming from Stuart and wondered if he had drifted off too. He hesitated to wake him; he knew how important and scarce sleep was during this kind of ordeal. He knocked softly on the wall he leant against. No response. In barely more than a whisper he called Stuart's name. Moments later he heard shuffling noises and a single knock.

"Hey, Stuart. Sorry if I woke you. Are you okay?" One knock.

"Has he been back?" Two knocks.

"Hang in there. We'll get out of this." Two knocks.

"Don't you give up, Stuart. Not know. We are going to get out. The police are coming for us, I promise you. There's this one cop, Jack—he's a stubborn shit. He won't stop looking for us, and he has a partner, Kate. She's smarter than Jack, but don't ever tell him I said that, and she's tough too. She won't give up either."

When Will stopped to take a breath, he could hear nothing but soft sobs coming from Stuart. "Shh, shh, it's okay," Will quietly crooned over and over, until the sobbing sounds stopped, and a single strong knock sounded. Will understood the tumult of emotions Stuart was experiencing and the mental fortitude that was needed. Last time, he had only his own fortitude to prop himself up during the lowest of times, but he and Stuart could brace each other when the storms of defeat raged through them.

Will didn't think there was any benefit to sharing his past with Stuart, but he needed to distract him. Sometimes distraction was a viable weapon in the war on sanity during a crisis. He decided to barrage him with yes-no questions about his likes and dislikes. It's surprising how much you can learn about a person, even when they can only respond to you with a nonverbal yes or a no. Will was starting to get a fairly thorough picture of Stuart Bates. He hoped they would have the chance to get to know each other better if they could make it out of there. No, when they made it out, he refused to think of it as *if* they made it out.

Just as he finished asking Stuart if he was a fan of *The Walking Dead*, and Daryl Dixon in particular, he heard a loud, creaking noise. It was almost unnaturally quiet where they were, and with Stuart unable to speak, it remained that way with only Will's soft questioning breaking the silence. The creaking noise was so out of place in the silence it was almost like cannon fire to Will. He knew instantly what it meant. Someone was coming.

Though he tried his hardest to remain positive, hoping it was Jack coming for him, he wasn't quite that naive. His entire body turned instantly cold and shaky. He felt weak, exactly like he did just before becoming violently ill. He admonished himself to calm down, to be ready, but he was shuddering so brutally now as he listened to footsteps approaching that he doubted he could do anything to help himself, let alone Stuart. Will lay on his side, not difficult, since he was already mostly in the foetal position thanks to the way he had been bound, and he couldn't stop shaking. He dug his fingernails into his palms, irritating some of the splinters embedded there. He concentrated on the pain to stop tears from falling, reaching for the anger he had felt earlier. He didn't want to cry in front of this fucker.

Bright light cut through the darkness, and Will quickly shut his eyes against it. He waited a moment until the light had filtered enough through his eyelids that it wouldn't be blinding for him when he did open his eyes. He turned his head towards the lightness and saw a medium-sized man, roughly thirty, if he had to guess, silhouetted by the light and leaning against the wall. Will didn't bother to look at the man's face; he wasn't interested in what he looked like. Besides, his interest had been drawn almost exclusively to the sawn-off shotgun held loosely in the man's arms, yet clearly pointed in his general direction. The man took one hand off the weapon and fished in his pocket. He pulled out something too small for Will to see. The man then grabbed the shotgun with both hands and aimed it far more accurately at Will.

"Sit up, back to me, head back, and mouth open," he stated as innocuously as if he had been giving Will instructions in a yoga class, for fuck's sake. What the hell was wrong with him? How could he be so composed when he was quite possibly about to take a life? With little choice, Will did as he was asked. He could hear footsteps approaching, and he felt the cold metal of the gun barrel pressed to the top of his head, as the monster loomed over him.

Will flashed back to one of the psychiatrists he had seen after he had escaped his monster. Much of what they had told him over the years had seemed useless, if not ridiculous to Will, but he remembered sitting in one cold, unwelcoming office in particular, while a self-important doctor looked down at him, as if Will were so far beneath him he barely warranted acknowledgment. Will couldn't even remember the man's name now, but he remembered the one thing he'd been told that Will believed then and now—the mind was mankind's greatest weapon against all kinds of adversity; a strong body was no good if the mind was weak. He had to keep his mind strong.

His entire body was jelly-like as the fear of the shotgun coiled its way through him, but Will's mind laughed, inappropriately perhaps, but he laughed at the thought of the Godawful mess the monster would make if the trigger was pulled. His mind fought, told him—ordered him—to believe that this was not it. This was not how he went out. His shaking eased, and his limbs seemed to solidify again.

With his head tipped back, Will could look up at the monster, and he watched as one of his hands moved toward his mouth. The monster shoved his fingers into Will's mouth in an effort to force what was no doubt a tablet down his throat. When the monster withdrew his fingers, Will's first reaction was to spit whatever it was out, but the barrel of the gun pressed harder to the top of his head, and the monster calmly told him to swallow. In the position he was in, he had no choice but to do as he was ordered. Will could hear the monster start to shuffle backwards, and though he knew the shotgun was no longer pressed to the top of his head, he could still feel it there like the phantom pain of a lost limb.

"Turn to me, back to the wall." Disobeying didn't even seem like a possibility. He would wait, biding his time. He could already feel the effect of the tablets, knowing he had been drugged again. As he pressed his back and bound hands to the wall, he felt his head start to loll.

Now, he didn't take his eyes off the man's face. He watched as the man stood there, shotgun held loosely at his side again. The monster was so remarkably calm, in control. The monster's face was ordinary. He was neither ugly, nor handsome. His lips were thin and pulled tight, and heavy stubble covered the lower half of his face. A slightly crooked nose centered between two of the emptiest-looking eyes Will had ever seen. There was nothing in the monster's eyes to give Will hope—no shred of sympathy or compassion, no indication that humanity resided inside the organic matter that made up this monster. And there was no hint of fear either. The monster wasn't worried about being discovered anytime soon. This last thought disturbed Will the most as he drifted into unconsciousness.

THIRTY-SEVEN HOURS and nine minutes had passed since Jack had lost Will. His body ached from his various injuries, but it was the pain in his heart that threatened to incapacitate him. If this was what loving someone got you, then Jack wasn't sure he was strong enough for it. Every time he imagined Will's beautiful face, every time he heard the sounds of pleasure Will had made in his arms, every time he remembered the intimacy and contentment he had experienced in Will's presence, he knew that he wanted it back. He wanted Will back with a desperation he knew would tear him apart. He knew that he wanted God or the universe or fate or who-the-fuck-ever to allow him to love Will...to give him another chance to be with Will again. He knew that loving Will was worth the pain he was now enduring. He refused to allow himself to imagine what Will was possibly suffering; he knew it would sweep him under, and he'd be useless to help his lover.

Pete had physically escorted him home twenty minutes ago, demanding that Jack get some rest. He had argued to just curl up in the staff room, but Pete wouldn't allow it. Mosley had been dropping by

Jack's place to check in on Henley so Jack hadn't needed to get home to the dog. The simple truth was he didn't know if he could face his home, with its ghosts of Will. Phil had been called in by Pete to drag Kate home when she too had refused to leave. Jack would be forever grateful to everyone who was trying to get Will back for him. That didn't assuage the anger he felt at being forced to rest, though.

When he dropped him at his home, Pete had offered to come up with him, but Jack had refused. He couldn't allow Pete to be with him as he walked into his home because he wasn't at all certain that he could keep it together, knowing that Will wasn't there and may never be there again. Twenty minutes later, he still hadn't made it inside. Instead, he was sitting at his front door trying to find the courage to go in where he had to face memories of Will. To face Henley, who despite his age, seemed to be uncannily aware when something was wrong. Soft snorting noises coming from under the door warned Jack that Henley had discovered his presence. A growing fondness for the stinky animal prevented Jack from staying out any longer. It was time to pay the furry piper. He rose on his still achy legs, slowly. Shakily inserting the key in the door, he rested his forehead against it, taking one last breath to steady himself before finally opening the door.

Henley was lying in the entryway, front paws outstretched, head laying on them. He was the picture of misery. Jack couldn't lift his eyes to look around the room, knowing the one person he wanted to see curled up on his couch with a book in his lap wouldn't be there. He slid to the floor instead, pulling his knees up and resting his head sideways on them so his gaze could remain on Henley. Soft whimpering sounds were puffing out of the canine's grim-looking jowls. Jack tenderly reached for his scruff and scratched through the thick fur in a consoling gesture. "I know, boy. I know... I miss him too." God he wanted Will. He wanted him back in his arms; he wanted to watch him wake up in the mornings with his hair sticking up all over and a thin trail of drool crusting his chin. He wanted to fall asleep with him at night, listening for when his breath evened out and his body softened into slumber. He wanted to talk to him about anything and everything. He wanted to know what Will thought about everything—did he like his leftover pizza cold the next day? Did he have a favourite Beatle—Lennon, McCartney, Ringo, or maybe even George? Did he have names picked out for his children? Was he Labour or Liberal or did he donkey vote? Oh God, he hurt. He hurt all over.

Several hours later, Jack had not moved from his silent vigil beside Henley. They had both drifted off a few times, but he didn't think either had found true rest. He couldn't stay here anymore. He had to get back to the station, had to be doing something. Steeling himself, he walked towards his bedroom, gaze never veering from the path in front of him. Like a robot, he grabbed a change of clothes and showered in record time. He took Henley out to do his business and left the dog with a bowl of food and one of the giant bones Will loved to spoil him with. In minutes he was out the door, apologising to Henley for leaving him, but promising to bring his master home.

They had released a grainy image of their suspect, captured by the hospital's CCTV cameras, to the media, and the story of Will's kidnapping had knocked the latest Taylor Swift love fiasco right off the top spot during news bulletins. The media was in frenzy about Will being kidnapped by the copycat, and the image of the suspect was being shown everywhere. It wasn't a clear picture, but Jack hoped that together with the police sketch, it was recognisable in that not-quite-tangible way to anyone who knew the suspect. He and Kate had been to the council to follow up with their CCTV cameras. They had been able to follow the dark SUV to the outskirts of Windsor, a distance of about thirty kilometres. The registration had come back to James Andrews of the same address they had gotten from his TAFE file, so nothing had helped them there. They had lost the SUV when the cameras ran out on the more rural roads. Swarms of officers were out canvassing local residents in the hopes some of them may have security cameras that had caught the vehicle as it had passed their property. They hadn't heard from any of the officers for a while, and Jack was getting antsy; too much time was passing, leaving him feeling as though he was doing nothing. His traitorous mind was beginning to think the worst.

Jack had slept maybe four hours since Will had been taken, including the brief nap he had managed with Henley at his front door. His sleep had been pervaded with nightmares. Half an hour ago, Kate had returned to the station, likewise unable to stay asleep. She had tried to convince Jack to at least lie down in the break room and rest some more, given that he was injured. She was unashamed to try a bit of guilt on him, but Jack had remained steadfast. He was afraid to close his eyes, afraid of the nightmares that would follow him into sleep. So Kate had received the same glare he had levelled at Pete earlier when he scolded Jack for coming back to the station.

Jack's gaze fell on Kate now as she took a call. He watched as her eyes rose to meet his own while she nodded, perhaps forgetting the caller couldn't see her response. It was a quick call, and as soon as she put the phone down, she came to Jack where he stood looking at the map they had up on a monitor of the area where the SUV was last seen. She looked hopeful.

"Jill Tucker just called, and she said a resident on Percival Street may have caught the SUV on their home-security cameras. They are the corner house on Percival and Hawkesbury Valley Road, and they could see a dark SUV turn into Percival from Hawkesbury Valley. They are pretty big blocks out there, so Jill is going to head a few houses down, and see if she can pick it up again. It's risky skipping houses, but I think we're running out of time, Jack," Kate finished quietly.

"Yeah, no, you're right. She should skip a few." Jack knew his response was lackluster, but just the hint of Will running out of time nearly broke him.

"You love him, Jack." It was a statement, not a question.

"Yep. I do." It didn't take any effort at all to admit it anymore, and he was too damn proud of Will to bother trying to keep his feelings to himself. "Had to happen, didn't you tell me?" He had to snap out of this funk. He was no good to anyone like this. "Well it did happen, and it is wonderful and terrifying and amazing and nerve-wracking, and I just can't lose him, Kate. He doesn't deserve this; he's already been through so much. Fuck. Fuck. Fuck. Why didn't I stop him? What kind of fucking cop am I that I let the man I love be taken from me right under my fucking nose?"

"Jesus, Jack, you had been shot, and you were drugged to shit. Doctor said he wasn't sure how you even got yourself out of that bed with the drugs you had in your system, so don't you dare beat yourself up about this. If you want to get angry, get angry at the prick who did this, and use that to get Will back." Kate was one formidable lady, and Jack was glad she was on his side. Her words got to him, brought him back from the brink. He was done sitting around waiting.

THE SMELL AND the cold was the same as when he had first woken in his prison, but he could tell he wasn't in the dark now. His body still ached, and he was nauseous on top of everything. Will thought it was likely the drugs making his stomach roil, though an unhealthy dose of fear could also do it. For just a moment, he considered not opening his eyes; perhaps if he couldn't see whatever was happening, then it wouldn't actually be happening. It was a childish thought in a desperate moment. His logical mind countered that he had to see where he was and what was happening so he could deal with it and do something about it. He gave himself another brief moment of despair before he ordered himself to open his eyes and confront his reality.

Will opened them quickly, just like ripping off a bandage. He was in a large wooden room with a dirt floor and no windows. It must have been some sort of shed, likely an industrial one, given the size. The light was coming from two large spotlights, much like they used for temporary lighting for roadwork. One of the spotlights was to his right, facing towards the middle of the room. The other light was further back and to his left, and it was pointed to what Will knew to be a surgical table directly opposite him. Lying on the table, held down by straps, was a young man of average size. Will could see the man's face in profile; his mouth was still covered with masking tape. His stillness would have made Will fear he may already be dead if it wasn't for his chest gently rising and falling. Will assumed the man was Stuart Bates. Will himself was sitting in a wooden chair, hands bound behind the chair and ankles bound to the legs of the chair. Without looking, Will knew he would find tools on a table against the wall to his left. It was just as it had been six years ago. The sick fuck had done his research.

"Welcome back, Will. It's been a long time." Did this monster actually think he was Russell Coburn? What should he do? Should he engage him or stay silent? Would it matter either way? It hadn't last time.

The man finally moved into Will's field of vision. He had a predatory look on his face and a mallet in his left hand. Will remembered the mallet, remembered the damage it could do, and he could feel himself sliding into panic again. He tried to picture Jack as he had looked after their first kiss, with his pupils blown wide and a feral look of want in his eyes. Will had never believed anyone would ever want him, as broken and wrecked as he was, but Jack had, and he would damn well get through this for Jack.

The monster was watching him almost as if he knew the thoughts going through his head, and it seemed to anger him. He stalked toward Will with the mallet raised to shoulder height. Will braced himself for the blow. But it didn't come. Struggling sounds as Stuart fought against his restraints drew the monster's attention.

The monster watched Stuart for a few moments, before turning back to Will, a look so malicious crossing his face that it made Will tremble. He had a brief flicker of selfishness, hoping the monster would be drawn back to Stuart, leaving him alone, but it didn't last. He tried desperately to decide what to say, what words he could use to buy them time. He knew begging would likely only excite the monster, but what about anger? Would that inflame the monster's fury or sidetrack him? Any interaction could be dangerous—he didn't want to antagonise him into further irrational violence—but he had to try something. He would use his anger, showing he wasn't afraid, and maybe that would help him somehow. It was utter bullshit, and Will was trembling with fear, but he had to try something.

"You're doing it wrong." Will managed to force out. Confusion warred with anger on the monster's face.

"What is it you think I am doing wrong, Will?"

"Well, there should be two of them. One for you, and one for me. That was the plan you know." He tried to keep his voice even, though he couldn't stop his words from coming out shaky and broken. The monster stared at him for a seemingly unending period of time. Will wasn't able to read him at all. Had it worked? Or did he not care for the rules at all, and he would simply go ahead and kill Stuart before his eyes? Will could hear Stuart still sobbing and struggling behind the monster, but he didn't dare look at him in case it drew the man's attention back to Stuart. Instead, he fought his own instincts and feelings of revulsion to continue meeting the monster's eyes.

"You're right." The monster seemed agitated. Was he angry? Should Will keep pushing? He just didn't know, feeling as though he were walking on broken glass. One false move and he'd bleed. The monster continued staring at him, the wheels clearly turning in his damaged brain. He had been silent so long that Will jumped when he at last spoke.

"Though there's no reason why we can't play a little until I can get us another friend." Will wouldn't allow himself to feel the guilt that perhaps he had doomed another young man to a violent death. He had bought himself and Stuart time, though he suspected it was not going to be an easy time, as the man closed in on him, mallet in hand.

SIXTEEN

OH JESUS, WILL knew he would never get tired of looking at Jack's body, naked or clothed. Although only a couple of inches taller, Jack had muscles on his muscles. His flawless skin tasted mildly of sweat and citrus and something uniquely Jack. Will couldn't get enough of it as he licked a line from Jack's clavicle down to his belly button. He swirled his tongue once around the navel before gliding down towards the base of Jack's gorgeous erect cock. The flavour of Jack's precome burst onto Will's tongue as he licked the head, and Will swore his own cock got harder just from the taste. Above him, he could hear Jack's soft moans and whimpers, and he could feel Jack's body involuntarily start to thrust, seeking out the friction that would allow him to come. God, he didn't know what he would do if he could never have Jack like this, so close, so intimate. He wanted Jack, needed him with a fierceness that made him dizzy. He couldn't wait for Jack to be inside of him again. He pulled his mouth from Jack's cock and reached out with his hands to trail them over Jack's taut abs.

But he couldn't find him, so he reached further...searching but could feel only coldness and something else... Was that dirt? Jack's warm body should have been there. Where was he? Slowly his thoughts were piecing together to form an image of cold, hard truth. When the true picture of his reality formed in his mind, Will choked on the sob as it ripped from his throat.

The realisation Jack was not there, and he was still a captive, was a psychological agony far greater than the physical pain starting to seep into Will's body as consciousness returned. Had he ever gotten away in the first place? Could the last six years of freedom have been a dream? Surely if his freedom was only a dream he would have dreamt of more time with Jack, rather than all those years of loneliness. And, if it had been a dream, he wanted to go back...desperately wanted to go back to Jack.

He moved around in the dark, trying to get more comfortable. At least his hands and feet weren't bound this time. He knew from the smell that he was bleeding, though he wasn't losing enough blood to worry about—superficial wounds only. Laughter bubbled up from deep inside... *This monster was an amateur compared to Coburn.* He couldn't decide if his thoughts and his laughter were healthy or perhaps the first indication of insanity. This monster had done some damage, for sure, but he didn't have the same flair as Coburn when he had inflicted pain on Will. Jesus, he potentially was losing his sanity if his thoughts were heading in this direction.

Had Stuart been spared any further injuries? Will hoped Stuart had been out of danger this time. The monster had focused solely on Will when Will had made him believe things weren't quite as they should be with only one victim there. He felt the sharp barb of guilt again because he may have condemned another man to death, but he had to buy some time for Jack to find him.

It was surprising and comforting to Will that he didn't doubt for a minute Jack would come for him. It didn't mean he was going to sit around like a damsel in distress waiting for the knight in shining armour to come rescue him, though. No fucking way. Will was going to do anything he could to get himself and Stuart, if not out of here, at least ready for when Jack came.

Realising there was no going back to the sweet relief of sleep, or forced unconsciousness, Will wanted to check on Stuart.

"Stuart? Are you awake, mate?" Will spoke softly, not wanting to alert the monster should he be around. He was pleasantly surprised when, instead of his usual single knock, Stuart used words to reply.

"Will. Are you okay?"

"Yeah, I think so. I can't see anything, but nothing feels broken or too badly hurt. How about you?"

"No, no, I'm fine. He never touched me this time." After a few moments silence, Will caught a murmured "I'm sorry" from Stuart.

"Not your fault. I'm glad he left you alone. Have you got any serious injuries?"

"Is it true?" Stuart ignored Will's question, asking one of his own instead.

"I'm not his helper, Stuart. It's a long story, but six years ago I was kidnapped by Russell Coburn. He killed twelve men, but I survived. He became...fixated on me and wanted to train me to be his partner. I survived and this guy—he's a copycat. I promise you I just used that to buy us some time."

"Shit. I...I'm...fuck. Will, I don't know what I'm doing or saying or... I'm so scared. I just want to go home."

Will knew that feeling. All he wanted was to go home, to Jack. That was home now, wherever Jack was. He could feel tears coming, but they were unwelcome; they wouldn't help him. He needed to distract them both.

"Tell me about your family, Stuart," Will demanded. He waited patiently as Stuart seemed to collect himself and then listened as Stuart talked, his mind floating away from his brutal reality the more Stuart spoke.

It seemed like many hours later, but was probably only about two, and Will felt that he knew Stuart almost as well as anyone. He had listened as Stuart told him about his dick of a father who treated him like shit because he was gay and his spineless mother who had never stood up for him, choosing instead to live as though she were in an alternate world where they were the perfect family—her husband was a gentleman, and Stuart was most assuredly not gay. As always, Will marvelled at a parent's ability to disregard or openly despise their children simply because of who they loved. Unconditional love was clearly not a prerequisite to becoming a parent. Stuart had also spoken with endearing fondness about his friends, in particular someone named Kyle. Hopefully Stuart would get the chance to tell Kyle how he felt about him once he figured it out himself. Stuart was a nice guy, a good guy, and he sure as hell didn't deserve what was happening to him.

Will wanted to save him—them—so bad he could taste it. Now he just had to figure out how. Stuart had asked him a little about his experience with Coburn, but neither of them seemed to want to rehash a nightmare when they were currently living one. Will hoped that he had given Stuart some measure of faith that he could survive this.

SEVERAL HOURS AGO, Jack had begun calling in every person who had been questioned in regards to this case. For all he cared, they could sit here, no doubt rather impatiently, and wait to be reinterviewed. Several had initially refused to come in, claiming they had nothing further to offer, but they soon changed their tune when Jack either guilted them or outright bullied them into coming in. He knew Pete would tear him a new one when this was over, but he couldn't allow himself to care about that now. He had planned to speak to them himself, but then a call came through to Kate and everything changed.

Jack had just gotten off the phone with Lyndsay Bordin when he looked across to where Kate was on a call of her own. Her eyes were narrowed in that way she had, telling Jack either someone was in deep shit, or she was right on the verge of figuring something out. Kate ended the call and immediately signalled for Jack to follow her. They walked towards one of the empty interview rooms and met Shane at the door.

An elderly woman was standing with him, Shane's hand clasped too tightly around her bicep. The top of her head barely reached Shane's chest, and her body was stick thin and folded over like it had caved in on itself. Her hair was mostly grey and looked unbrushed. Her face was wizened and leathery, but it looked like the damage was from hard living rather than old age. Despite the rest of her appearance, her hands told Jack that she was probably only in her midsixties, if that. Something had prematurely aged her. If Jack had ever seen anyone so visibly pale and in a state of shock, he couldn't remember it; the woman looked like she was one step from a tango with the reaper. Shane, despite being an exasperating dick at times, was also a well-mannered and professional man, so Jack was taken aback by his overtly rude treatment of the frail woman beside him.

"Tell them." Shane's tone was icy. And when she didn't immediately start talking, he gave her a little shake.

"I think my son...no, I know my son is the man you're looking for."

Jack watched her as she spoke, and he would swear it looked like she had to reach down and heave the words out of her body. He and Kate were shocked into silence before sanity returned, and they ushered her into the interview room. Shane practically dragged her into the room, throwing her an annoyed glare before turning to leave.

"You okay, Shane?" Kate asked.

"Yeah...bitch knew, Kate. Told me she knew it was him before Jack was shot and Will..." Shane gave a disgusted shake of his head and walked out.

For a moment, Jack considered closing his fist around the woman's throat, tightening it until her breath was cut off. She had let this happen.

He saw Kate glance at the two-way mirror, no doubt signalling to Pete that perhaps Jack should leave the room. Fuck that, he wasn't going anywhere. "Tell us," he demanded.

"My...my name is Mary Ferrante. Twenty-eight years ago I had an affair with Russell Coburn, which resulted in the birth of my son. My son's name is James Andrews, my maiden name. I never told Russell, because by the time I realised I was pregnant, he had already started to...scare me. He was violent and I don't know...crazy." She looked so frail Jack almost...*almost* felt badly for her. "A little over a year ago, James found out about his father. I was talking to my husband, and he...he overheard. James had always been difficult, prone to violent outbursts like his father, but..." Tears came in a steady flow now. Mrs Ferrante reached that point in crying where she was unable to get coherent words out. Kate moved to the other side of the table to sit with her, quietly speaking in an effort to calm her. Jack wanted to jump the table, reach down her throat, and pull the fucking words out. He was barely containing his anger when Pete walked in.

"Mrs Ferrante, here's a glass of water. Can we get you a cup of tea or coffee?" Pete was cool as a cucumber, but Jack wanted to scream with indignant rage for her to just tell them where Will was. Mary Ferrante shook her head and went back to sobbing. Pete stepped closer to Jack. "We have a doctor on the way who can give her something to calm down—"

"No, no way, Pete. She needs to talk. She has to tell us where they are." Jack and frustration were old friends, but this was something entirely new. He was so damn close.

"Jack, she's no good to us if she gets hysterical, and I'd say she's not far off. This is her son. She's here to tell us she thinks her *son* is a killer."

"No, she's here to tell us where Will is. That's all I care about. She doesn't leave, doesn't get fucking tea or coffee or cake or any-fucking-thing else until she tells us." Jack was incandescent with rage.

Pete pulled up to his full height, all Captain Delaney now, not his friend Pete. "You need to step outside, Detective." It was an order. Jack left, his seething temper his only companion.

Through the two-way mirror, Jack could see Kate and Pete calming Mary Ferrante. The doctor had arrived, but to her credit, she refused his offer of a calmative. The doctor stayed in the room, with her permission, just in case. Meanwhile, Jack was going out of his ever-loving mind. If the old woman didn't start talking soon, Jack would not be held responsible for his actions.

Inside the room, Kate suddenly turned to the window and gave a quick thumbs up. Hopefully, that meant the woman was ready to talk again.

"Mrs Ferrante, please go on," Pete encouraged.

"Well, he found out about his father, and I thought everything would be okay. A sort of calmness came over him. He was very angry with me, though, for keeping it from him. One day..." Mary took in a deep breath, and Jack sensed they were getting to the heart of it. "One day, while my husband was out, he beat me. Told me I had kept him from his legacy. I didn't understand then."

"What did he mean?" Kate, always so calm.

"His legacy was killing. I considered it after the second man was found, when the media started calling him a copycat. But...but...he's my son, please...please understand. He's my son." The old woman was crying again.

Jack didn't have time for this. He stalked into the interview room, ignoring the almost panicked looks of Kate and Pete and went straight to Mary. Jack knelt before her and took her hand. He was calling on every ounce of his willpower to stay calm rather than rage at the old woman. "Mrs Ferrante... I know how hard this must be, but please... He...he has my Will. He has Will, and I love him, and I want him back. Please. Where are they?"

As frail as she was, there was still a little fire in Mary Ferrante, who reached out to stroke Jack's hair. She had no idea she was stroking a coiled asp ready to strike if she didn't tell him what he needed to know. There were no lengths Jack wouldn't go to for Will.

"I'm so sorry," she whispered. "James had a place, an industrial site out on Cornwallis Road at Windsor. Thirteen to nineteen I think." She clutched at Jack's hand. "Please don't hurt him."

Jack had exhausted his patience and his compassion, so rather than answer her, he turned and fled the room. Kate was right on his heels, already on the phone. They ran to their car, Kate still relaying the address and instructions to officers already in the area.

"This has got to be him, Jack. I called Kassel. He and Holmes are still in the area, so they're heading over there now with some uniforms. Shall we join them?"

"Bet your fucking arse we shall." For the first time in almost fifty hours, Jack felt as though he could breathe.

WHEN THEY ARRIVED an hour ago, they found Kassel and Holmes already engaged in a heated dispute with quite possibly the most unhealthy-looking man Jack had ever seen. The man was so red in the face from the exchange that Jack honestly expected him to clutch at his chest and drop at any moment. Kate and Jack quickly ascertained that this man was the onsite custodian and was refusing to allow the officers entry, despite the situation being explained to him. He also claimed to have never met the actual owner but had been hired and was dealt with by a leasing firm. After listening to the ignorant fuck prattle on about privacy and warrants and heavy-handed police tactics, Jack had grabbed him by his throat, shoving him back against the rickety fence they stood near so hard Jack worried they may actually go through it. The irony of his heavy-handed actions was not lost on him. He had hissed in the man's face that if he didn't open the door in the next three seconds, he would break it down but not before breaking his fucking nose. In times to come, Jack would no doubt be ashamed of his words, but these were not normal times, and Jack could think of nothing but Will's sweet face. Kate had hauled Jack away and immediately called Pete, who had called back about three minutes later advising Kate that a warrant would be emailed within the hour.

For the next forty-three minutes, Kate had stood behind Jack as he faced the wall of the building, her small hands holding him in place with a surprising strength each time he had turned to argue some more with the custodian.

Jack squirmed and twitched as he stood waiting. His impatience was reaching into new and somewhat frightening territory. Even now, as the man finally opened the door and moved aside to let them pass, Jack could almost imagine himself popping this fucker right in his smug face.

He and Kate entered first, weapons drawn, with a small team of about five uniformed officers backing them up. Holmes and Kassel had the perimeter. They spread throughout the building, a well-oiled machine, each one of them a tendril moving to every corner. Each knew their job and where they were expected to be and what they were expected to do. With each moment that passed with repeated calls of 'clear', Jack's hope sank. It seemed the building was empty. In fact, the only part of the building containing anything at all was the small one-room apartment that housed the custodian.

Jack's frustration had been simmering for hours, and now it boiled over into an ill-advised punch that put Jack's fist right through the gyprock, splitting his knuckles in the process. Several of the officers moved as if to either comfort or restrain Jack before registering the look of utter despair on Jack's face. Rather than approach, his team was quickly moving away, perhaps wanting to avoid the embarrassing emotional Vesuvius Jack could feel about to erupt from him. Then there was Kate, who did not turn and hide from the rawness of Jack's emotions but was standing with him as they flooded through his body. It was her calm stoicism that finally reined in Jack's behaviour. He dropped his head, disheartened and exhausted to the point of collapsing.

"I'm sorry," he whispered.

"Oh, Jack, no. No worries at all. I wish..." Kate was either unsure of what she wished for or unsure if voicing it would further wound Jack. As he had seen her do many times, Kate straightened, visibly collecting herself and pushing on. "You take a minute; get your head back in the game. I'm going to go see if there's anyone at the property up the road. Maybe they know something." Kate squeezed Jack's shoulder in solidarity, comfort, friendship, love, all those wonderful things that Jack so desperately needed right now.

As soon as Kate left the room, Jack sank to the floor, pulling his knees to his chest, wrapping his arms around himself in comfort. Physically holding himself together in an effort to stop his sanity from being as lost to him as Will was. The wounds in his leg and shoulder pulled and ached, but they were tickles to the pain in Jack's heart.

SEVENTEEN

SINCE ESCAPING FROM his monster six years ago, Will had sought treatment with a variety of therapists. Some of it was useless and some of it helpful. He was thinking now about one of his therapists, who had the unlikely name of Gilbert Valentine, but had strongly encouraged Will to call him Bluey, the typical Australian nickname for those blessed with red hair and blue eyes and skin so white that ten minutes in the sun turned it a colour to match their hair. As a rule, Will did not do nicknames and had obstinately stuck with Gilbert, much to Gilbert's dismay. Gilbert had been one of Will's favourite therapists, and he would have stuck with him had Gilbert not fallen in love with a rather flighty lady who simply could not live in one place longer than a year. Last Will heard, Gilbert and the whimsical Marina had left Sydney for the hustle and bustle of Mitchell, Queensland, a mere 567 kilometres from Brisbane, population approximately one thousand. Will had often thought of Gilbert and what the hell he would do in an outback town of that size. Apparently the annual camel and pig races were not to be missed. The places love would lead you defied imagination.

Will ruthlessly stomped down thoughts of Jack and concentrated on the words Gilbert had shared with him during their sessions. Will had never thought of himself as heroic after what had happened to him—all he had done was live—but Gilbert had taught him all about positivity and how it could change your life. Gilbert had had a poster on the wall behind his chair so you couldn't help but see it during every session. It said *When shit happens...turn it to fertilizer*. Somewhat unorthodox for a professional therapist, but that was what Will had liked about him.

Will could be sitting here bitterly thinking about the unfairness of his life, but he wasn't there yet. That time may come, but for now, he would think of Gilbert and the positivity he had taught him, so he'd try to make fertilizer. One of the things he'd liked best about Gilbert had been his unassuming manner and straightforward way of speaking. Will had met many therapists who had spoken in such a complex way that often Will found he was lost and unable to grasp what they were asking. Despite its simplicity, Gilbert lived by the mantra of 'She'll be right, mate,' always clamping his hand on Will's shoulder as they stood at the end of each session and speaking those words with an absolute confidence that defied fate to prove him wrong. Will had never thought of it as shallow or simplistic because Gilbert sincerely believed that 'She'll be right,' and Will found himself repeating it to himself over and over now as he had once done with his times tables when learning them as a child. Learning by rote, repeating it constantly until you knew it in the very core of yourself. *She'll be right, mate.* After all, it had to be, didn't it?

Stuart had fallen silent some time ago. Will was unsure if he was asleep or perhaps conducting his own mental inventory, shoring up his own defences. Will was entirely absorbed in his thoughts but still straightened instantly when he heard the trill of a doorbell. He suspected it was one of those doorbells that relayed from the main house or building as he had not heard any signs of life apart from Stuart and the monster since he had arrived here. Regardless, he knew there was somebody else around, someone who may be able to help them. The monster wouldn't ring the doorbell. He immediately began yelling, screaming till his throat hurt for help. He was so loud he could barely hear Stuart next to him calling his name.

"Stuart, that was a bloody doorbell. Yell, mate." Within seconds Stuart's voice joined his own in a conflicting chorus of hope and desperation.

JACK HAD ALLOWED himself exactly five more minutes of self-pity before figuratively kicking himself in the arse and storming outside to interrogate that custodian fucker. He approached the group that consisted of the custodian, whose name Jack still hadn't bothered to find out, and three officers who stood virtually surrounding him in an intimidating fashion. Jack couldn't believe the man did not look more intimidated with the imposing officers around him. Cocky fucker. He could see Officer Tucker talking on the phone to the side of the group, and she broke away to approach Jack or perhaps intercept him before he could attack again. There was no risk of that; Jack had himself together now. Falling apart again would do no good for Will.

"Hey, Detective, I've just been on the blower to the captain and he's called through to Grindmill, the company that hired old mate over there. They're emailing all the information they have on the owner, and they're sending a representative out to speak with us. He should be here in about fifteen minutes."

"Thanks. Has he said anything useful?" Jack asked, nodding towards the man in question.

"Nah. Says he doesn't know anything, and why would he tell some pig cops if he did. Especially ones that swore at him and threatened to break his nose," Tucker said with a laugh. Jack rolled his eyes and groaned. Though he couldn't give a fuck right now, he knew his earlier behaviour would bite him in the arse one day.

"Where's Kate?" Jack looked around as he spoke, seeking out his partner.

"She went to the property down the road to question them as soon as she came out. Holmes and Kassel went to the turf company on the other side."

Fuck, how did he forget? Christ, he was so fucking messed up that he was making mistakes, and these mistakes could be fatal. He should have gone with Kate or at least headed straight there when he got his head on right again.

"Of course, yeah. Listen, I'm going to head over there and catch up with her. Let me know when the rep from Grindmill shows up, okay?"

"Will do," Tucker replied, walking back to the other officers who still surrounded the custodian like a school of circling sharks.

The neighbouring property was visible from where Jack stood, so rather than ask for a lift, he decided to walk, taking a little extra time to clear his head. His and Kate's car was missing, so Kate must have driven down there, and Jack thought they could drive back together when the call came in about the Grindmill rep.

It was beautiful out here, the flat green landscape broken up by the pale purple of the blooming Jacaranda trees. The Hawkesbury River flowed just a few hundred metres away, and Jack could see a cottage-like house on the other side of the river looking as though it had stepped right out of the pages of a fairy tale. As he neared the neighbouring property, Jack wondered what it must be like to live with so much space around you. He'd lived all his life in the suburbs of Sydney, the walls of neighbouring houses or unit blocks almost touching as people tried to build the biggest house they could squeeze onto their tiny blocks. In the house he had grown up in, he and Lisa Jones, the girl next door, could reach out of their bedroom windows, and their fingers could almost brush against each other. Their friendship had died when she was old enough to realise that Jack could hear every argument that went on in the Jones's household, and the shame of her parents' behaviour taught her to hide from anyone who could see into the truth of her home life. After becoming a cop, he realised that some drunken arguments and name-calling weren't so bad in the scheme of things, but it could often be the first step to something much worse and much more destructive. He sometimes thought about what might have happened to Lisa after she had moved away. Hopefully, she'd made it through her childhood relatively unscathed.

Their car was parked within metres of what appeared to be the front entrance of a small shed-like building that may have doubled as both living space and site manager's office. There were several other sheds of various sizes spread across the property. None of them looked to be in use. The properties along this section of road seemed to be mostly industrial, though most were empty. The turf company on the other side of the Andrews property was in business, but the Andrews place and this one seemed to be paused, waiting for the next business to come along. He could hear the low tones of a conversation just out of reach of being clearly understood. Rather than knocking on the screen door, he called out his name and asked if he may enter. Kate replied, telling him to come on in an unmistakably fake cheery voice, which was abruptly cut off with an almost shriek, scuffling noises, and then silence. Jack drew his weapon.

He cautiously entered and swept the room just as he had been taught and had executed so many times before. He walked towards the doorway that led into the next room and entered cautiously, gun high, finger ready but not on the trigger—he didn't want to shoot Kate. He wasn't sure what he had heard, but Jack trusted his gut, and it was roaring danger at him. He turned a blind corner into what looked like a makeshift kitchen and stopped, looking down into the wide eyes of Kate.

She stood with her head slightly tipped back, and a gleaming twenty-five-centimetre kitchen knife kissing the skin of her exposed throat. But the look on her face was pure anger—she was pissed. Behind her stood James Andrews, his face just visible, a cruel snarl lifting one side of his thin lips. The knife in one hand and Kate's weapon dangling carelessly from the other suggested that he preferred the intimacy of knife work to the less personal use of a gun. It also suggested the overconfidence of many killers: that although he had a gun, he wouldn't need it.

Jack had met murderers before, and they all shared a common trait, something in their eyes. People described it as having dead eyes, but to Jack dead suggested nothing, and he wasn't so sure it was a nothingness. There was an absolute blackness to their eyes, but it housed the living evil that formed their soul. He was looking right into one of those souls now.

"You can't control this situation, James." Jack was proud of how steady his voice came out. There was a slight shake in his hands, but he wasn't James fucking Bond; he was only human and had found himself in a terrifying situation. "My team know where we are, and they'll be here in minutes to join us. Put the knife down." His tone brooked no argument, but normal social conventions meant little when dealing with a psychopath.

"I don't think I'm going to do that, Jack, but you're going to put down your gun, and then we're all going to visit with a mutual friend." James was confident and smooth, like most psychopaths, but the mention of Will turned Jack's mouth dry with a fear unlike anything he had experienced before.

Fuck, what did he do? He could shoot this fucker, but there was a chance he would kill Kate in the process; his aim was good, but there wasn't much of Andrew poking out from behind the barrier of Kate's body to target. As much as he cared for Will, could he risk Kate's life? If he put the gun down, they could all be fucked, but it may buy them some time. His mind raced, looking for an out, a third option.

"Shoot the hostage, Jack." Kate's voice was calm, resigned, but steely.

Jack stared at her, unblinking. "It's not a fucking movie, Kate," Jack roared back. There was no way he was going full Keanu on her. For one, he didn't have a clear shot of her legs with the table in the way, and second, there was no guarantee this fucker wouldn't just finish her off for shits and giggles before Jack could take him down. And there was just no fucking way he was shooting his partner. Kate's option three was off the table, and any other ideas eluded him, so reluctantly, he carefully placed the gun on the table.

"Step back," Andrews's command came immediately. "Now you, Kate, who is so very angry with me"—he continued, smugness oozing from him as he pressed the knife deeper into her neck—"you stand up over next to your partner." Kate moved carefully but quickly to Jack. Andrews shoved Kate's gun into the waistband of his jeans, and then picked up Jack's weapon with a look that could only be described as gleeful delight. "You know, Jack, I was just thinking what it's going to be like when I kill Kate here and our friend Will with your gun. It's not quite as I planned, but we must adapt, and there's a certain…appropriateness about using your gun to kill them. Now both of you, out the back door there." He pointed to where he wanted them to go, using the gun. James Andrews didn't bother to bind their hands or cover their mouths, and his hubris gave Jack hope that was how they would beat him, using his own overconfidence to foil his plans.

EIGHTEEN

IT HAD BEEN maybe half an hour since they had heard the doorbell, and no one had come; no one had responded to their shouts. Will and Stuart sat quietly now, both straining to hear noise of any sort that might indicate someone was around, someone who could help them. In the darkness they had no idea if it was day or night, but it felt like daytime to Will.

Out of the silence, Will suddenly heard the sound of more than one set of footsteps. His stomach dropped instantly when he imagined that the monster was bringing in another victim. Before Will could even decide whether or not to call out, he heard Stuart's shaky voice rise in hope rather than fear. With nothing to lose, Will joined him. During a break in their cries, Will heard a voice calling out in response, a voice he knew well. Sobbing with relief, he listened to Jack calling to him.

"Will, Will, baby, I'm here. You're going to be okay. It's okay, it's okay," Jack repeated over and over again.

Will heard Jack getting closer and closer, so he started knocking gently on the walls, calling for him, desperate to feel his arms around him. Jack was here, Jack had come for him. He could *feel* Jack close by now, just on the other side of the wall. He could hear him talking softly to someone else, maybe Kate, and he could hear the lock on the door start to rattle around as Jack opened it.

Bright light reached his eyes, and Will only made out the outline of Jack as his eyes adjusted from pitch blackness to bright light. He stumbled toward Jack, desperate to touch him but mindful of Jack's injuries as well as his own. Last time he had seen Jack, he had recently been shot, and he had been unable to get to his feet to help Will when the monster had come. The last thing Will wanted to do was hurt him more, but he could no more stop himself from throwing himself into Jack's arms than he could stop the earth from spinning. Jack's strong arms came up around Will's body, engulfing him in safety and comfort. Both men were trembling.

Will took in the familiar scent of sweat and Jack and knew he needed to taste him, needed to touch his lips to Jack's to know this was real, not another dream leading to heartbreak when he awoke from it. He lifted his head from where he had rested it on Jack's shoulder and moved to take Jack's full, soft lips with his own. A voice cut chillingly through the moment and shattered Will's illusion of safety.

"Enough!" the monster boomed. Will jumped back from Jack as though he had gone up in flames. It was only then that Will took in the reality of the situation. Yes, Jack was here, and so was Kate, but the monster was there, and the monster held a gun and a knife in his hands. *No, no, no. No.* This could not be happening, not Jack, not like this. *Oh please, please, no.* He looked up at Jack then and witnessed the complementary emotions visible in Jack's eyes showing in his own: fear, anger, sadness. These were the trifecta of awful emotions. Experienced in a significant dose, they were enough to break the strongest spirit.

"Move away, Jack. Now." The monster waited for Jack to comply. "Will, join us please." The monster motioned with his gun, and all three captives turned and walked in the direction pointed out. Will could hear Stuart calling, asking what was happening, but he ignored him, hoping that the monster would too.

They didn't need to walk far to reach the room the monster had brought Will and Stuart to before. Will couldn't, or wouldn't, look around. He needed to sharpen his focus, wait for his chance. There was no way he was going to allow Jack to die here, even if it meant he had to.

JACK WAS WAITING, watching. He knew this fucker would slip up, and he would be ready. Will was not dying here; Jack would see to that. This would be his last chance to protect Will. If he failed here, that would be it—he'd lose Will forever. He wouldn't allow that. It had felt so good to have him in his arms again, if only briefly, and Jack knew at the first sight of Will, when he'd stumbled out of that dark room, Jack would gladly die rather than let more harm come to Will.

Jack had quickly inventoried Will's injuries as he'd stumbled toward him. His face had been badly bruised and swollen. There was a dried cut on his left cheek, and he was limping, though Jack could see no obvious injuries to Will's legs. He was barefoot, and there was some dried blood on both feet.

For that brief moment when Will had thought Jack had rescued him, he'd given Jack a look of such jubilation, such adoration, Jack thought he would never again witness anything more beautiful than Will's face in that moment. However, that moment had been brief and cut bitterly short, when Will realised the true situation, leaving his face a mask of such utter devastation Jack hadn't been sure he would not collapse with anguish.

They came to a halt when they reached a dead end and turned to face Andrews. Jack positioning himself in front, trying to shield both Will and Kate, who had remained silent since the standoff earlier in the kitchen. Jack knew, without question, that Kate was waiting for an opportunity of her own. There was no way she would give up either, and he also knew she wouldn't appreciate him trying to protect her, but fuck it, that's just what he did, especially for people he cared about. Andrews stood glaring at all three as if trying to work out what to do next. He hadn't planned for this, and as a copycat, perhaps he would have trouble thinking on his feet, giving them another advantage. As if reading Jack's mind, Andrews smirked at him, seeming to have come to a decision.

"Will. Here. Now." Will stepped out from behind Jack who tried to hold him back. He grabbed onto Will's arm trying to push him back behind his own body, and a small tussle ensued until the crack of a gunshot broke them apart. Andrews stood with the smoking gun still aimed at the roof where he had fired the shot.

"Now, Will," he commanded again. It took everything Jack had in him to hold himself back from reaching for Will again. He watched as Will unsteadily walked the four or so metres to where Andrews wanted him. Will stopped as far from Andrews as he would allow. Andrews motioned for Will to turn and face Jack with a twirl of his hand. Kate had moved herself out from behind Jack using the distraction of Will's movement so that she now stood shoulder to shoulder with him, letting him know that they were in this together.

Unlike the movies where the evil villain insists on delivering an extended monologue to explain their actions, allowing the hero time to get out of trouble, Andrews moved quickly and immediately lashed out at Will, striking him hard on the right side of his head. Will stumbled to his knees, blood flowing from the cut on his right cheek where the handle of the knife had struck him. Jack could tell that the blow had left Will dizzy, but he was still conscious and on his knees, leaning forward heavily on his arms to prevent himself from falling to the ground. Jack's blood thundered in his ears, and he would have sworn right then the entire world had been tinted a vibrant red. Jack had been angry before, but never had he been so wholly and overwhelmingly enraged. Will was his and there was no way he was going to let that fucker touch him again.

"I am going to fucking take you apart if you touch him again." He did not yell or shout or rant. Instead, Jack's voice was ice-cold steel gritted out between clenched teeth, cutting through the air and the cloak of confidence that had been wrapped around James Andrews. For the first time, Jack could see a tendril of doubt creep into Andrews's features.

Jack could see the knife in Andrews's hand now. He wasn't sure where the guns were, but there was no way that was going to stop him now; Andrews had just waved a red flag in front of Jack, and Jack attacked. To his right he could see Kate also moving, and though his eyes were fixed on Andrews, he could also peripherally see Will tumbling out of the way. Andrews lunged and struck out with the knife, but Jack could tell it had been a glancing blow to Will, who had lifted his forearm in defence, and was now practically rolling to get out of reach. Kate was almost at Will so Jack kept his focus on Andrews, who had clearly also decided Jack was the bigger threat to be dealt with. He lunged at Jack, the knife held straight out in front of him. Jack still didn't know where the guns were, having lost track of them. He reacted to what he could see, and the threat right now was the knife.

James Andrews was not an experienced knife fighter, so Jack easily dodged the blow and reached for the wrist holding the knife. Andrews saw him coming and pulled his arm back before Jack could grab his wrist. Jack's hand closed over the blade of the knife instead, immediately slicing his skin. The pain of the cut was nothing; in his rage Jack felt it as a pinprick. Jack held on, bringing his other hand up, this time clamping onto Andrews's wrist. He viciously wrenched Andrews's wrist back, waiting for the satisfying snap of bone before releasing it. He knew that instinct would force Andrews to drop the knife, and when he did so, Jack rounded on him with a sickening knee to the crotch, doubling Andrews over instantly. Jack finished him off with another knee to his head, and even as Andrews fell unconscious to the ground, Jack followed him down, wanting to deliver the killing blow.

Fury was the only emotion riding him now. He pulled at Andrews's collar, cocking back his arm to deliver what would be a devastating right hook to the head of the unconscious man when two voices broke through his rage. He could hear them both—the two people he cared about most in the world trying to bring him back. Kate was telling him that they had him and it was over, and Will—sweet, sweet Will—pleading with him to stop, to come back to him, that he needed Jack.

Jack's breath was heaving, but he released Andrews, who flopped back, and then he stood and turned to see Kate, just to the right, covering Andrews with a gun, the other gun poking out of the waistband of her slacks. And he could see Will, so strong and brave in the face of such horror, sitting at Kate's feet, the hem of his shirt pulled up to stem the flow of blood from his cheek. Jack took two paces to reach him and dropped to his knees in front of his lover. He tenderly reached out to touch Will's other cheek, his shoulder aching with the movement.

"I'm so sorry," he whispered over and over again, pressing their foreheads together, too damn frightened to grab at him the way he wanted for fear of hurting him more.

"Your hand," Will murmured, his voice as cracked and broken as his body appeared. Jack could see blood spilling from a nasty gash that split the length of Will's arm almost from elbow to wrist where Will had fended off the knife earlier. Jack removed his button-up shirt, ripping the buttons rather than wasting time undoing it properly. The cut to the palm of his hand was starting to throb. He knew it would be deep, but the best he could hope for was that no serious and permanent damage had been done. Jack leant forward to tie his shirt around Will's bleeding arm.

"You too," Will said and motioned to Jack's cut and bleeding hand. Jack could hear Kate talking on her mobile, no doubt calling it in; in fact, he was fairly sure he could already hear the sirens. Thankfully, they didn't have far to come. Jack had neither the strength nor the patience to try to rip his shirt, so he continued tying it around Will's arm.

"I'll do me once I've fixed this up, okay?" Jack cajoled.

"No you won't." Will smirked.

Jack adored this man, his fight, his humour, the dignified and moral way he lived his life. Will was everything to Jack, and it became crystal clear to him at that moment that he wanted Will in his life forever. He leaned closer and pressed a gentle kiss to the tip of Will's nose. "God, I fucking love you," he whispered.

NINETEEN

WILL HADN'T BEEN able to see Jack in nearly three hours, and despite the mild sedative they had given him at the hospital, he was practically jumping out of his skin, impatient to see Jack again. Immediately after Jack's whispered confession at the monster's dungeon, complete chaos had broken out with the arrival of more police, followed by ambulances, the fire brigade, other assorted emergency personnel, and finally the media. Will had wanted to go back to Stuart, but until the backup had arrived, Jack had refused to leave Kate alone with the monster, and he had refused to let Will out of his sight.

As people rushed in and through the building they were in, Will had been separated from Jack by ambulance officers who insisted they both receive treatment immediately. Will heard Jack attempting to argue with one of his paramedics, who was a tiny slip of a thing standing about five foot tall and looking like she'd have blown away in a light wind. Her voice, though, when she turned on Jack, sounded like it came out of a six-foot-five mountain of a human being, and Will had actually seen Jack cower in the face of the tiny woman's stubborn refusal to allow him to go untreated. Jack endured her ministrations with ill grace bordering on actual pouting, which Will found surprisingly endearing.

As Will's own wounds were being tended to, he'd watched as Stuart Bates was taken out on a stretcher. The team of medics passed by Will, and Stuart had asked them to stop while he shook Will's hand. It was awkward, as Stuart was lying on the stretcher, and Will's right arm was being treated, but it was a warm and necessary closure of a sort for them both. Stuart looked battered and bruised and as though he would pass out at any moment, but behind that, Will could see a flicker of life returning with his renewed freedom—especially, Will thought, if he had the support of Kyle to go home to. Kate was uninjured and had barked orders at everyone who set foot into what had been Will's temporary prison. She had overseen the monster being taken away, the crime scene units who had poured in like ants at a picnic, and he had heard her demanding the media be removed from the immediate area or quote 'heads will roll'. She was an amazing woman, and Will was thrilled at the prospect of getting to know her even better.

It was Kate who entered his hospital room now and drew him from his memories. She looked pale and tired, but the fire continued to burn in her eyes.

"Hey, Will. How are you holding up?" Her soft voice belied her steely expression.

"I'm okay, Kate, thanks. How's Jack? Can I see him?" The few butterflies that had been dancing in Will's stomach turned into a kaleidoscope when he caught agitation flick over Kate's expression so fast he almost missed it. Had something happened? Where *was* Jack?

"Sure. I'm sure he'll be here as soon as he can. Lots of loose ends to tie up though. He has to give his statement and whatnot, so I guess he could be a while." Kate's words didn't ring true to Will, and her evasiveness just plain frightened him. What the fuck was wrong? Then it hit him. Oh, God. Had Jack not meant what he said? Had the 'I love you' been an adrenaline-induced reaction? Were he and Jack over now that the case was over? Oh fuck, that hurt. It couldn't be.

"Ah Jesus, I'm not doing this." Kate groaned at his side. "Listen, Will, I love Jack like an annoying-as-shit younger brother, but the man is a complete idiot when it comes to people." Will could hear Kate's affection for Jack despite her words. "He has got this stupid, fucking notion that you won't want him because he didn't protect you. I tried to tell him that was complete bullshit, and if he couldn't see the way you looked at him then he was a sightless bastard who didn't deserve you."

Will didn't try to stop the laughter that burst from him, regardless of the subject matter. Fucking hell, Jack *was* an idiot if he thought Will didn't want him. Well, he wasn't going to put up with this shit. That was for damn sure.

"Where is he, Kate?"

"Two rooms down. Pete won't let him out despite him claiming he is perfectly fine. When I left his room, I believe Pete's exact words to him were 'You stupid son of a dick, you are staying if I have to cuff you to the fucking bed,'" Kate quoted with a huge grin on her face. He hoped Jack realised just how much he was cared about by Kate and Pete.

Every part of Will's body ached despite the drugs, but there was no way in hell he wasn't going to Jack right this fucking minute to set him straight. *Not want him, my arse, the fucking idiot.* He gingerly sat on the side of the bed, and ever so slowly stood, testing the waters and hoping he didn't fall on his arse. Kate came to his side and offered her arm, which Will wasn't too proud to take, and together they made their way to Jack's room.

As they walked through the door, he could hear Pete yelling at Jack that he "didn't have a fucking handcuff kink." But Will's focus was zeroed in on Jack, who seemed to be likewise focused on him. The tension in the room was uncomfortable, to put it mildly, and Kate and Pete couldn't seem to get out quick enough. Kate walked him to the bed, squeezed his shoulder, and turned away. Neither she nor Pete said a word as they practically bolted from the room, leaving Jack and Will eyeing each other, two circling wild animals, each waiting for the other to make the first move.

"Will."

"Jack."

Silence.

"You look good. Considering what..." Jack broke the silence hesitantly. Outright rudeness hadn't been his style with Will since that day in the police station, yet his cold and detached manner was supposed to have the same effect on Will. Jack was trying to make him leave; he was trying to get rid of him. Well, fuck that.

"You look fucking hot, Jack, as you always do."

"Will, I—"

"Shut up, Jack." Jack's eyes were as large as saucers at Will's aggressive tone. "Let me guess. It's been fun, but we're done now. Don't call me, I'll call you. It wasn't meant to be. We were in a tense situation, and one thing led to another. Please stop me when I get to the correct line here, Jack." Will was working himself up to outright anger. Jack slumped in his bed, his beautiful eyes no longer on Will's, but rather, he seemed to be fascinated by the view of his own hands clenched tightly in his lap.

"I just don't see how you could want this...me," Jack murmured.

"You're right, Jack I don't want you."

HE KNEW IT. Jack had fucking known Will wouldn't want him now, and he knew it was going to hurt, but Jesus, Will's confession knocked the wind right out of him. His chest felt like Will had punched a hole straight through it. He wasn't going to make it through this, and he needed to get Will to leave now before he lost it and made an even bigger fool of himself.

He didn't know what to say. What words did you use on someone who had just broken your heart, ripped it still beating right out of your chest? He couldn't use anger—he wasn't angry. Not at Will, not yet. He raised his gaze, determined to look into Will's beautiful dark-chocolate eyes one last time before Will wasn't his anymore. God, they were stunning; Will was stunning. He was watching Jack closely, and Jack looked for pity, disgust even, but he couldn't see it in Will's eyes.

So slowly, as if he was fearful Jack may startle and bolt, Will reached out to grab Jack's good hand, gently rubbing his thumb backwards and forwards over the smooth skin. He was offering comfort.

"Jack, I don't just want you. I *need* you, so don't you dare try some bullshit to get me to leave because I am not going any-fucking-where. Do you hear me?" Will spoke with an absolute confidence that was positively turning Jack's shit on. "I heard you back there, Jack. I heard you, and I fucking love you too. And I just... I just need you. Okay?" Will was losing the wind from his sails, deflating right before Jack's eyes.

"You heard me?"

"Yes."

"And you love me too?"

"Yes."

"Is this real?"

"Yes."

"What do we do now?"

"Fucked if I know." Will laughed. "We're like the blind leading the blind when it comes to relationships, Jack. But I want to try...with you. You don't know what it was like before. I was so alone and so afraid. I was only existing, and I was never sure if that was okay or not, but you helped me. You made me want to get back to the world, Jack. You make me want to live, not just exist."

"I let him get you, Will," Jack whispered.

"You stood between him and me, more than once. You saved me, Jack. Not just from him...you *saved* me." Will's tone brooked no argument.

"C'mere." Jack pulled Will down by their entwined hands until he was resting on Jack's chest. They were both battered and bruised all over, but they didn't care, touching each other as gently as they could, wherever they could, carding fingers through hair, rubbing soothing circles into backs, tracing lips with thumbs. Neither spoke, just touched, finding absolute comfort, absolute peace in the feel of each other beneath their hands, until they eventually fell asleep, to be found by a nurse a short time later, snuggled together as close as they could get.

MUCH TO JACK'S annoyance, Will was released the next day while he remained in hospital for another week. Jack suspected Pete had something to do with that. Till his dying day, he would swear he overheard something about 'keeping him out of my hair' when Pete had been talking to Jack's doctor one morning. Pete denied it, but there was, without doubt, a smug grin on his face. Will came to visit every day, overtly delighted to be eating hospital food regularly. Kate was usually the one to bring Will in and take him home. Occasionally Nathan Mosley escorted him, and even Jim Moore had popped in.

Things were moving surprisingly swiftly with the case against James Andrews, who Jack had discovered was in a room just down the hall under heavy police guard. A hospital bedside hearing had resulted in him being denied bail, and he would be moved directly to Silverwater Prison once he was released from the hospital. Jack dreaded the trial, for Will's sake, but he knew they would get through it. Jack was learning that they were even stronger together. Stuart Bates remained in the room directly across from Jack. With his myriad injuries, he was looking at a lengthy stay. The day after his rescue, Jack had been privy to a heated discussion between Stuart and his parents, which resulted in an enraged Roger Bates fleeing the hospital, glaring at Jack as he'd passed him by on the way out. Mrs Bates had apparently grown some balls and stayed with her son. Stuart's most frequent and constant visitor, however, was Kyle Sandler.

Jack was sitting with Stuart and Kyle now, waiting for Will and Kate who were on their way to pick him up. Finally, he was going home.

"Yeah I get it, Will, but come on, without Rick they would be fucked." *Oh here we go.* Kate and Will were involved in yet another *The Walking Dead* debate as they entered the room.

"But the arms, Kate. Daryl's arms are worth at least the value of two Ricks."

"Arm porn, Will. Really?"

Looking at Jack, with the hint of a smile as they entered the room, Will replied, "Yeah. It's a recent thing."

"Jack, your boyfriend is very shallow, my friend." Kate was tapping out of this debate. She continued into the room, giving both Stuart and Kyle hugs, unaware of Will and Jack both frozen behind her.

Boyfriend. How casually the word had fallen from Kate's lips, and yet, incredibly, the word had not been mentioned by either Will or Jack.

Boyfriend.

They continued staring at each other, a silent conversation between two men whose intimacy had grown to the point where a look could convey...everything. They smiled together.

Yes. Boyfriend.

Will walked forward, taking ahold of Jack's hand and giving a little squeeze. "You ready to get out of here?"

"Hell yeah, I've been ready for a week. Are you... I mean, you will be staying tonight won't you?" It was ridiculous how vulnerable Will made him feel at times. There was no question that Will had the power to slay Jack.

"That's the plan." Will beamed. "Stuart, are you on for tomorrow?" Will turned to the other three people in the room.

Kyle was already nodding before Stuart could even answer. "I am...definitely." Will had arranged for Dr Granger to come in and see Stuart. Jack had met the doctor when he had popped in with Will one day, and though he was a little stiff, Jack had no doubt he knew what he was doing and would be a great help to Stuart's recovery.

Jack quickly said their goodbyes and headed towards Kate's car, his bag slung over one shoulder and Will's hand held firmly in his. Twenty-five minutes later, they were standing at the door of Jack's unit, having waved goodbye to Kate, who did not want to come up and 'bear witness to the ick-fest homecoming' that he and Will would no doubt engage in. Last time he had been here, just a week ago, Jack thought he had lost Will forever. Incredibly, he was coming home with a very much alive Will—his boyfriend.

"Jack?"

"Yeah, sorry, Will. I zoned out for a minute there."

"Well, unless you want a very excited Henley to scratch right through your door, may I suggest we go in?"

He could hear the desperate clawing now as Henley tried to get to his master. Jack opened the door quickly, putting the dog out of his misery. The furry beast launched himself, as much as an arthritic twelve-year-old dog could, at Will, favouring Jack with a sniff and a lick on his way by. Several minutes later, Jack was not ashamed to say that he was a little envious of the attention Henley was getting from Will. It was time to get a little of that attention for himself; after all, Henley had had Will all to himself for the last week. It had been too long since the last time he'd been able to get his hands on Will the way he craved to be able to touch him.

As he walked into the kitchen, Jack headed toward the fridge. He opened it and found exactly what he needed. He grabbed the large bone and headed back to find Henley.

Jack wasn't sure if Henley smelt it first or saw Jack waving the bone around first, but regardless, the dog left Will's lap immediately and trotted after Jack. Jack left Henley and his bone on the floor of his bedroom. If not for the arthritis, Jack was certain Henley would have been up on his bed smearing bone debris and saliva all over his cotton sheets. Jack stalked back to Will and found him standing now, watching intently as Jack approached him, his eyes wide, pink tongue peeking out to lick a trail across his bottom lip. Jack couldn't stifle his groan.

"You really are '*Pony*'." Will inexplicably commented.

"What?"

"Never mind. Whatcha doin' there, Jack?"

Continuing to peel his shirt off, Jack came to a stop inches from Will. Their breath mingling, heartbeats aligning. Jack's shoulder still ached, and his hand was bandaged and still throbbed at times, but he was damn well going to have Will Blaikie. "I need you, Will."

"You have me, Jack, always." Reaching for each other, their lips sealed in their most tender kiss yet. The sweetness of the kiss soon gave way to blistering passion. The now familiar feeling of not being able to get close enough to Will overwhelmed Jack, shredding his control.

"Jesus, Will. I love you so much. I planned to make love to you, slowly and tenderly, but you're making it hard," Jack gasped out, hands now working on the buttons of Will's shirt.

"That's the idea isn't it?" Will laughed at his own joke. "Slow later, Jack. I love you too, but I've missed you, and I need you now."

"What do you want?" Jack's hands continued to pull at Will's clothes, his lips at Will's ear.

"You. I want you in me, Jack. Here."

Jack looked around the room for the best surface he could find, and then he dragged Will to the couch. It would be more awkward than a bed perhaps, but they would make it work. Will pulled away from Jack's hands and stopped. Thinking perhaps he had hurt Will, he turned and found his man, shirt off, belt and zipper hanging open, and in the process of kicking off his shoes. It wasn't exactly a striptease, but Jack stopped to enjoy the show anyway. When he was naked, Will winked and walked to the back of the couch, before folding himself over it. He tipped his head up to Jack, a heated look in his eyes and groaned out, "Like this."

For half a beat, Jack couldn't move. Never had he wanted someone so desperately. He ran from the room, no doubt leaving a startled Will in his wake. After grabbing the supplies he would need from the bathroom, he headed back down the hall, attempting to disrobe as he went. He hopped, fumbled, fell into the wall, dropped the supplies, and stumbled again. He was making a hell of a racket.

"Jack?" Will's voice was half concerned, half amused.

"Yep, coming," he managed to splutter around the tube of lube that now hung from his mouth, his hands twisted in the muddle of jeans and underwear he was trying to shuck.

"You better not be," Will called back.

Jesus Christ, he would be the death of Jack. After finally ridding himself of everything but the lube and condom, Jack walked back into the living room. Coming from this direction, Jack got his first view from behind Will's body as he lay draped over the low back of the couch. His long, toned legs spread wide, perfect arse exposed, strong scarred back curled over. Jack's mouth was watering, desperate for a taste, wanting to savour every sensual pleasure Will offered. He was so fucking hard it hurt. He balanced the lube and condom on the back of the couch beside Will before he reached out and gently traced the scars, flashing to the night in the laundry room when he had first seen them. "So beautiful." The words he had thought that night echoing from his mouth now, unstoppable. Pressing his lower half to Will's, he leaned over and nibbled at Will's ear. "You are so Goddamn beautiful, Will." He licked a line down Will's neck, working his way down his back, tracing the scars as he went.

"Please, Jack." Will moaned.

Jack couldn't deny him. He grabbed the lube, coated his fingers, and eased first one, and then another, into Will's tight hole. He played a while, stretching and tormenting until Will was incoherently babbling. Jack withdrew his fingers and reached for the condom, quickly rolling it on, desperate to be inside Will.

JACK WAS GOING to kill him if he didn't hurry up and get inside of him. Surely people could die from being pleasured to death. After some googling and wading through some rather unfortunate porn he had found, Will had become obsessed with Jack fucking him over the back of the couch. He had gathered his courage and put himself on display to get this little fantasy happening, and Jack was making damn sure it was exceeding his expectations. Now if Jack would just hurry up before he exploded from the pleasure...

The rip of the condom packet and snick of the lube bottle closing were music to Will's ears. One of Jack's hands was holding onto Will's hip, and he could feel the head of Jack's cock pushing at his entrance. Will's own dick was rock-hard, pressed between his stomach and the soft back of the couch. He relaxed, helping his muscle to loosen and allow Jack in. The pleasant burn of being stretched inflamed him and then the exquisite feeling of fullness. Perfect.

His entire body felt amazing. Jack draped his body over Will's so they were chest to back, and then he started moving, slowly. Jack was rotating his hips, pushing his pelvis into Will's arse. It was leisurely and sensual and it was blowing Will's fucking mind. This was unhurried, grinding more than thrusting, and it had Will panting embarrassingly loud.

Every roll of Jack's hips emphasised his complete dominance of Will's body as he ground his cock into Will, ensuring he knew Jack had given him every inch of himself, and Will had taken it. Jack's lips were nibbling at Will's neck and up to his ear, his earlobe sucked into Jack's hot mouth, and Will was lost. He was overwhelmed with sensation, whimpering uncontrollably.

"Ready?" Jack breathed into his ear. All Will could do was nod. "Then hold on."

It was the only warning Will was given before Jack raised himself from Will's back, grabbing his hips and pulling his cock out almost to the tip before slamming back in. And he did it again and again and again. Jack was thrusting into him over and over. It was hard, desperate thrusting as though he was claiming Will, and it was so Goddamn good. Jack leaned forward, again covering Will's back with his chest, not an inch between them, wrapping his arms around Will's chest and raising him slightly. The thrusting continued, but the angle changed. With every shove of his cock, Jack was hitting Will's prostate. The pleasure intensifying, until Will knew he was going to come, his own cock untouched but getting enough friction from the couch and his belly.

"I can feel you, Will. I can feel you're about to come," Jack panted into his ear. "Do it. Come all over yourself. I'll lick you clean, baby."

Jack's words were too much, and Will came, crying out his pleasure, emptying his come all over himself and the couch. He could hear Jack groaning, feel his movements falter moments before he felt Jack come inside him, roaring out his pleasure.

They were sweaty and messy, panting hard, collapsing together over the back of the couch, and it was fucking amazing.

Eventually Jack moved, standing up and pulling out before turning Will around and then dropping to his knees. He tenderly licked at Will's come-stained belly. It was tickling, and Will was laughing, and he felt wonderful.

"I'll get a cloth, Jack." Chuckling, he pushed Jack away. He left Jack kneeling on the floor and headed for the bathroom, stopping along the way to grab some boxer briefs to put on. After turning on the water, he wet the flannel and washed away the evidence of his pleasure. Bending down once he was done, he began pulling on his briefs. He hadn't heard Jack come in behind him.

"Don't bother with those. I haven't finished with you yet, Will."

"Well I need some sustenance after that, and I'd say Henley will be just about finished with his bone, so unless you want your balls licked by a thirty-kilo dog, I suggest you get something on while we make some dinner." Will watched as Jack paled and reached for a towel to wrap around himself, no doubt disturbed by the image of Henley and his wayward tongue. Chuckling, he left Jack in the bathroom and went to the kitchen in search of food.

Rifling through Jack's freezer, Will found some chops, which he put on to defrost while he was working on a salad. He had the music playing on Jack's Bose speakers, and he was swaying to the smooth sound of Van Morrison's "Days Like This." Looking up at the sound of a slight intake of breath, he came face to face with Jack, who was leaning against the door frame, watching him intently.

Jack held his hand out. "Dance with me?"

"Always."

EPILOGUE

SIX MONTHS LATER...

"Fucking hell, isn't that thing dead yet, Jack?"

"Christ, Kate, don't let Will hear you talk like that. He loves that smelly fleabag almost as much as he loves me."

"Almost?"

"Yeah, yeah, you're hilarious." Life was so damn good for Jack today. He was moving in with Will after much cajoling and pleading—by him—and he was being helped by people who had become family to him and Will. Kate and her husband, Phil, even her rug rats were helping out of a sort. Pete was here and several others from work. It was true, many hands made light work, and they were just about done with the big move. Will had pizzas ordered and cold beers on ice.

He still pinched himself at least once a day to be sure he wasn't dreaming his life. Every single day he was amazed that Will was still his. The first month or so after Will had been kidnapped had been tough. Both of them had nightmares, but they were easing.

Jack's hand injury had left him desk-bound for almost four months until he had full range of movement back and could hold his weapon, and needless to say he had driven everybody crazy while he was desk-bound.

Things were good now though, better than good, and tonight they would share a bed for the first time as live-in lovers or whatever the fuck the politically correct term was. Jack didn't give a shit as long as he got to go to sleep every night with Will in his arms and wake up to his beautiful face every morning.

Jack was proud of how well Will was doing. He was in full-time therapy again, but he was getting out of the house far more than he had previously. Even if most times Jack was with him, it was a start. With Dr Granger's encouragement, Will had plans to go back to his university studies next year, and even though he'd intended to go back strictly as an online student, he was still making progress. Will's brother, Sean, had come back shortly after Jack had been released from the hospital, having finally been found and notified about what his brother had gone through. A quiet but stern word in his ear from Jack had left no uncertainty that Jack would not tolerate Sean abandoning his brother again. Sean had stayed for a month, and then left to go back to Scotland to tie things up there before moving back home permanently to be closer to Will. He would be here later this evening after completing his shift at the fire station.

Jack had also met cousin Del, who had laughed uproariously when Jack had threatened to put her in cuffs after she offered Will one of her 'special' cookies. He thought her a cracker; she thought him a dork; and they both adored Will, so they couldn't help but be friends. He called her at least once a week.

Will had remained close to Stuart Bates, and they even attended some therapy sessions together. Stuart and his partner, Kyle, would be arriving shortly for pizza. Stuart had wanted to help with the move, but his left arm still hung virtually useless at his side as a result of a shoulder injury from the monster. It would get better with time—though never as it had been before—but Will didn't want him to do further damage by trying to help.

He could see Will sitting on the couch, talking earnestly with little Bailey, and he wondered what on earth an almost three-year-old could talk about so seriously. Both heads turned to him and Kate, a beaming smile on Will's face and a frown on Bailey's. Taking Bailey's hand, Will walked over to him and Kate.

Pulling Kate into a warm hug, Will spoke quietly. "I hear congratulations are in order, Kate. Though I believe Bailey would much prefer a puppy to be in Mummy's belly than a, and I quote, 'stupid, crying baby.'"

Kate pulled back, chuckling. "I knew he wouldn't be able to keep it quiet from you, Will. We're having some problems convincing him this is a good thing, but we've got six months to talk it up."

"Oh, Jesus, you're pregnant?" Jack slapped his forehead. "You promised, Kate. You said no more. You know what happened last time." How could she do this to him again?

"I promised Pete and the rest of the station, Jack, not you. They were the ones who had to deal with you while I was on maternity leave."

"I'm the one who had to put up with Robinson as a partner." His indignation was gaining steam. "Rob-in-son, Kate," he elucidated in case she missed it the first time.

Pete, obviously overhearing the conversation from across the room, weighed in. "Christ, Kate, you promised. Do you have any idea what we had to deal with last time? He was intolerable, the whingeing, the moods...ack. How could you?"

"Hey, I am the one who had to put up with Robinson—"

"Brian Robinson is a model cop, Jack," Pete countered.

"He exfoliates, Pete; he exfoliates, and he suggested I might like to try it. Who does that?"

"Lots of men exfoliate, Mitchell," Pete bellowed.

"Na-ah, no, no exfoli— Oh God, you exfoliate, don't you, Pete?"

"Well I think I hear...someone calling me." Kate attempted to make her escape, Bailey trailing after her.

"Oh no, Kate, you get back here. You promised me." Pete stormed after her, leaving Jack and Will alone. Jack watched them walk away, joining the others who were now relaxing throughout Will's house, the move complete.

Turning to Will, who was likewise watching the scene, Jack asked. "Happy?"

Will turned to face him, his gorgeous dark-chocolate eyes on Jack's. "I don't think I could be happier, Jack. I have you and I have family. It's...perfect."

Jack leant forward, dropping a kiss on the tip of his nose. "Maybe one day we'll even be expecting kids of our own?" Jack was rarely shy, especially with Will, but he felt hesitant saying this, despite knowing Will wanted kids one day. He was opening himself up completely to a world he had thought would never be his, and it felt amazing.

"Maybe." Will's eyes glowed...happiness, contentment, love, all of those emotions reflected there. "I hope you won't lose your boyish figure though, Jack."

Jack smacked Will's arse as he ran off laughing.

ABOUT THE AUTHOR

Karrie lives in Australia's sunshine state with her husband and two sons, though she hates the sun with a passion. She dreams of one day living in the wettest and coldest habitable place she can find. She's been writing stories in her head for years but has finally managed to pull the words out of her head and share them with others. She spends her days trying to type her stories on the computer without disturbing her beloved cat, Lu, curled up on the keyboard. She probably reads far too much.

Twitter: http://www.twitter.com/karrie_roman
Website: http://www.karrieroman.com
Email: author@karrieroman.com

Also Available from NineStar Press

WWW.NINESTARPRESS.COM

www.ingramcontent.com/pod-product-compliance
Lightning Source LLC
Chambersburg PA
CBHW050939120626
46552CB00001B/286